LEE ANN WARD

Evernight Teen ®

www.evernightteen.com

DEDICATION

For all the times you took me to the library and checked out the Nancy Drew mysteries I adored, and for unabashedly raising me to believe that having a crush on the Hardy Boys was pure perfection... This one is for you.
I love you, Mama.

ACKNOWLEDGEMENTS

I want to thank my husband, Joe; my children, Tim, Travis, Ben, and Austin; and my precious granddaughter, Lilliana Rose, for their faithful love and support. Without them, my life would be meaningless. I also want to thank my parents, Chester and Sharon Collier, for teaching me that I can accomplish anything, and for their unwavering support for my passion for writing. I love you, Mama and Daddy. I want to thank my sisters, my family, and my friends. And my best friend and the best editor in the world, Joyce Scarbrough. She's my literary sister and this story would not be complete without her support and guidance. I want to thank Carrie, Sandi, Candice, and Stephanie for being beta readers for *Shadow Lilies* and the best "write club" any girl could ask for. I also want to thank Sheliah, Lady, Andrew, Christa, Farica, Sheri, Joan, and several other beta readers and friends who have supported this story. It means the world to me. And, lastly, I want to thank the Evernight Teen family, especially my editor, Audrey, from the bottom of my heart.

LEE ANN WARD

SHADOW LILIES

The Shadow Lilies, 1

Lee Ann Ward

Copyright © 2017

Prologue

When someone tells you the worst news in your life,
it's not with screams. No, the screams are what cut
through your house like scissors through paper. Ripping.
Tearing. Creating torn pieces that will never be whole
again. The actual words are calm, quiet—so quiet you
can still hear her voice, smell her hair, visualize the
wilted flower still tucked behind her ear like the last time
you saw her.

"But where is she?" I'd repeated over and over.
Repetition never bothered me when I was twelve.

"We don't know," Mom had explained for the
hundredth time. "Aubree is just … missing."

"Is she dead?"

"Don't say that, Julia!"

It was rare for Mom to yell, but the day my sixteen-
year-old cousin disappeared, so did normalcy … if you
can call how we live normal.

"Well?" I'd urged again.

"I don't think she's dead, Julia. Can't think it." Mom
never looked me in the eyes that day. "Maybe she just

found a better future, more than your Aunt Beth could offer her…"

I decided that day never to ask my mom about Aubree again. My cousin wouldn't just disappear … wouldn't up and leave us. Leave me. Maybe my family had stopped searching just to move on with life. But not me. No matter what, I'm finding Aubree.

Chapter One

You don't forget the promises you make in the dark. Cold. Hungry. Holding hands and huddled close for body heat. People think it never gets cold in New Orleans, but it gets real frosty in December when your heat's been out for a month because the folks couldn't pay the gas bill. But Aubree and I didn't care. It gave us an excuse to sleep in the same bed. That way we could talk a while before falling asleep. We'd talk about nothing, about everything. And she always had a secret stash of saltines in the nightstand just in case supper didn't stretch that far. Aubree promised it wouldn't always be like this. Both of us would do well in school, go to college. Make a better way for our futures.

"I'll make sure of it," she'd said. "And you can have the last cracker, Julia." She always gave me the last saltine. Every single time. We'd pinky swore to always be there for each other, no matter what. You don't forget those kinds of promises, even if the one you made them with is missing. Lost. Gone.

Three years can feel like forever, or no time at all. That's how long it's been since we've lived in New Orleans, since my cousin and I made those promises— since she's been missing. But now we're back, and I never thought excitement could mingle so well with sheer terror. I need to be in New Orleans. It'll make looking for Aubree a lot easier. I know that. But remembering *this* is the city that lost her—devoured her—ties my stomach in knots that won't loosen. This is the place that shattered me, nearly broke my family apart. I take a deep breath.

Almost home.

I'm blinded by the glowing, neon naked lady as soon

as I step from behind the U-Haul.

"Women take off their clothes in this place, don't they? Is this where we're gonna live? Please say yes!" Jesse looks like a lottery winner who's hit a mega jackpot. My little brother's such a troll.

"But I thought we were moving into our old apartment complex in Oak Park," I say. "Why are we *here*?"

"Nope, this is it," Dad replies. "Surprise."

"Are you freakin' kidding me?" I drop my backpack and stand next to Mom. Dad could've mentioned a strip club when he said we were moving back to New Orleans. This is an all-time low, even for us.

"Put a cork in it, son," Dad replies, as nonchalant as if he'd just pulled us up to the drive-thru at McDonald's.

"Unbelievable." I look at Mom. "Sure, it's no biggie. I mean, people move into the third-floor apartment over a strip joint every day, right?"

"Living here's gonna rock," Jesse adds, and I actually feel sorry for the little toad. I mean, it's really sad to drool in public. I've never been more grossed out.

I drape an arm over my brother's shoulder. "Sure, living here will rock, Jess. It's all good. I mean, STDs can't be transmitted through touching door handles or walls. Right, Dad?"

"Julia Reynolds! Don't you talk like that."

I roll my eyes. "Seriously, Dad? It's okay for your kids to live here, but you're offended by simple sarcasm? And how exactly did you talk Mom into this one anyway? What planet am I living on?"

But I know the answer. I'm living on the same planet I've inhabited since birth, the one with frozen dinners on Thanksgiving because that's all we can afford. The one with scratch-off lotto tickets for Christmas because Matt and Erin Reynolds believe banking on "lady-luck" could possibly give us a way out. The one with a father who believes that living above a strip joint on Bourbon Street just might be that fresh start for all of us.

"Exactly how *did* you manage this?" I glare at Dad again and throw my hands to my hips for effect. "Why here? Please don't say this is the only place you could find on short notice, because I'm telling you now I won't buy it. What gives?"

He walks behind the U-Haul and fiddles with the door. "Your mom said she talked to you and Jesse before we ever left Mobile. You're the one who wants to be the hotshot TV reporter one day. Figure it out."

When I look at Mom, she diverts her eyes, but I ask anyway, "Why don't you just tell me? I know you didn't really have anything to do with this location, right? You wanted to live in Oak Park again."

Dad cuts in front of us. "Look, the guy who owns this club is an old buddy of mine from when we lived in New Orleans before. Said if I did some bouncing, he'd let us live here for little to nothing. He said it would be a good deal for both of us, since his previous renters were heavy partiers and tore the place up on a regular basis. Will be a lot cheaper living here than in Oak Park."

Cheaper than Oak Park? How is that even possible? But I say instead, "I thought you had a job at the shipyard?"

"Shipyard's job number one, but the club here's job number two. It's a sweet gig."

I can't believe this. "Sweet for who? Besides the fact that everything about this is completely gross, let's look at the facts, shall we?"

"Here we go again," Jesse says. "Miss Reporter comin' out to play."

"Shut up," I say in the toad's direction, and ask Dad

my questions anyway. "What about the noise? And the type of people who'll always be hanging around outside?"

Dad pushes the U-Haul door up in one swift shove. "Listen," he says, "I don't need your mumbo-jumbo evening news crap, girlie. The way I see it, you and Jesse keep your earbuds in twenty-four-seven anyway, so noise shouldn't be an issue. And we're on the third floor, not the second, so we'll have something of a buffer. As far as safety, you two will be the only kids on Bourbon Street who'll have bouncers standing right outside your front door at all times. You'll be plenty safe, especially when I tell everyone that you're my kids."

And there it is, the one thing I knew he'd say in his feeble attempts to ease me into acceptance, but it's the last thing I need reminding of. I know I'm his kid, like I know I'm allergic to penicillin, and that dandelions make me sneeze, and that I usually had to wear a pair of shoes until my toes pinched for a good six months before he'd let Mom buy me new ones. And before I can even think to mock by repeating it with him, he throws in the only mention of love I ever hear from the man.

"Now let's get to these boxes, 'cuz you know it's not what you do that counts, it's what you do with the people you love that counts."

Dad is so far off the mark about love, it's painful. Personally, I think it's rarely ever what you do *with* the people you love that counts, but what you do *to* the people you love that counts. But when I see the sadness in my mother's eyes, I grab a box and take a deep breath. I've gotten really good at deep breathing.

Mom touches my shoulder. "I have a job lined up too, Julia. Things will be okay, you'll see."

"Seriously? A *real* job?" I ask with probably more

excitement than is appreciated.

"Yes, Julia, a *real* job."

"Where?"

When she fiddles with her ear, I know I'm not going to like the answer.

"Did Aunt Beth help you get it?"

She nods. "Yep, at the same place she works … the casino. I'm going to be a server."

"A casino? And what are they gonna make you wear for that job?"

She turns her back like she can't look at me. "What difference does it make? I know you like it that your mom's hot and not some old hag."

"I do. I'm sorry." She *is* right, after all. You *shouldn't* look like an old hag when you're only thirty-two. Yeah, my mom became a teenaged mother, not long after she met my dad. I was the accident, although she swears I was "simply the added bonus". Yeah, right—the kind of bonus responsible for the two of them not finishing high school. People usually think we're sisters instead of mother and daughter. Mom looks like me. We're both lean like a dancer, but Lord knows we couldn't afford dance classes even if I were the least bit interested. I have her blue eyes and fair skin, but my dad's black hair. Killer combo according to Mom.

But I still wish I didn't have to endure her perfect body paraded around my peers as punishment for my birth. But I suppose it *could* be worse. One poor girl at my school in Mobile has a mom who reads palms in an old FEMA trailer left over from Hurricane Katrina. Calls herself Madame Zora or something. Brutal.

"And it's not like any new friends you make will see me dressed for work, Julia," Mom adds. "I made sure of it this time. I mean, y'all aren't exactly old enough to gamble, now are you?" She winks.

Oh, but I beg to differ. Sixteen is plenty old enough to gamble. Every new move my dad makes is a gamble I'm forced into, whether she realizes it or not. Jesse and I are simply pulled right along with them. But at least she's right about one thing, it is a good chance that any new friends I make won't have to know her new occupation. Too many kids at my last school saw her waiting tables in the local Hooters with her orange micro-mini shorts and leave-nothing-to-the-imagination tank top. It was grounds for me to pop one chick in the mouth for calling her a skank. I mean, who the hell was she to judge? My mom's awesome, and she's good to me, like when I was little and she'd go inside the bank and tell the lady that her sister's kids were out in the car, too, so I'd get three free suckers instead of one. I love her to pieces.

As we start up the stairs, Dad says, "Hey, this place even has three bedrooms. It's real nice."

Now *that* I can handle. The only thing that prevented Jesse and me from sharing a bedroom at our other apartment was an old wall divider Dad scrounged from a junk room at his last job. I could hear every move my brother made, but at least I didn't actually have to *see* what he was doing. Somehow the idea of knowing what a thirteen-year-old boy is doing behind some cheap divider makes me want to gag.

Jesse chimes in. "Our own rooms, huh? Sweet."

I smile, but it's fake. I'm still trying to net the butterflies in my stomach. Sometimes I wonder what's really going on in my brother's awkward, greasy little head. But, then again, maybe it's best I don't try to figure him out. You know, that gag-reflex thing again. And, honestly, I am happy to be back in New Orleans. *Very happy.* We left here a couple of months after Aubree's disappearance. Mom said it had nothing to do with us leaving, but I know better. I'm actually shocked we're back, seeing that Mom said she'd never live in the Devil's Playground again. Well, devil or not, now I can start looking for Aubree again.

When Dad turns the key in the lock and opens the door, an odor that can only be described as road-kill hits me in the face.

"Open all the windows," he says, unaffected by the stench.

Mom and Jesse start shoving the windows up, but I just stand there, not moving. Not breathing. Everything about the display before me is wretched: the peeling paint, dirty walls, disgusting shag carpet that looks matted down by only God knows what. This is the worst place yet. I look at Dad again with one word on my tongue. "Why?"

He stands in front of me, his massive shoulders in all their glory, thanks to the white wife-beater he wears no matter the season. He shadows me like a grizzly bear, but I stand my ground.

"This is your definition of nice? Things weren't this bad in Mobile. If we can't live where we lived before, we could at least live with Aunt Beth—"

"I already told you, girlie, and I ain't explaining myself again. Now get your shit to your room and stop complaining. I've had enough of your mouth today."

I push past him and head to the small hallway. Jesse's eyeballing the room on the right, so I scoot in front of him to get a look before he claims it.

"Hey, I saw it first!" he yells.

"I'm just looking," I say.

"Let your sister see it," Mom says. "She is the oldest, after all."

"No fair," my brother replies.

I claim the room since it's a little bigger, and Jesse drags his box across the hall, making as much noise as possible.

"This room's too little," he notes.

"It's fine," Mom says.

My new room needs painting worse than the graffitied alleys in the French Quarter, but at least the smell isn't as strong in here. I try rationalizing our latest failure by picturing where my bed and desk will be. I hold tight to the knowledge that I can actually beat the streets for Aubree now, not just research everything I can about her disappearance online. I drop the box in my hand when a rat the size of a dog runs past my flip-flopped foot. I scream like a B-movie actress.

That's it!

I storm into the living room with Jesse at my heels.

"Mom, there's a rat in my room!"

"What?"

Jesse laughs in my face. "Ha, guess you picked the wrong room."

Dad shrugs his hairy, hulkish shoulders. "Don't worry about it. I'll take care of it."

"Yeah," I say, "like you take care of everything." I grab my backpack and bolt out the door before they can see the tears.

****

I'm not sure how far I've walked, but it doesn't matter. I still haven't walked long enough for the bubble in my chest to shrink. Instead, it tightens with each step, smothering me from the inside out. I know the feeling as well as my own reflection, the fear of living in a new place … again. And I hate it. As much as I've wanted to find my cousin, I don't know why it always has to be like this, living in a total dump, too embarrassed to make real friends from fear of them finding out. Aubree felt it, too, way back when. I was just a kid, but she told me everything ... until that one crazy day she just never came home. She and Aunt Beth had been living with us for about six months when it happened. I'd say that Aubree was like my sister, but that wouldn't be true. No, not a sister. She was my best friend.

You can face the same obstacle a dozen times and think you know the deal, but it's the variations that suffocate you. Always the variations. We lived in Florida, Georgia, and South Carolina when I was really little. North Carolina happened when I was eight. That's where flat-faced Cari Logan noticed the key dangling from the chain around my neck on the playground. She called me Latchkey until we moved a year later, and when we made it to Texas, I made damn sure never to expose my house key again.

Dumpster Diva was my nine-year-old nickname, although I wasn't actually in the dumpster with Dad when Margo Tillman saw him fishing out the not-too-beat-to-hell coffee table. She told everyone my house was furnished with trash. Living in New Orleans for three years after that was much better because I had Aubree. We had each other. But we left for Alabama when she went missing. I was almost thirteen then. Thank God I finally got some boobs to cover my broken heart. A pretty face and the shallowness of teens everywhere keeps me fairly okay for now. Until some random kid finds out I live above a strip joint. I can't even begin to imagine the nickname I'll be pegged with then ... don't want to imagine.

You'll graduate high school one day. Go to college. Finally be on your own. Just stick it out a little longer.

I've gotten really good at recalling Aubree's encouragements. I just wish *a little longer* didn't feel like *a lot longer*. Aubree was right. College is my only ticket out of Gypsyville, and it has to happen no matter what it takes. Thank God I have a brain, and nothing's more important than my grades. No way in hell the folks can afford higher education, so a scholarship—a broadcast journalism scholarship to be exact—is a must.

But since a news desk is still several years away, I do the next best thing: blog. I write about the different cities we move to. Reason one, because I never lack for material. Reason two, because blogging is cheaper than therapy—and it could help me find out what really happened to my cousin. She's been missing now for three years, four months, and six days. The cops stopped looking for Aubree a long time ago. I mean, a sixteen-year-old girl missing in New Orleans. That's rare, right? "A needle in a haystack" were the detective's exact words to my aunt. But, he didn't know Aubree, not like me. That girl was all about the paranormal: ghosts, vampires, voodoo curses making zombies walk among living people. She lived for it, although as much as we searched for clues that the Shadow People—that's what Aubree called them—were real, we never found any. At least, I didn't.

So I use my blog, *A Little Mystery In Between*, to dig up local mysteries in the cities we move to and try solving them. Aubree loved ghost stories—I love fact-finding. And my blog readers appreciate it. I'm up to twenty thousand followers now—twenty thousand more ways to search out what really happened to Aubree. I wipe the tear streaks from my face and pull my journal from my backpack. New Orleans—the murder capital of the country. A budding reporter's paradise. My cousin's worst nightmare.

Exhaust fumes from a bus hit me in the face, so I take a moment to familiarize myself with the surroundings.

"You gettin' on?" a woman beside me asks.

I shake my head and keep walking. I stare at every cast-iron apartment balcony I pass, most of them lined with flowers, and the quaint, inviting courtyards in front of the outdoor cafés and shops make me want to stop and go inside. My stomach growls when I catch a whiff of gumbo a man is stirring in a big pot right on the sidewalk. I wish he was giving out free samples. I'm starving. I need to find a map, get reacquainted with the city. I see someone I can ask.

"What street is this?" I ask the man. He seems like a safe informant. After all, he's standing on a silver box, and he's silver too—every inch of him. Even his eyelashes are painted. He's holding a silver guitar that looks more like a prop than something he can actually play. When he's silent, I feel stupid, like maybe he's a glitzed-up mime or something … and that I should know that. But as I'm walking away, I hear "Chartres Street."

It's almost four, and I know I should head back in the direction of the apartment, but a building up ahead catches my eye. It's nestled inside a concrete wall, and all I can see from the street are shuttered windows, like they're closed up tight in preparation of a hurricane or something. It's weird. I can't resist the urge to get a little closer.

Near the entrance is a sign that reads, *Old Ursuline Convent, New Orleans's Oldest and Most Historic Building, Erected in 1745.* Oldest? Sweet! Maybe today won't completely suck. One thing I've learned from blogging about the historical buildings I've encountered, the oldest of anything is either the most haunted, has the most secrets, or tells the most interesting story. I jot the words *Old Ursuline Convent* in my journal and pull my camera from my backpack.

"So, convent," I mumble, "what's your deal?"

But before I take the first picture, I notice another sign. You can actually tour the place, and it closes at four. Damn. I have five minutes. I speed walk through the entrance and inside the main doors. I'm hit in the face with nostalgic majesty in two seconds, disappointed that I can't look around. I spot a table with what appears to be flyers. Excellent. At least I can go back to my rat bedroom with a little reading material. People are already leaving, so I join them. But I'll definitely be back. This place is wicked awesome.

I stick the flyer in a pocket in my backpack and head in the direction I came from. After several minutes, I'm on Bourbon Street again. Then I spot the strip joint. Home Rat Home.

"Excuse me, Miss?"

"What?" I'm taken off guard. I clutch my backpack a little tighter and glance about to see exactly who's talking to me.

"I'm sorry, did I frighten you?"

My initial response is to make a smart remark, remind him that a young woman is *supposed* to practice a certain degree of caution when some old guy randomly talks to her. But I refrain after getting a good look at him. He's kind of charming, in a creepy old man sort of way. And he's seated in front of an outdoor coffee shop dressed like he stepped out of the antebellum period or something, his get-up complete with bow tie, white suit jacket and pants, and a handkerchief in his pocket. I'm surprised his shirt isn't ruffled too. How dangerous can he be?

"No, you didn't frighten me." But I glance around and make eye contact with one of the bouncers in front of my "new home" for a little added comfort. "So, can I help you with something, or—"

"Not at all, child," he replies. "I take my afternoon tea at this café on certain occasion, and I couldn't help but notice you leaving that adult establishment earlier this evening." He nods down the street. "And you were crying. Are you all right, child?"

Panic stalls my words for a second or two. He couldn't possibly think I *work* there, could he? Nervous laughter passes over my teeth before I can stop it. "Oh, you ... well, it's not what you think, sir. You see, my family and I just moved into the third floor above the club." I point to a window in our apartment. "See?"

"Oh yes." He smiles. "I do see that, and I actually feel like an old fool for asking now. I should have realized that. Sorry to have bothered you, my dear. I suppose curiosity can get the better of us from time to time, am I right?"

"It's okay." I watch the older gentleman sip his tea and can't help but feel sort of curious myself. I've never met anyone like him, the way he talks, the way he dresses, and I'm itching to know his story. Unusual people fascinate me. Yeah, I'm the girl who imagines how cool it would be to interview someone like Colonel Sanders every time my folks pull into a KFC. But I'm pretty sure my mysterious stranger wouldn't appreciate the comparison. I'll resist the urge to pull out my notebook and interview him right here on the street, but I'm not leaving without talking to him.

"So, you're not from New Orleans, are you?"

"I've lived here most of my life, child." He takes a sip of tea. "Why would you think any differently?"

"Well, for starters, you're having afternoon tea. And you really don't talk like a southerner."

"Is there something wrong with the way I talk?"

Oh crap, I've offended him. "There's absolutely nothing wrong with the way you talk. It's quite charming really."

"So you find me charming?" He winks.

"No—"

"No?"

"I mean, yes, but not in that way. I mean…"

The older gentleman breaks into raucous laughter, and I'm glad I can't see my own face this very moment. I'm sure it's red enough to taunt a bull into a full charge. This is not turning into the interview I'd anticipated. Better cut my losses while I still have a shred of dignity intact.

"Well, it was nice chatting with you, sir. Enjoy your tea."

"I will, and no more tears, okay?" he replies.

But when I start walking again, he says, "You visited the Ursuline?"

The hairs on my arms stand on end and I turn around. "How do you know that?"

"A leaflet from the convent is sticking out of your bag, dear."

There goes my last sliver of pride. "Oh, I guess I'm a little paranoid. I just moved back here." I feel like an idiot, so I add, "And I plan to be a broadcast journalist in the future, so suspicion is a fairly decent friend of mine too."

"There's nothing wrong with a healthy dose of caution. Would have kept many a young soul out of trouble in this town, I can assure you, especially when it comes to the Ursuline. My name is James, by the way."

"Julia." *The Ursuline*. Now I'm intrigued. "What do

you mean *when it comes to the Ursuline?*"

"So, you want to be a reporter, huh? Then how is it you don't know the stories regarding the convent?"

"Stories?"

His gaze never leaves my face as I sit in the empty chair beside him. "Bad things happen to those who attempt to enter its forbidden third floor. Whatever's up there wishes to remain a secret … forever."

"Whatever's up there?"

James downs his last mouthful of tea as I pull the pamphlet from my backpack. "That's just folklore, right? A ghost story?"

"Perhaps," he replies. "Perhaps not."

"I'd like to find out," I say. "A forbidden third floor? Major mysterious, and cool."

"I guess that means you don't agree with the old saying then?"

"What saying?" I ask.

"That curiosity killed the cat."

I'm positive he's senile or something at this point, but I play along. "Can't say that I do, James. I mean, if it wasn't for curiosity, there would be no discovery. Would make for a rather boring world, wouldn't you say?"

James stares dead at me and smiles for what seems like a full five seconds, nodding in agreement the entire time. "I would say you are a very bright girl. And it has been a pleasure meeting you, Miss Julia. I can't suppose it has been easy for you, seeing the area your parents have selected for your upbringing, if you don't mind me saying."

He's already said it, so I guess it really doesn't matter what I think. He's a little late for tact. But honestly, I'm not the least bit offended. I can't put my finger on it exactly, but there's something about James that lets me know he's not putting me down. I think he admires me a little, and I like it, so I simply say, "I know what you mean."

He reaches into his shirt pocket. "I want you to have something, my dear."

I can't imagine what he's about to give me, and part of me feels apprehensive, yet another part of me feels like a little kid on Christmas morning.

"Here," James says, pointing the retrieved item in my direction. "It's for luck."

The stranger hands me a pen, but not any old pen. It looks to be an old-fashioned writing pen. It has a sharp, gold-pointed tip and a cork grip. The body of the pen is wooden but painted shiny black. It is totally beautiful, and the nicest gift anyone has ever given me. "Thank you," I mutter. "It's gorgeous."

"You're welcome, child. I have to warn you, though. It hasn't held ink for years, but it was too handsome to simply toss. And besides, I like the inscription."

I examine the pen closer to see what he's referring to, and written in the shiny black wood are the words *Discretion is the better part of valour.*

"Bravery is indeed a fine trait, my dear, but it is also good to be careful. If you're careful, then you will not put yourself in situations that require bravery. Understand?"

I understand more than he could possibly know. But I say instead, "Oh, I get it. It's from Shakespeare, and it's beautiful. Are you sure you want me to have this?"

"Absolutely." He smiles. "A little luck never hurt anyone."

He reaches for my hand and I allow it. He lifts it to his mouth and his lips graze my knuckles. I notice a gold pin on his jacket pocket. It looks like a bird.

"I like your pin."

James glances at his pocket and smiles again. "Thank you. Good day, dear Julia."

"Bye, and it was nice meeting you." I tuck the pen in my pants pocket and head for the club. That sweet old man is right. A little luck is exactly what I need.

****

After a few hours, my *new* room's almost bearable. I'm glad the parental units at least thought ahead and have the Internet up and running, and that Dad bested that damned rat. My cell phone's a piece of junk. It's technically a smartphone, but we don't have a data plan, just unlimited calls and text, so I depend on my computer for everything.

"Knock, knock," Mom says, setting a can of Coke in front of me. "Looks better in here."

She stares as I take a sip of the soda. "You know, Coca-Cola was originally green."

"I know, Mom. You've told me that about a billion times." My mom's the queen of useless trivia.

"Dad's taking us for burgers later, okay? I think he's trying to make up for the smell."

"I guess." I plop in front of my dinosaur of a computer.

"You're blogging already?" Mom asks. "I figured you'd be too busy unpacking to get online tonight."

"I'm trying to see what it takes to get into Ben Franklin High," I say.

"Oh, I should've guessed that one." She smiles. "Don't be too long, okay? Dad's hungry. I better go light a fire under Jesse. I bet his boxes aren't even unpacked yet."

I nod as she leaves, then strum my fingers on my just-about-to-fall-apart desk, a nasty habit I've acquired since waiting for a slow Internet connection and an even slower computer. When I'm finally on Google, I type in *Magnet Schools in New Orleans* and wait for another eternity. After about a billion worthless pop-ups, I finally hit pay dirt: Benjamin Franklin High School, home of the Falcons. That school has produced some influential people. It would be cool to go there, so I look up the testing schedule and criteria for enrollment.

"Hey, Mom, come here again please."

She pops her head in the door. "What?"

"Ben Franklin looks amazing."

She reads over my shoulder. "Yeah, that could be the one. We'll call on Monday and see if anyone's in the office. Wish I had your smarts. I would've loved going to a school like that."

"You're smart," I remind her. "You should go to night school. Get your GED or something."

"Ha! Your dad would shoot that down real quick. And besides, you know we can't afford it."

The guilt hits me again. She really should hate me. After all, I'm the reason she lost her choices in the first place. But instead of resenting my birth, she embarrassingly goes on and on about my "good noggin" and "killer looks". Well, I definitely get my curiosity from her, and one day I'm going to do something big, something she can be a part of too. Something to make her proud.

"We'll tell Dad about that school. He'll want to know."

"God, Mom. He won't care. It wouldn't matter to him if I finished high school or flipped burgers. All he cares about is Jesse."

"That's not true, Julia."

"Is so. He's always teaching Jesse stuff and fist-bumping him and crap. All he ever says to me is, 'You better marry well, girlie. It'll make your life a hell of a lot easier someday.' He's such a Neanderthal."

"He's a man." She winks. "Get used to it."

"If I ever get used to a man like Dad, just shoot me."

When she's out the door again, I shift gears. I can't stop thinking about the convent I saw today and the old man's words about the third floor. I type the words *Ursuline Convent in New Orleans* into the search line, and tons of factual material fills the screen. But when I type *Forbidden Third Floor of the Ursuline Convent* instead, the first logline I see makes my stomach do a backflip. *Was the Murder of an Ascension Parish Woman connected to the Old Ursuline?*

Within five minutes, I've already skimmed over every story related to the lady's sadistic killing, along with a couple of advertisements for voodoo supplies and a link to a website offering low-cost spell casting for those cowardly hearts who aren't brave enough to slay their own enemy or snare their own romantic interest. *Priceless*. I keep digging.

A few more clicks and something else about the murdered lady catches my eye. Some blogger totally believes the woman fell victim to a vampire. What? This chick says the Ursuline actually houses creatures of the night. Oh yeah, I can just picture a bunch of nuns doing that. Crazy, but I mark the page in my favorites. Aubree would've eaten that information up with a spoon. But why vampires? Why *there*? Where's the evidence? I reach in the box on my desk and pull out a framed picture of Aubree. I wonder how many new blog followers I'll get if I do a story on that convent? After all, it's all about the numbers. More followers means more people I can ask about Aubree. When my eyes lock with her photo, it's settled. The Ursuline is my first mystery for New Orleans.

****

I'm going on no sleep. I've been dreading this moment since yesterday, the seconds surrounded by new kids, new snobs, new torturers. But I tuck the negative thoughts far back into my exhausted brain. I know I'm crazy fortunate, being allowed to take the entrance exam and enroll in Ben Franklin High a week before Fall registration. I try focusing on the opportunity I've been given. Still, my stomach is twisting in a million knots.

Why am I freaking out? The school's ranked sixteenth in the nation by *U.S. News and World Report*. No way the kids here are even half as shallow or reckless as the losers in my last school. I mean, it's practically the Harvard of high schools. So I remind myself that usually in life you have to do the thing that scares you most if you ever want to be somebody.

A lady with blue hair held together in an iron-clad bun gives us lucky new students a map of the school and an overview of Ben Franklin High's rich history. She's almost as exciting as watching those progress bars when you're uploading. I fiddle with my name tag and try to ignore the heat rushing up my face. My choice of a V-neck baby doll t-shirt makes it look like I have the thing stuck directly over my boob. I don't, but I still can't help but think that everyone's eyes are hitting that area when they look at me.

I try not to be too obvious as I scan the new faces, trying to distinguish who's approachable and who's so incredibly privileged that they'd never talk to someone like me. I cross two chicks off my potential new friends list straightaway when one rudely points to my shoes and cups a hand around the other girl's ear. If they're going to talk about me, they could at least practice a little discretion.

I guess I should really feel sorry for them, though. After all, shoe shopping may be the only thing they're good at. But deep down, I know that's not true. The only real difference between me and those girls is the family I was born into and the opportunities we've been given. Well, I deserve to be here, cheap shoes or not. So I take a deep breath and stare in the opposite direction.

Another new student walks up to me. "Hey, I'm Macey."

Wow, someone actually spoke to me first. Sweet.

"I'm Julia, uh, Julia Reynolds. Nice to meet you."

"Same here. Ms. Loewn's lame, am I right?"

"Seriously," I say. "I wonder what subject she teaches so I can bypass her. You know?"

"She works in the office, so we're all safe. Well, except for the tour."

I smile. I like this girl. She's tiny and at least a couple of inches shorter than me, with curly blonde hair and eyes a lighter shade of blue than mine. "So tell me, how do you know so much about the staff? You're new too, right?"

Macey smiles. "Yeah, but my mom teaches here."

"Inside connection. Outstanding. What year are you?"

"Junior. You?"

"The same. I'm surprised your mom didn't have you here your freshman year."

"I failed the entrance exam two years straight. But hey, after enough ragging and studying, I finally passed the stupid thing, so here I am. Not a total disappointment after all, huh?"

I've managed to put my bad-shoed foot directly in my mouth in the first ten minutes. Not passing the entrance exam never occurred to me, and all I can think to do is paste a big, stupid smile on my face.

"Well, Julie, looks like the Loewnator is taking the tour down the hall," Macey says.

I try biting my tongue, especially after my screw-up all of three seconds ago, but I have to say something. "It's Julia. I kind of don't like for people to alter my name. I mean—"

"Oh, my bad. No problem, Julia. Relax. It's cool."

We make our way down the hall, skimming over trophy cases, photos of school events, and the *Welcome New Students* billboard, no doubt newly constructed yesterday for our benefit. Then I notice something else— an entire wall devoted to the school newspaper, *The Franklin Forum.*

Jackpot. I stop in front of a framed issue and read the headlines. Luckily, Ms. Loewn has stopped to pass around more handouts. I scan showcased issues that have won major awards and get chill bumps.

I actually won second place in a Young Journalists Community Project myself last year. But it still chaps my ass that Lindslee Jameson beat me. The girl can't report her way out of a paper bag, which begs the burning question, exactly who did her obnoxiously wealthy father pay off so his precious little poser could win? And what was his motivation? A seat on the school board perhaps? Or maybe he's thinking of running for another public office and his daughter's accolades bode nicely for him. Or maybe the little witch simply whined until Daddy came through for her. Well, regardless, the thousand dollar first prize was awarded to her, and of course, she had to flaunt *her* new laptop. I'm sure she already had a totally fab laptop, but knowing that was what I'd intended on buying with the first-place prize money was motivation for her to purchase a newer model to shove in my face. And I acted like it didn't bother me in the least, but the truth is I'd kill to be a somebody, anybody really. And what kind of name is Lindslee, anyway?

Oh yeah, signing up for Journalism is a definite. As the group starts up again, I notice a red door with the word *Journalism* neatly scrolled on the front. I can't resist peeking inside.

And that's where I see him.

Chapter Two

I've reread the blog post saved in my favorites five times already. This chick sounds like a total nut job, claiming that murdered woman was the victim of a bloodsucker. Turns out the Ursuline Convent is littered with mystery and has been for centuries. I've heard heaps of folklore and a gazillion ghost stories since moving back to the most haunted city in the country, but the convent ranks high in the amount of people who believe the legend surrounding it. I definitely hit the jackpot for awesome fodder for my blog, and pretty soon I can start posting questions about Aubree, too. Even though it's been a few years, someone in this city has to know something about her disappearance. And who knows? Aubree may have heard rumors about that convent herself back then. I wouldn't put it past her to check it out.

"Knock, knock." Mom pokes her head in my doorway. "I'm heading to work in a few minutes. Make sure Jesse leaves enough spaghetti for your dad, okay?"

"No problem." I glance at my computer again. "Hey, Mom, you ever heard of the Ursuline Convent?"

"Yeah, sure." She fiddles with her waistband. "That place is gorgeous. It was a girls' school at one time too. It's supposedly haunted or something. Why, you blogging about it?"

"Maybe." I take in a breath. "So, tell me, Mom. Do you believe any of the hype about that place? The haunted part, or bloodsuckers on the *forbidden* third floor?"

"If you're asking if I believe in vampires, no. But if you're thinking of doing a story about it or something, I'd choose a different location if I were you."

"Why?"

"Because after all these years, no one's ever gotten even remotely close to answering all the questions about that place. Know what I mean? I've read a lot about it over the years. It's like the unsolvable mystery or something. You wouldn't want to waste your time if you're doing it for your blog."

I snicker. "Oh, come on, Mom. The unsolvable mystery? Every situation has a rational explanation—all you have to do is find it. You know what a mystery is, right?"

We say in unison, "A mystery is simply well-hidden truth."

"You know, just because no one has found out the secrets of that place yet doesn't mean they *can't* be found." I wink. "And besides, I have mad skills."

She smiles. "I love your fire, baby, but your journalism skills would have to be beyond mad to crack that place. You would be doing something that's never been done before, know what I mean?" She looks at her wrist. "Oh, shoot, I have to get outta here. See you in the morning, Julia."

"Bye, Mom."

Doing something that's never been done before. Now that I can handle. I wonder how Mom would react if I *did* figure out the story of the Ursuline? Proud wouldn't even cut it. She'd be over the moon. And who knows, Dad might even notice too. And if the Ursuline is really the unsolvable mystery, and I solve it, I'd be a legend. Then everyone would be looking for Aubree...

I type *Ursuline Convent* and click on the first link that appears. This site is more informational, so I jot a few facts into my notebook, like the convent was completed in 1752 and is the oldest surviving example of

33

the French colonial period. It's actually the oldest building on record in New Orleans and the entire Mississippi River Valley, which is also crazy cool. Today the convent is used as an Archdiocesan archive, and people can pay to tour it, which I plan to do myself very soon. But what I read next is enough to give pause to even the biggest non-believer of the paranormal. It says the third floor of the Ursuline Convent has been off limits to the public since practically forever, and each window on that floor remains secured with shutters to this day. And check this out ... each of the shutters has been nailed down with thousands of nails blessed by the Pope in an effort to keep whatever is hidden away up there hidden for good. I bookmark the site. One thing's certain, even if there are no vampires tucked away in that convent, there are definitely some secrets stashed on that third floor. I mean, if the convent's sole purpose today is to be an archive, then what reason could there possibly be to block off an entire floor? There's a mystery here, and I aim to solve it. I have to check this place out.

"Hey!"

I jump nearly two feet. "God, Jesse! You scared the crap outta me."

"Sor-ree. I was just wondering if you've reconsidered on the Blastoise card. I'll trade you one of my Venusaurs. Not gonna get a better offer than that."

Good thing my back is to him or he'd see the goofy smile stretching across my face. My little brother is still way into Pokémon cards. I was too when I was younger, and I still have a stack of cards that he just foams at the mouth to snag from me. I really should give them to him, seeing that I'm really only sentimental about a couple of cards. But they hold too much bargaining power with the little disease—can get the little beast to do just about anything for the right card. Perfect timing.

"I'll tell you what, Jess. Agree to go somewhere with me right now, and I'll give you that Blastoise card. How's that for a deal?"

"Go where? Oh God, you're not already stalking some guy, are you?"

"Listen, troll bait, do you want the card or not?"

He sighs. "Yeah, I want it. So where are we going?"

"To that old convent on Chartres Street. It's only a few blocks from here. We don't have to go inside, I just want to get a good look at it and take a few pictures."

Jesse's eyes widen with revelation. "Hey, I know why you want to go there. I heard about the third floor. It'll be dark in a little while, and I wouldn't be caught dead snooping around that place at night. No way … not me."

Epic fail.

"Listen, we have a good hour before it gets dark, Jess. And if we leave now, I can snap a few pictures, and then we'll be back here in a flash. Come on, I really need to start some research on it, okay? And you're not actually scared to look at the place at night, are you? FYI, Mom said it's gorgeous."

"Well, scared or not, I'm not standing around that place at night. And if I do this with you, I think you need to throw in your Charizard card, too."

I knew the little dirt bag would go for the throat. Well, that's the deal breaker. My Charizard was always my favorite, and he's not getting his grimy little hands on it. "The offer was for Blastoise, but if you don't want it, then I guess I'll go alone."

"All right, I'll go. But I mean it. We're not hanging around that place after dark."

I can't control the smile that makes him grimace. "Deal."

"Just let me grab my game."

I retrieve a couple of extra batteries and my camera, then scribble a note for Dad. Good thing Mom works 'til the wee morning hours. She wouldn't be too thrilled about us venturing off this close to night time. That's why I didn't mention it to her before she left. And I feel a little guilty. I mean, something like this would practically have her drooling for every teeny tiny detail, but I really can't think about that now. I'll tell her more after I get pictures of the place. Oh yeah, I'm crazy excited to get another look at it.

"Hurry up, Jesse! Let's go!"

****

I yank Jesse by his shirt collar when I finally make it across the street. Why that boy can't use the crosswalks properly, I'll never know. Reason number four thousand and fifty for never wanting to go anywhere with him.

"What's your problem?" he says when I tug his shirt a little harder.

"You jumping in front of a moving car that has the right-of-way—that's my problem. Why do you have to do that? What are you, some kind of adrenaline junkie … or just a total moron?"

"God, Julia, unclench your butt cheeks for once. I mean, the way I see it, they can do one of two things— hit me or stop. My money's on the stopping every time."

I shake my head. What the little maggot doesn't understand is that I have weighed the options, and I just happen to be that person who questions why people are so trusting in a world filled with every imaginable reason not to trust anyone or anything at any time. And we trust at the most vulnerable moments, like crossing in front of a once-moving car at the slightest nod and wave of approval from the driver—a perfect stranger. What if that non-assuming person behind the wheel is really a psychopath? I'll tell you what … the once-trusting soul that crosses in front of that car would be dead, that's what. It never ceases to amaze me how we make ourselves such easy targets.

"So, where is this place?" Jesse asks, barely peeking over the screen of his video game. "Shouldn't we be there?"

"Cross the next street and keep walking. We'll turn a corner on the right and practically be in front of it."

"Great," he mumbles. "Freakin' third floor."

We keep a steady pace, but it seems like an eternity before I finally see the off-white cement of the convent. Chill bumps flood my arms immediately, but I ignore the creepy feeling now threatening my composure, and I aim my camera at the old building.

"This place even looks like it could be a vampire nest," Jesse says, slipping his game in his pocket and backing up to get a better look over the cement wall blocking our view of the bottom floor.

"And I guess you're an expert on vampire nests, huh?" I grin at him. "There's no such thing as vampires, Jess."

He nudges my shoulder. "I know, but it's still creepy. I mean, something has to be up there. Just hurry and take your stupid pictures. This place is creeping me out."

"This place is beautiful," I rebut. "Your imagination is what's creeping you out."

"Even so, just do what you have to so we can go."

"Wuss." But I know he's right. I need to hurry before it gets dark and my pictures are nothing but crap. Jesse leans against a lamppost, trying to act disinterested, but I know the boy better than that. Even though he'd rather eat a cockroach than admit it, he's curious. I think it runs in the family.

After a couple of minutes, I've already snapped several shots, first of the entire backside of the convent, then of different sections. I take a few pictures of a small second-story balcony and of a cross neatly positioned in the center of it all. But after the teaser shots, I focus on what I really came for—those third-floor shuttered windows.

"What do you see?" Jesse asks, glancing up from his game.

I shake my head. "I see a convent." *Dork.* "What do you think I see? A night crawler? A bloodsucker?"

"The way you're going to town with that camera, I thought maybe you were seeing something."

"I came to take pictures of the place, Jess. Let me finish up and then we'll go, okay?"

I start snapping the first shuttered window, zooming in as much as possible before any distortion becomes visible. I can actually see the nails, so I click the button wildly, getting as many shots as possible. I do the same with each one, hoping maybe I can blow up the pictures even more once I load them on my computer. I hate it that we can only see the back of the building from the street. I know from the photos I've discovered on a few search engines that there's this gorgeous maze-type garden in front of the convent, and even more third-floor windows on that side. You can bet your butt I'll be touring this place this weekend. I want to see it all. I point my camera to the last window on this side and press the zoom button. As I start my shots, I notice a slight gap in the shutter, as if someone on the inside had opened it just enough to peek out. I jump before I can calm myself. But luckily, my finger is still feverishly snapping away.

"What is it?" Jesse says. "You saw something this time, didn't you?"

"No, I thought I felt a bug on my leg."

"Liar."

I ignore my shaking hands and try steadying the camera. My eyes had to be playing tricks. That shutter wasn't really open a crack a second ago, was it? Maybe I'm losing it. Still, I can't wait to get a better look at my pictures. "I'm done, Jess. Let's go."

****

The street noise and chaos right outside my window is cranked into high gear, but I ignore it. Who would've thought a couple of weeks ago I would be practically immune to the insanity that frequents my doorstep? But surprisingly, I can block it from my existence like a punk on Facebook. Yes, I amaze myself.

I finish the last two sentences of my homework and then plug the cord for my camera into the USB slot in my dinosaur, making the poor sucker groan. My dad found the digital camera still in the case in a home he was remodeling at his last job. I was surprised when he gave it to me instead of selling it, but Mom convinced him that I really needed it for school. I love the camera, but I can't wait until I have a real computer. It takes a while, but my pictures finally load and I scroll through them as quickly as my ancient system will allow, until I'm staring at the ones of *that* window—the one with the slightly-opened shutter. Or so I thought. I zoom in on the photos almost to the point of distortion, and I still don't see the crack I would have bet my life was there this afternoon. This stupid shutter looks as tightly nailed down as the others. *Damn.* But I can't really say I'm that surprised—after all, my life has made me well-suited for disappointment.

Even though I'd been busting to get the pictures

loaded and scrutinized, I have no problem hitting the minimize button in light of my newest frustration. Why am I not seeing something that was so obvious to me a few short hours ago? Something doesn't add up. I pull out my notebook and jot down the few facts I *can* nail down, even if they make about as much sense as bowling in high heels. I need to know more, anything that will get me a little closer to the truth about the Ursuline, and that starts with a tour of the place. It would help to have a schedule.

My fingers fly over the keyboard, and in a few seconds I have *Ursuline Convent Tours in New Orleans* typed into Google. My eyes scan the choices of links for tour times when three words grab my attention like a thunderclap through a library: *Ursuline Intern Murders.* Chills tickle my arms as I click the link:

Two female interns for a local news station made a snap decision with disastrous results when they chose to stake out the Ursuline Convent on May 14, 1973. After touring the historic building and having been denied their request to see what was housed on the infamous third floor, the young ladies remained hidden on the premises after hours. They were found by a groundskeeper at sunrise the following morning, their lifeless bodies placed and overlapping on the front steps of the convent. Their wounds resembled simple scratches between their shoulder blades, but what baffles investigators to this day is the fact that nearly ninety percent of the blood had been drained from the victims, a scientific impossibility. Researchers are no closer to an explanation to this day, and the murders remain unsolved.

I sit up straighter, my head spinning like I've just exited a monster rollercoaster. Two women were actually murdered—and their blood was drained. There has to be an explanation, but what? Maybe some sicko was hanging out there after hours, lying in wait for his next victims. Those ladies made themselves easy prey … simple targets. But it did say that their only visible wounds were mere scratches, right? And investigators came up empty-handed, even to this day? It doesn't make sense. But I jot all the facts in my notebook anyway and mark the link in my favorites. This story just keeps getting juicer, and I'm not stopping 'til I taste the pulp.

In two seconds I'm staring at the photo of that shuttered third-floor window again. How could I have been so wrong this afternoon? Maybe I was so worked up that I *wanted* to see something, anything to validate my reasoning for dragging my unwilling brother and my own stupid ass on a wild goose chase. But then, I notice something, something I didn't see earlier. Blown up three times its size, there is a slight variation in the color of the line that runs down the center of the shutters. It's subtle, but it's there. It's a crack. I'm sure of it. And it's only in this photograph. Something had to make that crack, or someone. But who?

I lean back in my desk chair, exhausted from my own imagination and tiring search for answers. "Get a grip," I mumble when the chills pop over my arms again. "There has to be a logical explanation. All you have to do is find it."

Chapter Three

I'll never keep the cereal down, but I stick the spoon in my mouth anyway. I like breakfast, but I have to get used to eating this early again now that school's started. It was fine when I could sleep 'til ten and eat whenever, but waking up at six is torture. But I shove another bite in my mouth and hope for the best.

"Well, that's just great," Jesse says as his toast hits the floor. "And I don't even have time to make another piece. I'm late as it is."

"Better pick it up quick," Mom replies. "You know, Turkish people consider it unlucky to step on a piece of bread."

I tilt my cereal bowl and finish off the milk to hide my smile. I wonder how long she's been waiting to use that one.

"God, Mom," Jesse says. "It's probably just unlucky because some flaming moron dropped his bread. The fact that some Turk actually stepped on it doesn't mean crap."

"Well, maybe not, but I still think it's funny. And it made your sister smile." She flashes me a thumbs-up and then tosses a Pop Tart in his direction as he reaches the door. "Have fun on your first day, son, and hurry up or you'll miss the bus."

Mom turns to me when Jesse's out of sight. "Do you believe the mouth on that one? Smartbutt little wise guy." She shakes her head. "So what's your story?"

"No story, my school starts forty-five minutes later than his, that's all."

"All right. Well, if you don't mind, I'm going to lay down. Pulled an all-nighter 'cuz another girl called in sick."

"It's fine, Mom. I'll see you this afternoon."

She heads down the hallway but I can still hear her muffled words, "And give 'em hell today, chica."

Wanna know the sad thing? She truly believes with every fiber of her soul that I *can* give 'em hell. She has no idea that I'm secretly terrified by practically everything, like making friends, or making enemies, or making a complete fool of myself. I've had more "first days" in a single school year than most kids have in three, but I never get used to it. I hate first days.

****

Fortunately, Macey's waiting for me as I approach the front of the school, and I take my first real breath since stepping off the bus. It's always easier when you're not alone. I'm sure Macey feels the same way, otherwise she wouldn't be waiting around for me. And she has to know that she'll have whispers floating around about her, too—the teacher's daughter who failed the entrance exam two years in a row. That can't be easy, but she's likable and pretty, so it shouldn't last too long. Thank God for shallowness.

"Hey, Julia. I think we have our first class together."

I glance at my schedule. "I have English, Ms. Harper."

"Me too. Come on, I'll show you where her room is. We'll sit together, unless she assigns seats. That would suck. And listen, did you—"

Macey is one of those people my Aunt Beth would call a chatterbox, but I like it. She lightens the situation, keeps me from thinking about all the things that would be running through my head right now had I remained alone. And she knows the layout of the premises, another plus. This day might turn out decent after all.

Inside Ms. Harper's class, the walls are brightly

painted and cheery. A mock staircase decorates the back wall, and calligraphy-printed quotes from classic novels stretch from the bottom of the staircase to the top, ending with the phrase, "None of these authors would have climbed a single step toward immortality without proper English". High appreciation for the written word? I feel welcomed immediately. I choose a seat near the back so I can read the quotes.

"A back-row chick too, huh? Cool." Macey plops down beside me, and I smile. I almost tell her that my reason for sitting in the back is majorly cooler than hers, but I say nothing instead. She talks enough for the two of us anyway.

"Oh God, don't look now," Macey says, poking my arm and pointing at the door.

Why is she telling me *not* to look when I know she'll mutilate my arm if I don't? "So what am I not looking at?"

"Not *what*, *who*." She nods her head toward three girls. "That's Hannah Parker and the beyotches from hell. I hate those girls like vomit."

"How do you know them?" I try sounding more interested than I really am.

"Everyone knows Hannah. Her dad has more money than Bill Gates, and that chick on her left, that's Kimmie Jones. She follows Hannah around like a puppy dog. She's your typical clique girl—a poser to the extreme, if you ask me. Yep, nothing but air between those triple-pierced ears. No one's going to convince me that her dad's money didn't get her in this school. It's sad, really."

I shrug and read the wall quotes again. At least I know who to avoid now, but Macey didn't really elaborate on the third girl in the threesome, the one who was carrying such a behemoth purse that her posture resembled a blonde Quasimodo. "Well, what about her? What's her story?"

"Oh, that's Jasmine Seymour, but I don't really know a lot about her. She's a Hannah clone, and that's reason enough to hate her. I mean, why in the hell would anyone want to be Hannah? It's sick, really. And after the way she treated poor Ryan—"

Now I *am* intrigued. "Poor who? Ryan?"

Macey sighs and glances at the wall clock, obviously hoping she has time to dish out the dirt before the teacher starts class. "So here's the deal. Ryan Grandle is like the hottest guy in this school."

Doubt it. I saw the hottest guy in this school in the Journalism room.

"Hannah dated Ryan for like a year or something. But right before school let out last spring, he caught her in the field house making out with some jock. Just walked right in on them from what I heard. If you ask me, she'd have to be completely mental to cheat on him. Too much hair dye must've leaked in her ears and fried her brain or something. Anyway, you'd be smart to steer clear of that group. Wouldn't want to be infected."

I turn and focus on the back wall again. I can't help but smile. I mean, here's this chick— the one who actually waited for me to get to school this morning— warning *me* to stay away from the richest girl in school and her BFFs. I wonder what she'd say if she knew I was practically a gypsy, and my mom serves drinks in a way-too-low-cut top and a barely-there mini every night, and my dad is a weekend bouncer at a strip joint that I live two floors above? And that all I've wanted for a few years now is to find out what really happened to my missing cousin who's still considered a runaway? The irony makes my skin all prickly and I rub my arms. I face the front when the teacher starts talking and I make up my mind before she finishes her first sentence. To have any real chance of surviving this place, no one can find out where I live, or anything at all about the folks. Period.

****

I stand in front of the Journalism room and touch the red door like I'm about to enter a shrine. I'm actually glad Macey doesn't have this class, otherwise my ears would still be aching from her constant talking. My stomach is in a zillion knots, which is weird because I've actually been looking forward to this class since signing up last week. I breathe to release some of the tightness in my chest and step inside.

"Welcome, and take a seat anywhere." The teacher smiles. "You must be Julia Reynolds."

"That's right." I glance at the new faces around me, not recognizing anyone from my other classes. I sit in the second row and open my notebook.

"Well, for Julia's benefit, I'll introduce myself. I'm Ms. Dunkin, your Journalism teacher and sponsor of our award-winning newspaper, *The Franklin Forum*. You're our only new sign-up this year, Julia, and we're very glad to have you. From what I've read in your application, you're quite the budding reporter. And we love your blog, don't we, class?" She winks.

I feel a rush of heat flood my face, but I manage a smile and slight nod. *They've read my blog.*

"Now, if everyone would take a moment to fill out the sheets I'm about to pass around, that would be great. I need to know your focus for the paper this semester, whether it be reporting, photography, layout, or ad selling. And, Julia, why don't you take a moment to look through some of our past issues on the back table there? It'll give you an idea of what we're about."

She's way cool and actually treating us like adults. Oh yeah, Journalism rocks. A girl touches my arm when I pass her desk.

"Your blog is crazy intense. I love it." She's looking at me like I'm a rock star.

"Thank you." I practically float to the table as instructed and start thumbing through the newspapers.

"What'd I miss?" a guy's voice fills the room, and I lose my breath when I look up. I know it's him immediately.

"You didn't miss anything," Ms. Dunkin says when he drapes an arm over her shoulder. "Just fill out the sheet on your desk."

I'm not sure why I feel embarrassed. It's not like the hottest guy I've ever laid eyes on knows I'm recalling seeing him in here at registration, or that he's even vaguely aware I exist.

The words *don't stare* keep running through my brain. I crumple in my seat, as if crouching somehow makes the fact that I'm eyeing him from head-to-toe less obvious, then I peek over the edge of the newspaper. He's an Adonis in ripped black jeans and a button-front Old Navy shirt. His blond spiky hair and long bangs draped to one side remind me of an anime character, and his face is so perfect I should be staring at it between the pages of some teen heartthrob mag rather than slits between my limp hair and old newsprint. He's muscular, like a football player or something, but I saw him in here during registration and not in the field house with the other jocks. And he's here now, so he obviously does something with the school newspaper. God, who is this guy?

"Now," Ms. Dunkin says, "I'm going to break you up into groups according to your preferences." She glances my way. "You can keep browsing through our old issues, Julia. I know you signed up to be one of our reporters. You'll join Jordan's group in a few minutes." She points to a slender, average-looking girl who cracks me a half-smile and raises her hand slightly.

"But being a part of *The Franklin Forum* is more than just reporting and layout," Ms. Dunkin continues. "We also need advertisers to help defray the costs of production, so I want all of you who are interested in selling ads to join this fine gentleman right here."

She claps the shoulder of Mr. Hottie himself when a couple of kids whistle like he's a god or something. I look his way too now that I have public permission. So he sells ads for the newspaper. Makes sense. I'd buy anything he was selling. But before I can give him a full once-over yet again, I lose my breath. He's headed to the back table, straight toward me.

I sit up a little straighter, burying my nose in a paper again. Why do I feel like he knows I've been staring? Duh, because I *have* been staring. My pounding heart is crushing my chest from the inside out. I just hope I land in a graceful position when I keel over from the blows.

He leans slightly over the table when he reaches me and retrieves a couple of newspapers from the stack.

"Do you mind?" He flashes a ready smile.

I shake my head, pretending to be way too interested in the paper in my hands.

"So you really don't mind?" he asks again.

I wave a hand toward the stack, still focusing on the newsprint practically shoved up my nose.

He laughs. "Good thing this isn't our first date because this would be the spot where the awkward silence comes in."

My head pops up before I can stop it.

He smiles. "Gotcha."

I know I'm grinning like a big, goofy dork, but I can't control it. He actually made an effort to talk to *me*. The smile that's already making my cheeks ache gets even bigger and I look at him again before continuing my reading.

I make my way to the clump of desks reserved for the potential reporters when Ms. Dunkin tells everyone to pull out their notebooks. I force myself not to glance in Mr. Major Hottie's direction.

Ms. Dunkin asks, "What is the number one rule a good reporter must follow?"

"Always look for the story," the class repeats in unison. I move my lips like I know the answer too, falling victim to my dorkiness yet again.

"That's right," she says. "A good reporter always looks for the story. And I'm not referring to *a* story—a story is easy to find. There are stories all around us. No, what I'm referring to is *the* story, the one that requires you to dig deeper and search harder. I want you to look for the story that forces you take risks, obliges you to search your soul because that's where you'll find the passion to make it happen."

Chill bumps form on my arms immediately. God, she's so cool. I glance to see the other students' reactions, knowing that we're seated before sheer genius. The girl to the left of me is yawning. Yawning? I shake my head. She notices and throws me a look. I swear, if her eyes were blades, I'd be dead right now. How can she not realize how privileged she is to be in this class?

"Who can give me some examples in history where a reporter would have taken huge risks to get the story?"

A girl with dark hair and a mouthful of braces raises her hand. "From the onset of settling the colonies, a reporter trying to communicate with the Indians would have taken a huge risk for the story."

"Very good," Ms. Dunkin says. "That's exactly what I'm talking about. Anyone else?"

The eye-blade thrower raises her hand. This should be interesting.

"Yes, Holly."

"During the witch trials in Salem, a reporter trying to interview the girls accused of witchcraft would have taken a big risk talking to them. I mean, she could've been burned at the stake, too."

Well, Miss Yawning-Death-Stare had a good thought, but she's wrong about one thing. I raise my hand so high at first that I immediately lower it so as not to be too obviously enthusiastic.

"You have something to add about Holly's statement, Julia?"

"Yes, ma'am, I do. I agree that it would have been quite risky to interview those accused of witchcraft in Salem, but I can guarantee that a reporter would not have had to worry the least bit about being burned at the stake."

"Oh, really?" Holly folds her arms across her chest. "And why is that?"

I offer Holly a smile, hoping she's not too ticked that I spoke up. "Because none of the accused were ever burned at the stake in Salem. That is one of the largest misconceptions in history. There were twenty unfortunate souls executed for witchcraft in Salem, and nineteen of those people were hanged. The last one was pressed to death with large rocks placed on his chest until he was crushed of air—"

She cuts me off again. "Well, I know people were burned at the stake for practicing witchcraft."

"They were," I say, "but that happened in Europe during the Inquisition, not in Salem."

I can't help but glance in Mr. Hottie's direction after my spurt of brilliance. He knits his eyebrows together, then mouths the word *nice*. Oh yeah, he's impressed.

"Excellent fact-checking, Julia," Ms. Dunkin says. "I can already tell you're going to be a valued addition to the class. Now, let's talk about another—"

My thoughts fly in several directions at once, making it impossible to focus on her next pearls of wisdom. The hottest guy ever is conversing with me, the coolest teacher on the planet thinks I'm valuable, and I'm already investigating my equivalent of what Ms. Dunkin would consider *the story*. Yeah, I know vampires are totally bogus, but I can't shake the feeling that someone's hiding something on that third floor.

I gather my notebook and pen when the bell sounds and head for the door. That Holly girl scoots past me and bumps my shoulder pretty hard in her hasty exit.

"Oh, sorry," she says, giving me a good head-to-toe once-over, obviously still ticked that I'd corrected her in front of God and everybody.

I rub the spot on my shoulder. "No problem."

"Don't worry about her," a guy's voice says from behind, and I know it's the hottie even before I turn around.

"Hey, Holly," he calls to her. "What's the matter? You need some water for that burn?"

"Stick it, Ryan!" she yells back.

"Ryan," I mumble, something about that sounding familiar.

"Yeah," he says. "I'm Ryan ... uh, Ryan Grandle."

Ryan Grandle? Then it hits me. *Oh crap.*
****

Do I even dare to believe it for a second? This never happens. *But it did.* The hottest guy in school spoke to me, the girl with the way-too-dark-hair and thrift-store clothes. There has to be a catch, so I replay the facts in my still-whirling brain.

Fact number one: Ryan came to the back table and spoke to me first, but he did need to get a couple of newspapers. He was probably just being polite. But polite or not, he didn't have to joke with me or make the date reference. He didn't have to speak to me at all, truth be told. Fact number two: He mouthed the word *nice* after I put that Holly chick in her place, and actually pointed out that I burned her right to the girl's face. Maybe he really hates Holly, but then again...

I can't hold back the smile teasing my lips. The reporter in me knows exactly what the facts point to— that the hottest guy in school is interested in me, and I've decided to just go with it. I can't wait to get home this afternoon and talk to Mom. I'm dying to tell someone my theory about Ryan—that he actually likes me. I know I'm acting like a twelve-year-old girl crushing over the unattainable, but I really don't care. It's nice to feel good about something for a change, even if deep down I know Ryan Grandle wouldn't ask me out in a gazillion years.

"Aren't you going to eat anything?" Macey asks, her eyes focused off to the side instead of looking directly at me.

"I am eating," I say. No way I'm telling Macey about Ryan, so I unfold my schedule instead and check the room number for my next class. Fortunately, the cafeteria food at Ben Franklin is better than the nuclear waste they served at my last school, so I'm not lying about eating.

"Anyone in your classes so far look dateable?" Macey looks at me with a little too much enthusiasm, but I play along.

"Potentially." Definitely all I'm willing to divulge at the moment. "You?"

"I've scoped out a few prospects, but I'm still eager to see what the afternoon holds. But there was this one guy—"

It's hard to think through Macey's constant chatter, but somehow I manage. As grateful as I am for her friendship, I'll never again underestimate the value of a good set of earplugs.

"Oh my God, he is *so* walking straight toward us right now," Macey manages through a mouthful of pasta.

"Who?" But I see the who in question before I barely get the word out.

"Ryan Grandle, the guy I told you about—the one that Hannah the Witch cheated on, that's him. He is so hot." She leans into me. "And he is looking right at us. Oh God, he's coming over here."

I glance back to the schedule in my hands, and I know my face is red even before Macey declares it. Ryan is coming over to talk to *me*, not *us*. My thoughts drift to his first-date reference again, but I dismiss the notion as soon as I think it.

"Hi there, Miss Witch Trials," he says when he reaches our table. "Julia, right?"

"Right." I point toward my now not-so-talkative friend. It's amazing what a little shock can do. "And this is Macey."

"Hi," she replies, adding a mini-wave.

"I can honestly say I've never seen anyone put Holly in her place like that," Ryan says. "And I never thought the new girl would be the one to do it. So tell me, Jules—

"

"It's Julia," Macey jumps in. "She hates it when—"

"It's okay," I say through clenched teeth and totally in Macey's face. She should know that Ryan Grandle can call me anything he wants.

"Oh, I see how you're gonna be now." Macey grins so wide her face might actually crack. "Whatever."

He gives us a questioning look and then smiles more coyly than any little boy ever could. "Well, anyway, it was cool. I just wanted to tell you that. So, I guess I'll see you in class tomorrow."

"You bet," I say. But at the moment I think he should turn and walk away, he looks right at Macey.

"So, beautiful, what's your story? You new here, too?"

"Absolutely," Macey says. "My mom teaches here, so you and I have actually met."

"Oh, yeah," he says. "In the school parking lot that time, right?"

"Right," Macey says, looking more pleased than a bird at a worm wrestle. It's hard to watch.

They chat a few more seconds, and then Ryan makes his exit.

"He is so fine," Macey says.

"Yeah," I add, feeling like a complete idiot. No, an idiot wrapped in a moron. I should've guessed he was a ladies' man, should've known there was no way in hell he'd really be interested in me.

"All right, start talking. I need details. You didn't tell me you met Ryan this morning. Good God, talk about a totally fab first day. Now spill it. What did you do to … who was it … Holly?"

"There's nothing to spill. He's in my Journalism class, that's all."

"Oh, yeah? Well, if that's all, then why is your face so red, huh? If you ask me, you like him."

I don't need her adding to my self-loathing. I say the only thing that comes to mind. "He has potential." I bury my nose in my schedule again.

"Potential? Girl, please. See that guy over there in the blue polo? Him, the one with the brown, not-so-great hair but nice face? *He* has potential. Ryan, on the other hand, he's the entire package and then some. That guy is beyond fine." Macey glances at her phone. "Hey, we better get going. Bell's gonna ring soon."

I gather my things and make my way to the large metal counter and garbage cans to discard my remaining food, tray, and silverware. No way I'm ever being that gullible again, no matter how good Ryan looks in those jeans.

LEE ANN WARD

Chapter Four

"Shadow People? Like those dark, shadowy figures people say are ghosts?"

"No," Aubree replied that day. "Like those guys who staked out the vampire coven above that bar in the French Quarter last week. They call themselves Shadow People. They're really like paranormal investigators or something."

"Vampire coven?" I was doubtful.

"Well, it turned out to only be a few guys who slept in coffins and drank pig's blood, but they're self-proclaimed vampires. Still kinda cool, don't you think?" Aubree's hazel eyes were lit with wonder, and I loved her passion for folklore and mythology, how animated she was when we talked about it. God, I miss her.

I push my thoughts aside and shove my camera in my backpack. I plop on the couch and pull my shoes on.

"You're going where?" Mom's hanging on my every word. Yeah, she lives for juicy details when it comes to stuff like this. I swear, she's the only woman on the planet who's disappointed not to be called for jury duty.

"I'm going to the Ursuline Convent," I say. "I'm following up on the research I've started. I told you about it, remember?"

"Okay, well, if you're going against my better judgment, then you better tell me everything you figure out. I guess it will be cool to write about, huh? You know, I read that the windows are all nailed shut or something, and no one is allowed on the third floor. I wonder what's really up there. Can you imagine?"

Oh, I can imagine plenty, like every other thrill seeker and monster hunter who I'm sure has added their own version to the mystery surrounding that place. But I'm leaving my imagination at the door. All I want are the facts—the truth behind that historical building and those intern murders I stumbled across a few days ago. I want the *real* story.

Mom gets serious. "Please tell me you're not going to try anything stupid, like sneaking up to that third floor."

"God, Mom. I'm taking the tour, that's it. I'm not a total loon, you know. But speaking of loons, you and Dad are the ones who dragged us back to Looneyville in the first place, remember? Did you really expect someone like me not to check out all the twisted tales our fine city offers?"

And besides, I haven't devised a plan to get on that third floor yet.

Mom looks at me with inquisitive eyes and I'm sure she's about to spurt her version of brilliance. "There's a city in West Virginia that is actually called Looneyville, you know."

Figures.

"And no, I'm not the least bit surprised that you want to go check out some old convent on a Saturday morning. You are so different than I was at your age, Julia."

Yeah, at my age, you were pregnant. But I don't say it. I actually feel like a jerk for thinking it. At least she's interested in my day-to-day stuff.

"You put your camera in your bag ... do you have your notebook?"

"I have it, Mom. Thanks." Yep, I'm a total jerk.

"Yeah, I remember one time when you were little, your dad drove us down some back road we'd never traveled before, and it ended at this great little stream where there were these little purple flowers. They were gorgeous. You got so mad because you didn't have your pink notebook so you could write all about it. Do you remember that, honey?"

I wish I did, but I don't. "No, I'm sorry." It always makes me feel like dirt when Mom recalls an incident that I have no recollection of. It's actually hard to recall any childhood memories after Aubree disappeared, yet I remember things she and I did like it was yesterday. Once she and I walked to her new boyfriend's house. I'd never met him, and Aubree was all excited to introduce him to her "cool little cuz." She kept bragging that he was seventeen and had his own car. When we got to his place, he was in the yard trying to spray paint the undercarriage of his rusted out junk heap.

"You're not supposed to use spray paint on a car!" Aubree squealed, falling to the leaf-covered ground in a heap. It was fall, and the leaves were different hues of orange, yellow, and burnt browns. I watched as she laughed and rolled in the leaves, her long, auburn hair collecting a few stray leaves in her levity. She was beautiful that afternoon, and exactly who I wanted to be some day.

"Does the tour cost anything?"

"Huh?" I say.

"You were a million miles away," Mom says. "The tour, does it cost anything?"

"Oh, I have it, Mom. Don't worry about it."

She reaches in her jeans pocket. "Here, take this ten in case you want to go to McDonald's or something."

"Thanks, Mom. I appreciate it."

"Just be careful. You sure you don't want to take your brother?"

I grimace. "Very sure."

She smiles and heads into the kitchen. "All right, and I expect to hear all the sordid details when you get back, okay?"

"You got it."

I shove my phone in my pocket and put the chain with my apartment key around my neck, making sure to hide it inside my shirt before slinging my backpack on my shoulder. I've been so excited about touring the convent. I hope it lives up to my expectations. At least Mom's stoked about it.

****

Not sure why I'd pictured Shirley MacLaine playing a nun in that old Clint Eastwood movie when imagining what the tour guide would look like, but man, was I off. *Way off.* Our guide's a dude in dull khakis and a simple polo shirt. It's brutally disappointing, especially after he introduces himself as Steve and establishes that the Sisters of Ursula who'd once inhabited the Ursuline moved uptown in 1824 and have remained there ever since. I'm totally bummed but simply toss aside my misguided illusion of faithful nuns protecting the secret third floor and pull out my notebook instead. I need answers, so old Steve-O here will just have to do.

As disenchanted as I am about the non-existent nuns, the place in general doesn't disappoint. I will admit it seems to be nothing like the folklore that's bombarded me since moving here. Instead, it's the perfect combo of gorgeous and creepy. And not a scary creepy, but a nostalgic kind of creepy that comes in knowing you're strolling through something bigger than yourself. This place has existed throughout New Orleans's history as a silent observer, and I'd give anything to make it talk. But as hard as I wish it, the walls can't grow lips, so I focus once again on our guide.

Within ten minutes of the tour, Steve establishes that the Sisters were the first of many orders of religious women to arrive in the mud-hole that was the early colony of New Orleans in 1727. They founded schools, orphanages, and the convent itself here was once a school for girls, just like Mom said. *Interesting.* He talks endlessly about a nun who had a knack for medicine-making and actually grew herbs that later led her to be the first pharmacist in the United States. He describes how the nuns shaped the minds of many young women who graced these walls and how they saved countless lives in the colony itself, but I want desperately for the guy to describe something else. I'm waiting for the opportune moment to engage our guide to talk about the impossible things … the very existence of monsters lying in wait on a nailed-tight floor above us.

Steve continues the tour, explaining that the Ursuline is known as the treasure of the Archdiocese because it was the only building to survive a huge fire in 1788. The fire had swept through town and burned every structure but the convent. I write down the info and pay attention again as he stops in front of a huge glass case filled with old rosaries, brass-looking cups, and other churchy things. This stuff is cool, but not my reason for being here. Sooner or later, I'm asking about that third floor and the dead interns.

"You'll see that we have several religious artifacts and a few miscellaneous items here," Steve says, pointing to the stuff in the glass cases in front of us. "These pieces are well-preserved, and for the most part, were the personal items of the nuns. This particular rosary is over 250 years old and belonged to Sister Eugena—"

I'm trying to pay attention, but something else in the case catches my eye—and it doesn't look like anything that would ever belong to a bunch of nuns. It must've belonged to one of the girls, one of the students. It's a silver brush and mirror set, and it's old and amazing. I'm not sure I've ever seen anything as romantic, well, except for maybe my old fountain pen. I pull it out for a moment and glance at the inscription. Not sure why it makes me feel braver when I look at it, especially when the verbiage clearly instructs me to practice caution. But it's my good luck charm, and I'll be the one determining its purpose. I tuck the pen in my bag and pull out my camera instead. I snap a few close shots of the brush and mirror set before engaging in Steve's words again.

After several minutes, we move on and enter a new area, stopping in front of a wide, wooden staircase. My skin tingles. This is it, what I've been waiting for. I know we won't actually tour the third floor, but even the slightest, most dismal peek at it from the second would thrill me to the bone at this point. Just give me something—anything. But my enthusiasm is quickly shredded when buzzkill Steve makes one point very clear: the tour is restricted to the bottom floor only. *Crap.*

"Ugh, Mama, I wanna go up there," a little boy says, tugging his mom's shirt and pointing to the stairs.

"I know, honey, but we have to do what the man says," she whispers.

Well, maybe she and *honey* have to do what he says, but not me. I'm not sure how yet, but I'm going up those stairs before I leave here today. It's way too tempting. I mean, they're not even roped off or anything, just exposed for the climbing. But then I notice those velvety-looking ropes like the ones in the teller lines at banks, although they've been pushed aside for some reason. Someone has to be up there. Well, the way I see it, if a tourist takes a notion to go upstairs, then it's the convent's fault, really—should have taken better preventative measures.

Then it hits me! I wonder if the third floor's simply

blocked with cheap teller-line knock-offs, too? No way. It couldn't be that easy to get up there, could it? Well, I'll know soon enough. My chest tightens at the thought, but I don't let the fear deter me. In fact, I feed on it. In a while I'll simply slip away from the group and do what I really came here for.

We stroll fairly quickly through the next room and then enter a courtyard behind the convent. If I don't at least ask about the third floor soon, I'll lose my chance. And besides, when the opportune moment presents itself, I'm making a break for the second floor. But it's really hard to focus on my mystery-solving when I'm standing in the middle of lush hedges cut into an elaborate maze. I swear this place could be a scene from the movie *Labyrinth*. I feel like Sarah searching for the goblin king, doing whatever it takes to find her little brother, just like I'm doing for Aubree. The comparison gives me a slight chill and I shiver.

"If I can direct your attention to the statues on my left," Steve says, "I'll tell you a little about each one."

He points out the statues of the founding Ursuline Sisters gracing the courtyard like silent guards. I can't decide if they're regal or creepy, but the latter is probably a more accurate description. It's easy to see why so much folklore surrounds this place. It more than lends itself to that interpretation. When Steve finishes talking, I glance at the shutters on the third-floor windows and snap a few more pictures. I take a deep breath for courage and tap him on the shoulder.

"Excuse me, Steve, but is it true that the shutters on the third floor are nailed shut with nails blessed by the Pope?"

He smiles. "I guess you've heard the tales of woe surrounding our beautiful convent."

"You could say that."

"Are you going to ask me about the vampires next? Young lady, I'm asked this same question at least once in every group. And, no, there are no vampires on our third floor."

Young lady? Really? When he turns his back to me, I raise my voice. "Did I say a word about vampires? That's not what I asked at all. My question was about those shutters. Are they really nailed shut with thousands of blessed nails?"

Steve looks me dead in the eyes. "Yes, as a matter of fact, they are."

So I ask the obvious question. "Why?"

"Listen, Miss, I can assure you there is nothing on that third floor that even remotely resembles vampires, or monsters, or any other demonic thing you can think of. No one even steps foot on the third floor to my knowledge. The convent is basically an archive and a museum and nothing more. To think otherwise is preposterous, so may we please just move on?"

He seems adamant on convincing me to drop the subject, so naturally I push it even more. "Well, somebody has to go on the third floor sometime, because not too long ago, one of the shutters was cracked open a little. I took a picture—"

"That's impossible!"

Hmm, majorly defensive.

Steve takes a deep breath. "Look, for whatever reason the nuns saw fit back in the day, those windows were nailed shut with blessed nails. Lots of young women lived there. Maybe the nuns saw it as a way to keep out unwanted young men, who knows? But what I do know is there is no possible way one of those shutters was opened even so much as a crack. And except for a few old storage boxes or items, there is absolutely no one or anything up there." He turns to the group. "And we're moving on now."

I've never been a girl who enjoys being dismissed. "Well, sir, if you're asked about the third floor and the vampires daily, and if there truly is nothing of interest up there, then why not allow the public access so that fact can be documented once and for all? I'm sure there are several local reporters who would jump at the chance to view that floor."

Like me.

Steve ignores me completely. *Surprise, surprise.* Yeah, he's hiding something. I toss my bag over my shoulder and glance at the third floor again. I'll get my answers, sooner or later.

I jump when a guy from the group touches my arm.

"Hey," he says, "you do know why they say there are vampires on that third floor, right?"

"Because of the numerous unexplained deaths in this city involving significant blood loss?"

"Funny," he replies, "but no. I think it has more to do with the coffins."

"Coffins?" Now it's getting good.

The guy's eyebrows knit together as if he's about to engage in something intense. "Yep. Folks say the third floor is filled with coffins. They've been there since the settlement days or something. I guess they figure the only other use for coffins besides housing dead people would be accommodations for sleeping vampires." The guy laughs. "People believe the craziest stuff."

I smile. "I guess so, but you have to admit it's interesting. Coffins, huh? What else do you know about that third floor?"

"Me? Nothing really, just passing along a bunch of

legend." He winks. "Or BS, but that's for you to decide. Enjoy the rest of your day."

"Yeah, you too." I pull out my notebook when the guy leaves and write down what he said about coffins on the third floor. As much as I hate the thought of standing in a room filled with caskets containing only God knows what, I can't ignore the delicious thrill coursing through my tummy. This mystery is growing by whale proportions in casual conversation. Imagine what'll happen when I really start digging! I glance around and see that the crowd is breaking up and milling about the gardens. Time to make my exit, straight to the staircase.

Back inside, a few people are still lingering near the glass cases, but it seems like a slow day around here. I glance at the staircase and no one's there. I look around for Steve or anyone else who appears to work here, but the coast is clear. I take a fortifying breath and make my move.

Inching around the velvety ropes intended to keep me away from the second floor, and moving quicker than I normally would up the flight of stairs, I try not to think about the possibility of running face-to-face into someone. But trying not to think about it keeps the prospect fresh in my mind. I grasp for any ounce of reasoning I could pass on to anyone. I look touristy enough—not something I'm often proud of, so if I see anyone I'll simply lie and say I was looking for a bathroom or something. Yeah, that'll work.

I run my hand along the wall when I reach the last step, as if doing so makes it all right for me to be here somehow. I peek into the open space now in front of me, and no one's up here that I can see. There's a long hall and lots of doors on the second floor, like a hotel or something. I pull the camera from my bag and snap a few quick shots, fully aware that I need to keep moving before I'm caught. Hell, there could be security guards blocking the third-floor stairwell for all I know, and part of me kind of wishes there will be. Something worth guarding has a story worth revealing to the world. Part of me also knows that something far more horrifying than a few bulked-up dudes who talk like Stallone could be waiting for me on that third floor as well. There could be monsters—the very things that left two interns dead from their curiosity. And even though I should be near panic right now, I'm feeding on the rush. What does that say about me?

I push the thoughts deeper inside my racing brain and scan the room for the stairs leading to the third floor. After a few steps, I see an opened space at the end of the hall. It has to be the stairs. My hands are trembling now, but I ignore them. This is it. I move forward a couple of feet and then stop, my rational side stalling my movement like cement shoes on a gangster. Is this really dangerous? Like ending-up-dead dangerous? Or am I finally going to put to rest some beefed-up folklore that doesn't hold an ounce of truth? And if this is seriously dangerous, is it worth it? I think of Aubree and reach in my pocket. I grasp the fountain pen. *Discretion is the better part of valour.* Well, not today. I keep moving.

The stairs leading to the third floor are narrow, and I can tell there's no light at the top whatsoever. And there are no security guards. No ropes. Nothing. Maybe none of that is needed. After all, maybe whoever goes up there will be dead anyway. A chill makes my arms prickly, but I ignore it. My shoes suddenly feel heavy when I climb the first step, but I remind myself that I'm not supposed to be here so I need to move quickly. And I sure better hope I can run if need be. I fumble for my camera and turn on the flash. I'll definitely need it. I almost can't breathe when I reach the last few steps, but I know I won't make it onto the third floor. No wonder it's so freaking dark up here. There's a door at the end of the stairs. An ancient, no-doubt locked door.

I pull on the handle anyway and it doesn't budge. But the lock is so old it actually has a keyhole. I set my camera beside me and bend to look inside the hole. Maybe I can see something, anything. Old boxes? Cobwebs? Coffins? I squat and fit my eye to the hole.

"Hey!"

I scream before I realize it and bolt up like a jack-in-the-box.

"What're you doing up here? I told you the second floor is off limits!"

It's Steve, thank God, and I bite my tongue to stave off the snarkiness threatening to spill from my lips. *But this is the third floor, you twit*. I don't say it. I say instead, "I'm sorry. It's just, I have this school project and I really need an A. I really didn't mean any harm. And you scared me so bad. I've learned my lesson, I promise."

"Come down now, young lady, and calm down. You can research all you want on the first floor, just not up here."

His softer tone tells me he's buying it. I start back down, highly ticked that I've been caught but glad I'm still alive. Then it hits me. "Oh, my camera, I left it on the floor." I climb back up and grab it, and in one swift motion snap a picture of the lock, and then look back at Steve. "It just went off when I grabbed it."

He grimaces. "Sure it did."

"I swear."

I resist the urge to stomp down the stairs like a

disobedient child as the guide tugs the top of my arm to insure I'm following him. Great timing there, Steve-O. I hate this guy like dirt.

When he ushers me to the front doors like I need to leave, I turn and make my way to the glass cases again. After all, he said I could research to my heart's desire on the first floor. No way I'm giving him the satisfaction of an exit on his command. Plus, I need a moment just to breathe, calm down. I take out my camera and focus on the items in the cases again.

"I wish my students took as much interest in history as you do," someone says from behind me. I turn to see a nice-looking thirtyish guy with a smooth face and neatly trimmed hair.

"I teach at the middle school," he says, extending a hand. "The name's Brady Swinson."

I'm so taken aback I can't speak for a couple of seconds. Oh God! Brady Swinson. *Mr. Swinson...* "I know you," I say. "You were my cousin's favorite teacher when she was in middle school. She had the biggest crush on you back then."

His cheeks go pink. "Who's your cousin?"

"Aubree Turner."

He looks like I just slugged him. "Oh, Aubree. Yes, she was always such a sweet child, very inquisitive. I'm so sorry about what happened to her, uh—"

"Julia," I say. "Julia Reynolds."

"Nice to meet you, Julia. I've tried to keep up with it over the years, but did they ever find Aubree?"

"No, Mr. Swinson. We haven't."

"Please, call me Brady," he says. "No Mr. Swinson outside of school."

"All right, *Brady*," I say, instantly feeling weird doing so. I clear my throat and change the subject. "You must really practice what you preach. I always figured a history teacher would be as far away as possible from a place like this on a Saturday."

He smiles. "Just the opposite, I come here quite often. The Ursuline has a lot of secrets. Let's just say, she fascinates me."

Brady gives me a look and I know immediately. He's here for the same reason I am. He wants to tell her secrets as badly as I do. I'm not sure why I say it, probably because of the adrenaline rush I'm still feeling the effects of, but I blurt out, "I was just shooed down from the third floor."

His eyes widen. "You were on the third floor?"

"Well, not technically. There was a locked door at the top of the stairs on the second floor. I couldn't open it."

He rubs his chin. "Risky business there, Julia. Don't let them catch you doing that. They might revoke your Ursuline pass." He winks. "And, besides, I've found some interesting clues right here on this floor."

"I'll be more careful," I say, ...*not to get caught next time.* "Clues?" I add just to hear his reaction.

"Clues revealing what could really be on that third floor. That's why you're here, right? So, you researching something for school, or just a mystery junkie in general? You know, Aubree was a real mystery junkie, too."

"I know," I reply, loving the comparison. "Here for both, I guess. I take Journalism at Ben Franklin, and I blog. I haven't decided if I'm ready to share the Ursuline story on it just yet, but if you ever want to check it out, it's called *A Little Mystery In Between.*

"I'll do that," he says. "Nice to meet you, Julia. And be careful."

"Likewise." When Brady rounds the corner, I pull out my notebook and jot down the highpoints of our conversation. Maybe I can get to know him better if he comes here a lot, find out exactly what he's discovered about this place, if he'll divulge his sleuthing. But, in the meantime … a little friendly competition to see who figures out what the Ursuline's hiding? Well, bring it on. Guess I'll just have to get my answers first.

****

Ten seconds. That's all I needed. If Steve could've waited ten more seconds, I would have seen something through that keyhole, I just know it. But I suppose I got pretty far with no plan. Next time I'll be more discreet, and wear a disguise now that I'm on *The Ursuline Tour Guide's 10 Most Wanted List*.

I wipe the annoying powdered sugar from my bottom lip and set the remainder of my beignet on a napkin. I'm sure Café Beignet wasn't what Mom had in mind when she gave me money for lunch, but it's right down the street from the convent, and I prefer sweets when I'm ticked. Ugh, I can't seem to shake the frustration that's making my insides quiver. I was so damned close.

I pull out my notebook and skim over everything I've jotted down this morning, trying to decide if anything at all confirms a reason for anyone to think there are actual vampires on that third floor. The fire Steve talked about—the one that burned down the entire town except the convent—could vampires have kept it from burning somehow? No way, that's crazy. Vampires don't have power over fire, do they?

And the silver brush and comb set, it definitely belonged to one of the students—one of the young women. What better place for a vampire coven than a school for girls? Are the blessed nails a way to keep the vampires confined there somehow? Some unorthodox ritual the nuns discovered to keep the girls safe, perhaps?

I push the irrational thoughts from my head and focus on what few facts I have instead of playing into some wild fantasy. I flip to my notes about the intern murders back in the seventies. Someone killed those women—a real life, flesh and bone murderer. That's the only monster I need to be chasing.

I pop the last bite of doughy sweetness in my mouth. Oh, yeah, I'm definitely blogging about beignets tonight, and the fact that if you eat one too fast, powdered sugar could actually kill you … or at least make you *feel* like you're dying. No way I'm writing about the convent yet. It just feels like I need to keep it under wraps a little longer. There's a police station about a half mile from here. Time to resume my digging.

****

I'm still not sure what I'm going to say. They'll probably give me the boot within the first five seconds, but I really don't care. I need to do this, need to see if I can learn anything else about those dead interns. I take a fortifying breath and walk into the police station.

"Where's my son?" a woman is yelling to a lady seated at a desk near the entrance. "I need to see my son!"

"You need to take a seat."

"I'm not leaving until I find out what I need to know!" the insistent woman yells.

"You need to calm down, ma'am. Detective Johnson is on his way. Please have a seat until he gets here. He'll give you more information about your son, okay?"

The woman complies and I swallow hard. Desk lady looks annoyed now. Not good for me. I roll my shoulders to relieve some tension and approach her.

"Ma'am, I thought maybe you could help me."

"Yes, honey, what do you need?"

Oh, she threw out a *honey*. I can work with that. "I was wondering if you could tell me who I might speak to about two unsolved murders? Is there someone specifically in charge of those, or what?"

"Like cold cases?" she asks.

"Yes, you could say that."

"Well, do you have any information for the officer that might help in solving the murders?"

I take in a breath. "Oh ... um ... no ma'am, nothing like that. See, I was doing research for my Journalism class for school, and I stumbled on these old, unsolved murders—"

"Now you listen to me, young lady. This is a police station. The officers here are extremely busy. They don't have time for student reporters rehashing old murders. They have enough new crimes to work on that are still unsolved. Now, I respect your working on school stuff on a Saturday, but I suggest you do your research on the computer or the library like everyone else, okay, honey? Now have a good day."

Dismissing me. *Surprise, surprise.* I glance at the irate woman from earlier for inspiration and say, "Well, I'm not leaving until I find out what I need to know."

She cracks a crooked smile. "Is that right? Well, have a seat then." She points her pen in the direction of *Mad Mama*, but I sit on the opposite bench instead. I'm not sure how I'm going to get an officer to talk to me, but I can't just leave with my tail between my legs. Maybe they'll be less busy in a little while. Yeah, right. A police station in New Orleans less busy? I smile at the notion but stay planted in my seat anyway. I need to think of something.

After a few seconds, I notice a guy sitting in one of the rooms talking to an officer. Probably some delinquent. But then I notice him pointing to me, and the officer glances my way too. Get out! Could he be asking that cop to talk to me? The nameplate on the officer's desk says *Detective Elder*. Thank God for glass walls. The young man gives me a flirty look and I play on it. Hey, whatever it takes to get the story. I bat my eyes like I've seen girls do when they think a guy is cute in those Nickelodeon shows I watched in middle school. I hope it works. God, this is so humiliating. I better find some friggin' monsters for all this effort. My stomach tingles. The guy is headed straight for me. Maybe I'll get my answers.

He's a little lanky and looks to be about my age. His hair is honey blond, a very nice color, actually. He has a boyish smile and his hair is spiky and kind of everywhere. Different, but good different.

"Hi, I'm Tyler," he says and sits next to me on the bench.

Bold. I like it.

"I'm Julia. Nice to meet you. So, you hang out at police stations a lot?"

He throws me that boyish smile again. "I suppose I could ask you the same thing."

"You could, and my answer would be no."

"Good to know. Unfortunately, mine would be yes. See that officer over there? That's my dad, Detective Daniel Elder. He works homicide."

Homicide. Excellent.

"I heard you asking Gail about some old, unsolved murders," he continues.

"Really? You heard that? From *way* over there?"

He snaps his fingers in front of his ear. "I have ears all over this city, baby."

Cheesy, but it suits him somehow, and not in a bad

way.

"I can score you some answers, you know. But it'll cost ya."

"Cost me what?"

"Dinner and a movie with me tonight."

He's asking me out! Dang, that eye-batting stuff really works. How do I let him down without ticking him off? I still need to talk to his dad. My mom's words run through my head like they always do in situations like this. *When all else fails, try honesty. It usually gets you further anyway.*

Tyler squirms a little. "So, how 'bout it?"

"Well, Tyler—"

"Or you can call me Ty. Some people do."

"Okay, Ty. Listen, I really appreciate the invite, but I'm new in town and I'm really not ready for a full-out date-type situation. How about we go out as friends, though? I'd like that a lot. And, who knows? We can see where we go from there."

He jumps off the bench like he has a spring in his jeans and looks me dead in the eyes. "Wow, that's like the best rejection I've ever got, and believe me, I've gotten a lot. Wait, that didn't come out right. I mean, you're deep, Julia. You're cool. And, hey, I'm curious as hell to know what you're needing to talk to my dad about, looking at me all goo-goo eyed just to get at the old man. Slick, that's what you are. I thought you actually liked me or something."

Tyler's words are like his hair, all over the place and in every direction. And I already feel like a complete moron for not just saying yes to a *real* date night, especially because deep down I still want Ryan to ask me out. I'm so twisted.

"So, come on. I'll introduce you to my dad."

"Really?" I can't believe it. "You think he'll talk to me?"

"Only one way to find out."

I follow Tyler into his dad's office and plaster on my best smile.

"Dad, this is Julia. She needs to ask you something."

The officer extends a hand. He's a grown-up version of Tyler, minus the boyish smile. "I'm Detective Elder. Nice to meet you, Julia. Here, have a seat. I heard you asking Gail about a couple of unsolved murders, right?" He points to a small intercom on his desk.

I stifle a laugh and look at Tyler. "Ears all over the city, huh?"

He shrugs.

I clear my throat. "Well, sir, I appreciate you taking time out of your busy day. What I'm needing information on are two very old murders from 1973. They happened at the Ursuline Convent. Two interns were found dead, most of their blood had been drained. And their bodies were lying in the shape of a cross, one on top of the other. These murders were never solved. And I'm sure I don't have to tell you the rumors surrounding the convent and its third floor."

"No, unfortunately, you don't," Detective Elder says. "My question to you is, why do you want to know? Are you a relative of the deceased?"

"I'm a Journalism student at Ben Franklin High."

His eyebrows knit and his forehead tightens. "I see. And the best thing—"

"You go to Ben Franklin?" Tyler blurts out. "So that's why I've never seen you around. I go to the public school—"

"Tyler, if you don't mind," his dad says.

"Sorry."

"Like I was saying, Julia, the best thing you can do for your Journalism class is take a few pictures of the convent and do a historical account of it. It really is brimming with rich history—"

"I don't care about all that," I interject before I can stop myself. "I want to know about those murders. I want to know why people die when they snoop around that third floor, Detective. I want to know what's up there."

Detective Elder steps in front of his office door and pulls it shut. When he hits a button on the intercom, Tyler leans close to my ear and whispers, "Uh oh, here it comes."

"Young lady, I need to make one thing perfectly clear. I do not want you sticking your nose where it doesn't belong. You could end up in real jeopardy if you let your curiosity cloud your judgment about that place. Do you understand?"

I sit up straighter. "Quite frankly, I don't."

"Then let me make it crystal clear. I am very aware of those murders in 1973. The public has questioned for years how those young women were murdered and by whom, but there's something crucial that the public doesn't know. So how about I fill you in … for your own good."

I scoot to the edge of my seat.

"There were two main investigators assigned to that homicide in 1973. About three weeks into the investigation, both detectives were found dead. Their blood had been drained as well. Their bodies were in an almost identical state as the interns."

"What?" Chill bumps make my skin prickly. "How is that possible?"

"Because people die when they get too close to whatever is on the third floor of that convent. And those detectives losing their lives, well, they weren't the first officers to die after investigating that place. So, as it stands now, the third floor of the Ursuline is completely off limits to members of the police force."

I pull out my notebook, his words still spinning like a cyclone in my brain. I write down the info and mumble, "So the police just stopped trying to solve the murders, is that what you're saying?"

"Yes and no. We'll still do whatever we can if any new information comes through the office about the case, provided it doesn't involve actual contact with the third floor of the convent. But this case is so old that no new leads ever surface, except for the occasional reporter or Sherlock Holmes wanna-be, like yourself."

"Oh, coldblooded," Tyler says, diverting his eyes when his dad cuts him a look.

Elder thinks I'm a hack? Doesn't take me seriously? What if I let it slip to the good detective that I was almost on that third floor this morning. What would he say if he knew? No way I'm telling him, but I don't mind testing the waters a little.

I clear my throat. "So if someone actually called from that third floor needing help, you would what? Ignore the call?"

"Now you listen to me, young lady. If you have any ideas about that third floor, I suggest you forget about them now. You go poking your nose around that place and get in trouble, the NOPD will *not* come to your aid, do you understand me? This is your only warning." He leans over his desk and locks my eyes in a hard stare. "Do you understand that people are dead? No real explanation, just … dead."

It's hard to absorb his words. Exactly how big is this thing when a homicide detective is telling me that the entire police force will not aid anyone when it comes to the convent and its mystery? I suddenly feel sick to my stomach. Was I actually putting myself in mortal danger this morning?

"You can see your friend out now, Tyler," his dad says. "I think we're done here. Right, Julia?"

"Oh, yeah. Thanks for your time." I shove my notebook in my bag and follow Tyler to the door.

"Man, my dad … I'm sorry about that, Julia. He's kind of hardcore."

"Kinda," I reply. "Well, it was nice meeting you, Tyler. Thanks for not letting the lady at the front desk kick me to the curb."

"No problem. So, can I have your number?"

"Sure, here." I pull out a pen and grab his hand. "You don't have anything against ink do you?"

"Nope."

I scribble my number in his palm.

"Cool. How about a movie Friday night?" Tyler asks. "You know, as friends?"

"Sounds like a plan," I say. "Call me."

Ty glances at his newly inked palm and steps back inside his dad's office. My heart's beating so hard I should check my chest for holes. Hearing the dangers verbalized makes it all so real. It's easy to deny the danger when everything's in my head. But now, it's confirmed. That third floor is dangerous. But technically, I did make it to the third floor, and I'm still alive.

Then I think of something else—something Detective Elder said— and one question keeps running through my head. *How do you solve a string of murders where the victims are the investigators?* I feel the chill bumps again.

Chapter Five

Going on a date with Tyler comes with conditions. First, that I meet him at the movie theater. After all, this isn't a real date. Second, that I pay my own way. Again, this is a getting-to-know-each-other thing, not a true boy-meets-girl thing. And third, he's going to tell me everything he knows about the Ursuline, whether he's willing or not.

It took longer to get home from school today for some reason. Sometimes I think the bus driver purposely drives slower on Fridays just to get revenge on the delinquents who've driven her crazy all week. So I shower quickly and throw on a clean pair of black jeans and a red cami. Mom says a girl with black hair can't go wrong with red, so it's my definite "in a pinch" color. I have to get out of here quickly. I don't have enough money to ride the trolley to and from the movie theater, buy my ticket, and buy a snack, too, so I opt to walk now and ride the trolley home tonight.

I smear a dab of red on my lips and shove my notebook and phone in Mom's oversized purse. I'm out the door and on the street in front of the apartment when Dad catches me by the arm. *Bouncer Dad* is crazy annoying.

"Where you headed?" he asks.

"To the movies with a friend," I say.

"You walking?"

"Just this afternoon. Taking the trolley back tonight."

"Good," he says. "Just be careful, and don't miss curfew." He looks at Ronald, the other bouncer, and says, "Wouldn't want to have to break another arm if some guy messes with my girlie here."

Ronald laughs. "You know you don't mind breaking

arms."

I roll my eyes. "God, Dad. I won't miss curfew. Bye, guys."

"Julia," Ronald calls to me. "You look pretty."

Dad punches him in the arm.

"Ow!"

****

Tyler isn't here when I arrive, but it's still a little early. I don't have enough money for popcorn or a drink, so I sweet talk the guy behind the counter into giving me a cup of ice, and I buy a box of Milk Duds. I fill the cup from the water fountain and take a sip, not realizing just how thirsty I am until the liquid hits my appreciative throat. I sit on a bench inside the theater and wait for Ty.

A girl's laughter catches my attention and I almost choke on my water when I look in her direction. She's standing with a couple more girls and a few guys, and one of them is Ryan. I instinctively look away, not sure why I'm shielding my face. It's a free country, after all. But I don't want him to see me, don't want him to know that I can't resist staring at him in class, in the school parking lot, and now at the movies.

I glance at the front entrance. Still no Tyler. So I look at Ryan again. And he's magnificent. I know he doesn't play sports, well, unless skirt-chasing qualifies, but he has muscles for days. And they stretch and pull at the lightweight fabric of the blue, knit polo he's wearing. His hair is more unruly tonight, like he just showered and left out the gel he usually puts in it, but I like it. His eyes are smiling, animated, like the guy he's standing next to is telling the funniest story he's ever heard. I like his eyes. His hair. His muscles. His everything.

"Hey, Julia," Tyler says when he's standing in front of me.

"Oh, hey," I say, turning my face away from Ryan and his friends. "I'm glad you made it."

"Are you kidding me?" Ty says. "I've been looking forward to this all week. You look amazing, by the way."

"Thank you," I say. "You look nice, too." And he does, but he's not the guy I'm thinking of. I'm fighting the urge to look over at Ryan again, but I don't.

"So, did you buy a ticket already?" Tyler says when he notices my drink.

"No, just water and a snack," I say. "I guess we need to get in line."

Ryan and his crew are a few spots ahead of us in the ticket line. I try to hear which movie they're seeing, but it's impossible when Tyler starts talking. I'm more than a little disappointed when a guy hands Ryan and his friends their tickets and I'm left guessing their selection. God, I'm such a stalker. I remind myself that I'm here with Tyler and push the thoughts of Ryan to the back of my mind.

"So, what do you want to see?" Tyler says.

"I haven't seen anything that's playing here, so you pick," I reply. "I'm good with whatever."

"You sure?" he says.

"Absolutely," I assure him.

"Man, you're easy."

I cut him a look.

He bumps my shoulder with his. "Come on, Julia. I'm kidding. Lighten up."

He's right. That's exactly what I need to do. Lighten up and enjoy a movie and a night out. God knows any night away from our crummy apartment is a good night. We buy the tickets and head for the snack bar for his popcorn. Our movie's playing in theater number eleven, so we go inside and find a seat.

"Are you cold?" Tyler asks when I fold my arms across my lap.

"Not really," I say.

"Would you like some of my popcorn?"

It does smell incredible. I pull the Milk Duds from my purse. "Tell you what, you share your popcorn, and I'll share my candy."

"Deal," he says, and both of our hands dive into the popcorn bucket simultaneously.

After at least twenty minutes' worth of previews, and right before the movie's about to start, they play a soda commercial with the drink pouring slowly into a cup.

"Why do they do that?" Tyler asks. "Now I have to pee."

"Crude," I say, but I'm laughing. He's such a goofball.

"Excuse me, Julia. I'll be right back."

As Tyler makes his way into the aisle, the lighting is just bright enough that I can make out Ryan's face a couple of rows ahead of us. The lights dim just as he places his arm around the back of a girl's chair.

****

"Did you like the movie?" Tyler asks as we leave our seats and head into the lobby again.

"It was good," I reply.

No way I'm ever admitting that I barely watched any of it. I was too preoccupied with Ryan and Miss-Lucky-Girl-With-His-Arm-Around-Her to notice. I have no idea why I'm jealous. I have no right to be at all.

"Would you like to go somewhere else?" Tyler asks. "We can if you want to."

All I want to do is go home and forget all about Ryan and *the girl*. I need to focus on Aubree … on the convent, and the potential story with that place. I need to forget about him. Guys like that don't date girls like me anyway. They just don't.

"I really can't tonight, Ty. I have a curfew. But we can sit here and talk a few minutes if you want to. I wanted to ask you about something anyway."

He looks so pleased I actually feel guilty. *Man, this guy really likes me.*

"Fire away," he says.

"Well, when we met, I was asking your dad about the Ursuline Convent. What do you know about that place?"

"Enough to stay away from it. Why?"

"Well, that doesn't really tell me very much. I need details."

Tyler runs his fingers through his all-over-the-place hair. "My dad told you plenty of details. Wasn't that enough to let you know to stay the hell away from there?"

"Seriously, Tyler. Tell me what you know."

"I know you're pretty." He leans in and kisses me out of nowhere.

I push him back enough to break the kiss. "Look, this is a friendship thing, okay? Nothing more, nothing less. I wasn't expecting that, Tyler. It's too soon."

He looks so embarrassed I feel like a total jerk. I fumble with my purse and don't look him in the eyes for several seconds.

"I'm sorry, Julia. I just really like being with you. I shouldn't have done that."

"It's okay," I say. "I just really want us to be friends first, okay? You get what I mean, right?"

"Yeah, I get it," he says, looking so hurt I could climb under the bench. "Friends. Got it. I better go. Do you need me to walk you to the bus stop?"

"You don't have to leave, Ty. Please stay."

"It's cool, Julia. I'll call you, okay?"

"Okay," I say. "See you later."

God, what's the matter with me? I made that guy feel like dirt—that super sweet, take-him-as-he-is kind of guy feel like dirt. Maybe I need a lobotomy. I stand. What I definitely need is a bathroom.

As I step out of the restroom, I lose my breath. Ryan is coming out of the men's room at the same time, and he looks me dead in the face.

"Hey, Jules," he says. "What's up?"

"Just saw a movie," I blurt out. *Stay cool and breathe.* "The same one as you, actually. I saw you sitting in the same theater as me." *So not cool.*

"And you didn't speak? I see how you are."

"Well, you looked kinda … busy. And I didn't want to interrupt your date. Pretty girl, by the way."

He smiles. "Yes, she is pretty, but it wasn't a date. She's just a friend.

"Oh." It's all I can think to say.

"Well, see you around, Jules. And speak to me next time, okay?"

"Okay."

He rejoins his friends as I head for the main entrance and step onto the sidewalk, replaying our conversation as I walk to the trolley station. *Just a friend…*

Chapter Six

"There's always a rational reason for the impossible. That's why we gather facts. Search harder. Dig deeper. You have to question everything ... who, what, where, when, why, and how. I know it sounds cliché, and you've heard me say it a million times—"

Well, I haven't heard Ms. Dunkin say any of this, but I'm sure her lectures would never get old to me anyway. She's so passionate, so focused, standing in front of us with the same look in her eyes my mom gets when she tosses out another gem of useless trivia, the same look Aubree had when she talked about ghosts and Shadow People. It means something to her, means everything.

"Look for those moments, guys," she continues, pushing away a tuft of dark curls that has fallen into her left eye. "Our lives are made up of moments, after all. There's always that moment when innocence transforms into clarity—that's a given, and a very simple thing, actually. It's called growing, learning how to function in the world around us. But then there are those rare moments, the ones where that clarity turns into brilliance, and it's nothing short of magical. And it is in those moments that we discover what we're truly made of."

I'd die for that moment.

After a few minutes, I realize I've been so wrapped up in Ms. Dunkin's words that I haven't stared at the back of Ryan's head even once, 'til now. Man, she's good. As I'm appreciating the time obviously spent gelling his sun-kissed hair into those perfect little spikes, he turns and faces me. I ignore the urge to divert my eyes and simply stare and smile instead. I feel so empowered that someone should write me a theme-song right this second.

"Okay," Ms. Dunkin says, "let's partner up and start

throwing out ideas for our next issue."

Before I can move, Ryan is out of his seat and headed in my direction. He points to the back table, claiming it before anyone else can. He pulls out the chair beside him and motions for me to sit. My heart is in my throat, and I swallow hard before choking on it. So much for my super powers. I just hope I don't say something stupid.

"Have a seat." Ryan pats the empty chair beside him. "You don't mind partnering with me, do ya, Jules?"

Is he joking? "Not at all." I try not to sound sheepish.

"I know how serious you are about journalism, so I figure story ideas probably come easy to you. I saw your blog the other night, too. It's really good. And, twenty thousand followers. That's crazy."

I try to hide a smile. "You read my blog?"

"Yep. So, how long have you lived in New Orleans? I know you move around a lot."

"Since a week before school registration. I lived in Mobile before that, but actually, this isn't my first time living in New Orleans."

"Oh, so you're from here originally then?"

I cringe. Definitely the part I hate. "No. I was born in South Carolina."

"Your folks move around a lot because of your dad's job or something?"

"Yeah, something like that." Time to dodge the bullet. "What about you? You from New Orleans?"

"No, but I've lived here about ten years, so I'm practically a native. Don't hold it against me."

Hold it against him? If he's the product of this city, then all male children should be born here and properly dispersed throughout the planet!

"I know New Orleans gets a bad rap," he says, "but it's really—"

"A reporter's dream." *A family's nightmare.*

Ryan smiles. "Exactly." Then he looks at my journal that's open in front of me. "The Ursuline Convent?" His eyebrows knit. "You're not suggesting we do a story on the convent, are you?"

"Umm, no," I say, trying to backpedal. I'm not sharing the convent story or Aubree with him yet, not even if he looks like a god.

"Good," he says, "because we've covered it before. Absolutely nothing to tell, really. That place is just a bunch of hype."

I'm not sure why I'm suddenly defensive, but I can't stop from saying the words, "Well, I wouldn't say that. I've been researching it, and it's very interesting. I actually think there could be something to the hype about that place."

"Research? What kind of research?"

"The usual kind," I say. "Why?"

He smiles. "No reason. You know what? I like you, Jules. You're so different from other girls I've met."

He likes me! My face feels flush. I hope I'm still breathing. And as much as I want to sit here and let him like me, the side of me that always takes over kicks in. I have questions of my own, and I can't resist the urge to ask. "I've been wondering something, Ryan. No big deal, really, just curious."

"So you've been thinking about me?" He winks. "Cool. Go ahead, ask."

"Why are you in Journalism? I mean, you're as buff as any of the football players. You don't play sports of any kind? I don't mean to sound sexist or anything, but selling ads for the paper seems so—"

"Lame?"

Oh God! "No, not lame at all. I didn't mean to

87

imply—"

"Relax. I'm just kidding. I played a little football just to experience it. My stepdad was thrilled. But I got a concussion during a game my freshman year. It sucked. Made me wonder if I really wanted to have my head banged around on a regular basis just for *the experience*. Like I said, concussions suck. So, I quit. I never picked up another sport. Thought it was too late to start, I guess. But, I think my odds are much better for the business degree I'd like to have someday anyway. And selling ads for the paper will look good on a college résumé, you know."

Ah, beauty and brains.

"And," Ryan continues, "according to Ms. Dunkin, we've sold more ads than in previous years since I became the head of advertising, so I guess it's good all the way around."

"That's awesome," I reply. And it is. "I think you're smart for quitting the football team. Your head has too much going on inside it to be pummeled to mush."

"Thanks, Julia. I take that as a huge compliment coming from you. You're so epic, the way you took Holly down your first day in class with all that Salem Witch Trial stuff. No one ever questions Holly's intelligence in here—not that I think she's all that or anything. I'm just saying, it was brilliant."

"Thanks." It's all I can manage to say through his gushing.

"So, I was wondering. If you're not busy Saturday night, would you like to go to a movie or something?"

I know I'm smiling like a big, yellow happy face sign, but I don't care. "That would be great."

Now his smile matches mine. "Cool. What's your number so I can put it in my phone later?"

"You have anything against ink?"

"No."

I reach in my book bag for a pen and pull out my old fountain pen by mistake.

"Sweet," Ryan says. "Does that thing write?"

"No, I just like carrying it around. Kind of a good luck charm, I guess."

"Can I see it?"

He can see my pen, my notebook, and my cheap shoes if he wants to. "Sure."

Ryan rolls the pen into his line of vision. "*Discretion is the better part of valour*. Man, this thing is cool. It's Shakespeare, you know."

I swear this boy is crazy trying to make me fall in love with him.

He continues, "The actual line from the play is, 'The better part of valour is discretion, in the which better part I have saved my life.' It's from *Henry IV*, and Falstaff said it. What he meant in the play was at times he hid on the battlefield to keep from being killed. But now the meaning's interpreted as a reminder to practice caution in certain situations."

I'm sure my mouth is hanging open. "Wow, I'm impressed. How do you know that?"

"Well, quoting Shakespeare drives the ladies wild, and what the pen says, it's good advice."

I laugh. "I suppose I need reminding of that wisdom … frequently. That's why I carry it around." I can't believe my honesty, how comfortable I feel talking to him.

"Well, the pen's amazing. It looks really ancient, too. Do you have any idea how old is it?"

"Don't know. The guy who gave it to me—"

"Wait, hold up." Ryan sets the pen on the table.

"Some guy gave this to you?"

I cup a hand over my lips to keep from laughing in his face. "Not a *guy* guy. An older gentleman gave it to me after we met on the street, that's all. He told me that curiosity killed the cat and that a little luck never hurt anyone. Then he just handed it over. It's one of the coolest things that's ever happened to me."

That, and being asked out by Ryan Grandle. Looks like the pen's pretty lucky after all. I smile at the irony.

"Well, I guess that's okay, then." He stares into my eyes and I melt. "So, you going to take his advice? About the curiosity thing, I mean?"

I smile. "Probably not."

Ms. Dunkin pulls me from my stargazing. "Five minutes, people. Let's wrap it up."

"Five minutes already? That was fast." Ryan looks defeated. "And we don't have any article ideas, either."

"And you still don't have my cell number." I take his hand and turn his palm up. His jaw clenches and I know he likes his hand in mine. I write my number in his palm and release it. "You said you don't have a problem with ink, remember?"

"Hey, you can ink me wherever you want to."

I laugh. "I don't know about that. Oh, and here." I reach in my notebook and tear out a page with a few story possibilities I've jotted down since practically the first day of class. A couple of them are fairly good, actually, but nothing like the convent story. That one's remaining a mystery for now … until I solve it. "As far as article ideas go, will these do?" I hand him the page.

Ryan skims over it. "Amazing. I guess you do live up to the hype, huh?"

"Hype?"

"Kickass reporter extraordinaire. And in the

blogosphere, you're a legend."

I laugh. "I wouldn't go that far."

"I would."

The bell rings and Ryan writes our names at the top of the page of ideas before dropping it on Ms. Dunkin's desk. "You don't mind me writing my name on it, too, do you, Julia? I know they're really your ideas, and I'll tell Ms. Dunkin that if she picks one."

"Oh, I don't mind. It's perfectly fine." And so is he.

We walk out of Journalism class together. I know we'll be parting ways soon, but I wait for Ryan to verbalize that realization.

"So, my next class is in D-Hall," he says. "Guess I better head that way."

Knew it. "Okay. Well, maybe I'll see you at lunch, then?"

"Absolutely." He winks. "See you then, Jules."

Jules. It's funny, as much as I've always hated for my name to be altered in any way, the 'i' and the 'a' are completely endearing rolling off Ryan's lips as an 'e' and an 's' are. Thirty minutes with the guy, and I turn to a puddle of goo. But, hey, I have nothing against goo, and I'm going out on a date with Mr. Hottie himself. Someone needs to teach me how to do a back handspring right now. I force myself to stop ogling Ryan's back as he heads in the opposite direction and work my way down the hall instead. But before I become fully engrossed in my thoughts about the impending date, I notice Hannah Parker and her band of merry Barbie dolls. And she's eying me up and down. No doubt saw me leaving class with Ryan. But I'm ignoring her. No way she's ruining this high.

****

"You're not going to squeal like a girl if I tell you

something, are you?"

"Um, newsflash, Julia. I *am* a girl."

Macey pokes a piece of lettuce with a plastic fork and plops it in her mouth as I scan the cafeteria for Ryan.

"So, tell me already," Macey says. "I could use some good dirt right about now."

"Nothing scandalous, it's just that Ryan asked me out today."

"Shut up!" Macey blurts. "OMG, it's about time that boy made his move. This is like totally amazing."

"It is amazing, and don't say OMG."

Macey sticks her tongue out in my direction. "Miss Critical. So, when's the date, and where's he taking you?"

"Saturday night, and we're going to the movies. I gave him my number and everything so we can talk about it more. He's supposed to meet me in here."

"Sweet." I can see Macey weighing her climbing social status at the mere prospect of Ryan sitting at our lunch table in a few minutes.

"There he is," I say when I notice Ryan at the sandwich bar. "He's still getting his food."

"Oh, maybe I can come to your place Saturday and help you get ready. Pick out your clothes and do your hair and nails. That would be so awesome."

The sinking feeling punches me in the gut like a fist. "It does sound great, Macey, but you can't come over. My dad's been working long shifts and he'll be sleeping. He usually won't let me or my brother have company on Saturdays. I'm sorry."

"Well, that sucks," she replies, clearly disappointed. "Then you have to promise to call me the minute it's over and tell me all about it."

"I promise."

"Excellent." Macey smiles. "Oh, here he comes."

How am I ever going to pull this off? I've been so swept up in the prospect of going out with Ryan that I forgot one crucial factor. I'm such an idiot! What am I supposed to do? Have the guy of my dreams pick me up in front of the glowing neon signs of naked ladies and my bouncer dad saying, *"Hi, son. Welcome to our humble abode."* I have to think this through, work it out somehow. One thing is certain. Ryan can never find out where I live. It would ruin everything.

****

"Where you off to?" My dad shifts the toothpick to the other side of his mouth and clasps his hands in front of him, rocking back and forth on his heels. I call it his tough-guy stance. He always stands that way when he's working outside the club.

"Café Beignet. I have a date."

"Wait, hold up. What is the guy, a bum or something? He can't pick you up like a normal person?"

I hold my hands like Vanna White and move them up and down at the glowing naked lady in front of me. "Really, Dad, you think I'd let him pick me up *here*? No thank you. I don't have a problem meeting him there."

Dad elbows Ronald, who's working tonight too, and lets out a raucous laugh. "Get a load of my kid—too good to let a guy know where she lives. Where'd I get a classy girl like that from, huh?"

Ronald winks at me. "Don't know, Matt. Must take after her mother."

I smile. "Thanks, Ron. And, Dad, I won't be too late, okay?"

"Hey, make sure he walks you at least most of the way home tonight, Julia. I don't want you on the street alone after dark. All kind of crazies out on Saturday night."

He would know. "Got it, Dad. See you later."

Coming up with an excuse for Ryan not to meet me in front of my apartment turned out to be less daunting than expected. I simply told him that my dad worked crazy hours and was sleeping ... and that he's kind of a bear when he gets inadvertently awakened. 'Scary dad' stories always seem to work. So, there was no objection when I suggested meeting me for coffee at Café Beignet before the movie. Now if I can simply manage to surf the raging waves of nausea tumbling in my stomach, I'll be in the clear. I don't know why I'm so nervous.

I spent most of the afternoon on the phone with Macey trying to decide what outfit to wear. After a gazillion suggestions, I settled for my favorite black ruffled cami, skinny jeans, and red Converse kicks. When in doubt, go for comfort. I got the blouse from the Goodwill Store while we were still living in Mobile, and I *do* love it. But, most of my clothes are from secondhand shops, so every time I wore an outfit around my friends in Mobile, I was secretly afraid that something I had on would be recognized as one of their hand-me-downs. But, the minute I found out we were moving back here, I made one final shopping spree. At least in New Orleans I won't be stressing about wearing any of my peers' rejects.

I clutch my oversized purse a little tighter when I reach the crosswalk and press the button on the sign. I figured my backpack would look kinda stupid on a date, and I needed something big enough to hold my notebook. Not that I think I'll need to take notes on Ryan or anything, but I just don't leave the house without it.

And I do have to pass the convent.

After a few minutes, I'm on the street in front of the

Ursuline, resisting the urge to stare at the third-floor windows, forcing my racing thoughts to stick to Ryan and not the subject that has possessed my racing brain since the day Aubree never came home. Besides, I pressed my luck far enough the other day that I could actually be dead right now if New Orleans's twisted history had decided to repeat itself. I try to imagine myself stiff and cold in one of those infamous aboveground crypts. Gross. Yeah, meeting a total hottie for a date is way better. I smile at how ridiculously dramatic this town has made me and walk away from the convent without so much as a glance.

I reach the café and immediately start scanning the tables for Ryan. After a couple of seconds, I spot him. He's already seated, and a waitress is eyeing him like the last piece of chocolate in a Valentine's Day assortment, not that I blame her. He looks even yummier than the first time I saw him in the Journalism room. But I hesitate when I notice the girl's obvious flirting. I step behind a column and watch as the waitress *accidently* brushes his hand while filling a water glass. I hate being sneaky with Ryan, but I have to know if he'll respond. After all, I know his reputation. *The Ladies' Man…* When he doesn't acknowledge her in any way, I approach the table. Our eyes meet and he flashes a ready smile. I return it without hesitation. Oh, yeah, this is major. The panic waves in my tummy surge again as he pulls out the chair beside him and motions for me to sit. I take a couple of deep breaths for courage, and then it hits me.

I remember exactly why I'm nervous.

"Oh my God, Julia, you look amazing."

I'm sure my cheeks are pink. "I don't look any different than I do at school."

"Exactly. You always look amazing."

Someone needs to pull me back to the ground right about now. This boy totally slays me. "Thanks," I manage to squeak out. "So, been waiting long?"

"No, just got here, really. Should I order our coffee now? The movie starts in like forty-five minutes."

"Sure."

I realize I'm practically ogling him as he gets the flirty waitress's attention and she pours us some coffee. He's wearing a hunter-green V-neck t-shirt that matches his eyes and complements his skin tone so perfectly that I'd swear he saves it exclusively for first dates just to drive helpless girls into a frenzy.

"So," Ryan says, "I hope your dad's catching some Z's. I feel really bad not picking you up. I wouldn't mind meeting you outside your building, you know."

"Don't feel bad. It's no big deal, really. I like walking."

"Okay, if you say so." He stares at me a few seconds before speaking again. "Now, the way I see it, it's time for a little Q&A with you."

I take in a breath. "What do you mean?"

"Well, I told you my reason for selling ads for the paper, so tell me, Jules, what drives you to be such a kickass reporter? I mean, when you whipped out those story ideas the other day right on the spot like that, well, it was crazy epic. You take journalism seriously, don't you?"

I want to tell him the real reason, wish I could. But Aubree isn't something I'm comfortable talking about with someone face-to-face. I know it's selfish, but she was my family, my best friend. I'm the one who cried myself to sleep night after night when I realized she really wasn't coming home—was more than likely dead somewhere. So I blog and beg total strangers for any information they may have about her. But here, looking in Ryan's eyes, I just can't share her with him. Whatever small pieces I have left of Aubree in that way are mine. So I say instead, "It's all I've ever wanted to be … a broadcast journalist. It's like, in life, there's the truth, and then there's everything else. No gray areas, really, just black and white, true-to-the-bone facts. Sure, you have to question everything and shovel out tons of gray matter to find the black and white, but at the end of the day, it's there. And that's what I love about reporting the facts. The truth is always hidden somewhere. All we have to do is find it."

Ryan's smiling so wide his face probably hurts. I feel like a rambling idiot. I can't believe how freely I talk to him.

"Wow, that's deep. I like it. Your folks must be really proud of you. Tell me about your family. Any brothers or sisters?"

God, the question I've been dreading. At least I've learned how to play it cool. "I have a younger brother, Jesse. He's thirteen."

Ryan smiles. "Nice."

"Not really."

"Hey, be glad you have a sibling. I'm an only child, and it sucks sometimes."

An only child! Why would people capable of creating perfection stop at one offspring? Total lunacy, if you ask me.

"Yeah, my mom almost died when I was born, so I'm Mr. One and Only."

Thank God I didn't verbalize what I was thinking. I swear, Open-Mouth-Insert-Foot Disease is rampant with me sometimes. I say instead, "That's too bad, that your parents couldn't have more kids, I mean."

"Yeah, it is. But that's life, I guess. And my mom's great. My real dad is out of the picture, so it was me and her for a while 'til we moved to New Orleans and she met my stepdad. She's overprotective at times, but what mom isn't, right?"

I nod and sip my coffee.

"So, Jules, I want to know more about you. You said you've moved around a lot, because of your dad's job, right? What does he do?"

I hesitate for a moment, searching for details I can safely share. Why does Ryan have to be so great, so interested in my life? It's going to make hiding my living situation even tougher. "He works at the shipyard. He's an electrician." *And at the moment, he's tossing unruly drunks from the strip club I live above*, but I don't say it. No way I'm ever saying that.

"Oh," he replies. "I'd wondered if he was military or something, since you said you've moved around so much—"

My phone chirps and I'm actually relieved. Maybe I can use the interruption to change the subject. "I'm sorry, Ryan. Excuse me a sec." I answer the call and it's my mom, reminding me to be careful walking home tonight. It's too bad she'll still be at work when I do get in later. She was so excited when I told her about my date that I thought she was going to do a cartwheel or something. The only guy she ever dated was my dad. Poor Mom.

I shove my phone back in my purse. Ryan has sort of a weird look. "What?" I ask.

"Nothing, it's just, I think that's the same model phone I had in middle school. You've never upgraded? Not that it matters or anything."

I feel flush. Damn, I forgot about my ragged-out

phone. I backpedal. "Um, well, I never bothered upgrading because I'm used to it. And it holds a charge for a couple of days. You know, if it ain't broke, don't fix it." I divert my eyes and focus on my coffee cup instead.

"Oh, I didn't mean anything by it, Julia. I think it's awesome that you don't care about things like fancy cell phones. You're so real, not—"

"What?" I say before I can stop myself. "Plastic, like Hannah?"

Ryan looks defeated and I regret the words a millisecond after spilling them. "You know about me and Hannah?"

"Everyone knows about you and Hannah."

"Ouch, no need to be vicious. Look, Hannah was a mistake. And I know how she acts at school, but she was different when we were alone. Don't hold dating her against me, okay? I mean, you have to have some past boyfriend that you regret, right?"

There go my nerves again. What would Ryan say if I confessed that he's the first real date I've ever had? How pathetic is that? I've never even kissed a guy. I keep wondering what I'll do if he tries to kiss me goodnight or something. Then I remember Ty's feeble attempt and feel a pang of guilt. I fight the nausea waves again. "Sure," I say instead, "I have regrets. No harm, no foul, right?"

"Exactly."

****

"Your car is so amazing," I say as Ryan opens the passenger side door for me." I can't believe you own a Mustang."

"Well, technically, my stepdad owns the Mustang," Ryan interjects, "and he reminds me of that fact … frequently. If I fall outta line just once, he'll take my keys away so fast, Houdini would be impressed. And I can't count how many times my mom's said, 'Don't ever speed. If you get even one ticket, we'll never be able to afford the insurance.' But, hey, no pressure. Just forgive me if I tend to drive like a grandma."

Ryan's hilarious, another totally fab quality to add to the growing list of reasons I should fall face-first in love with him. All night I've been looking for some flaw, anything at all to put me on high alert—some clue to rationalize why a guy like him would be the least bit interested in a girl like me. Maybe he really is just tired of plastic.

****

"I'm sorry the movie was so bad," he says as we pull away from the theater. "It got decent reviews, though."

"It's okay." I want to tell him that I had barely followed the plot anyway. I was too interested in his hand on top of mine for an amazing two hours, and also trying to sound convincing when I persuaded him to drop me off in front of the convent instead of taking me home.

"You're sure you want me to leave you *here*?" he says when we reach the Ursuline. "This place is kind of creepy at night, don't you think?"

Absolutely. "Well, it's not like I'm going inside. I told you, I'm meeting my little brother here in a bit. He's coming from a friend's house, and my mom can't pick him up. So I have to walk him the rest of the way home." I try to look indifferent. "He'll be here in a few minutes, you know. It's really no big deal."

Ryan takes my cue and starts fumbling. He covers both of my hands with his and my insides melt like an ice cube in soup. We stay this way for a few seconds, and my tummy feels tingly and hard as stone in the same moment. I think I'm shaking, but he doesn't notice.

"Is it okay if I kiss you, Julia?"

I can't breathe. I simply nod instead. He brushes the top of my hand with a finger before taking it in a gentle grip. I tilt my head upward and our noses graze. The warmth of his freshly-shaven cheek molds to mine as our lips touch. I'm shy to respond at first, but open my mouth slightly and welcome the kiss when I feel his other hand touch my cheek. The waves in my stomach are replaced with mini-fireworks.

"Goodnight, Julia," Ryan says when the kiss is over.

As I struggle to calm my racing insides, I'm bombarded with thoughts of all the ways we handle our breaths. We can take one, hold one, run out of one, lose one. Well, in this moment, Ryan had stolen mine.

"Goodnight."

"Look," he says, "I can wait for your brother to get here and drive you both home."

"No," I say a little louder than desired. "It's really not necessary, Ryan. And I have to be brutally honest here … Jesse is a total dork. If you drove us home, he'd just be making kissy noises and crap like that. And then I'd have to resort to bodily injury. I have to say, it's not pretty."

Ryan smiles. "Okay, I get it." He gives me another peck on the cheek. "You said he'll be here soon, right?"

"Right."

Ryan's expression is suddenly serious. "You know, if there's any other reason at all that you don't want me to drive you home, you can tell me, Julia. Really, it's okay."

Waves of guilt toss my stomach like an ocean. "Yeah, I know." I glance at the sidewalk and down the street. I notice some people a good distance away and point. "I see him coming now. I better go."

Ryan sighs. "I'll get the door for you."

In a few seconds I'm standing on the street watching his car pull away, thank God. I was afraid he'd want to meet Jesse. Next time we go out, I have to come up with a better story. This was way too risky. I make sure he's out of sight before taking a single step. Every moment of our date is now racing around my head. Minus my white lies—okay, my big ginormous black lies—it was perfect. Totally perfect.

So, why do I stop when I'm dead center with the Ursuline and stare hard at the third-floor windows again? I know what Detective Elder said, that people who investigate this place wind up dead. Well, technically, I did reach the third floor, and I'm still alive. Why am I just standing here? Better not press my luck. I walk away from the convent but pull out my notebook to skim over my notes as I head in the direction of home. I keep wondering about the picture I took of the lock and the keyhole. Maybe if I blow it up, I'll see something through that keyhole. I wonder if there's a way to pick the lock.

Real fear hits me when Aubree's face floods my thoughts. What would I do if there really was some murderer up on that third floor and I'm poking around where I don't belong? What if I were ever cornered by someone? How could I possibly defend myself? Then I think of Ryan. Is it really worth the risks involved in reporting this story? Solving this mystery? I mean, would my blog actually blow up if I solved it? Is this mystery famous enough for that? And what would Ryan think if he knew? There's no way he would want me poking around such a dangerous place. I mean, look at his reaction tonight when I simply asked him to drop me off here. Maybe I'll never tell him just how dedicated I am to solving the mystery. But, that would mean this could never be my story.

I flip to the notes I jotted down the other day, the ones with Ms. Dunkin talking about a rational reason for everything. I think about the fire and the convent being the only surviving structure. There has to be a reasonable explanation for that, I just have to find it. I'll start there when I get home in a little while. I mean, where's the danger in that? And Aubree disappeared in New Orleans. I know deep down that when it comes to mysteries in The Big Easy, this place is it. I smile as I head toward home.

Yeah, this *is* my story.

Chapter Seven

I make it into the front of the school just as the rain starts pouring harder. I hate beginning the day in damp clothes, especially now that I have someone to impress. But I still have a few minutes to check myself before the bell rings, thank God. I push the restroom door open and slip in front of an empty mirror. At least I had the foresight to wear my hair in a ponytail today—the less collateral damage, the better. I twist the bottom of my lipstick and smear it on my top lip when I notice Hannah, Kimmie, and Jasmine standing behind me. Oh yeah, this should be good.

"FYI," Hannah says, "Ryan prefers pink lipstick, not that nude, barely-there color."

It takes all my strength not to laugh in her face, so I play along instead. "Thanks for the 411. I'll keep that in mind."

When I turn and face the mirror again, she actually looks insulted, like she was expecting me to lay into her like some jealous little girlie-girl or something. Total insanity.

"Well," she says, "it's just because—"

Here it comes.

"—we used to date."

Now I do allow the laughter to drift from my nude, barely-there lips. Fact Number One: Hannah Parker is jealous because I'm dating Ryan—jealous of *me*. Fact Number Two: This chick really needs to take a lesson in tactfulness. "Newsflash, Hannah. I know."

Kimmie steps in front of her, like her bleached-blonde head will explode if she doesn't jump to *Barbie's* defense. "They didn't just date! They were famous at this school."

"That's right," Hannah chimes in. "We *were* famous. And that's what I can't figure out about Ryan's apparent new taste in girls here lately." She eyes me from head to toe and then adds, "His taste has changed ... a lot. But you're simply the flavor of the month anyway, I'm sure."

Giggles drift from Kimmie and Jasmine. "Nice one, Hannah."

Nice one? Give me a break. I shove my lipstick in my backpack and step close enough to Hannah to smell her no-doubt expensive perfume. "To be brutally honest, Hannah, I know all about your and Ryan's infamy. And I also know about your last claim-to-fame right before Ryan broke up with you. It involved some jock in the field house, right? Do I have my facts straight? I mean, I wouldn't want to misrepresent you or anything, since you're such a huge celebrity and all."

Hannah's face is so red that I'm not sure if she's pissed or embarrassed, but neither reason matters an eyelash's width to me. My mom's tidbit of useless trivia about Barbie pops in my head, how if Barbie were life-size, her real measurements would be 39-23-33, and I chuckle again. Better get out of here before I come down with Plastic-Shock-Syndrome.

I push past Hannah. "Excuse me, ladies."

"He'll never get serious with you!" Hannah shouts as I exit the bathroom.

"Bite me!" I yell back and head to homeroom. What difference does it make to her anyway? Could she actually want him back? And what makes her think Ryan would even consider it after catching her snogging with another guy right in front of God and everybody? Is she really that self-absorbed? Or is she acting psycho because Ryan's dating me? It's almost surreal. A girl like Hannah Parker actually knowing I exist—caring about who I'm dating because he's the hottest male enrolled in this school—and he used to be hers. But now he's mine. Hannah Parker is jealous of *me*. And I almost forgot about my clothes being wet.

****

I'm glad my Math teacher's cool. I finished my test early, so he let me come to the library for the remainder of class. The computers in here are beasts compared to mine. I type in the logline for my blog and hit search. In a couple of seconds I'm staring at a post from last night. I wrote about the trolleys in New Orleans and how I'm falling in love with public transportation. Since I was only twelve when we left New Orleans before, I'm new to "public transit" in general, and it's crazy convenient.

I notice a new comment on a story I did a few months ago about the Oakleigh Mansion in Mobile, and the username is bradyhistory411. Ha! The cute history teacher read my blog. I'm suddenly nervous, like letting-someone-read-your-diary nervous, but I look at his comment anyway. *Very well-thought-out and researched.* Kinda clinical sounding. Teacher sounding, actually. But I'll take it.

My phone vibrates and I check it. Ryan. **Ask your mom if you can come to my place after school. Meet me in D-Hall.**

His place after school? Nerves and tingles tighten my stomach as I send Mom a text.

****

"So, what did your mom say?" Ryan asks as he meets me in the hall after school.

"She said it's okay."

"Outstanding. Let's get outta here then."

He takes my hand as we exit the building and head to his car. I notice a couple of chicks staring and pointing.

Yep, he's off the market, but I don't say it. I wonder if they're thinking the same thing as Hannah, wondering why in God's name Ryan's with me. I push the thought out as quickly as it surfaces. Why not me? But I'm not allowing my brain to go there either.

"Here," Ryan says when we reach the car, "let me get the door for you."

I smile. "Sweet. Thanks."

We're on our way to his house to watch a movie, and my legs feel like Jell-O. I've been more than a little curious about his family and where he lives, but being faced with actually going there feels like standing naked on a stage in front of a million people. So I try focusing instead on his smell that's wafting around my nose as he gets in his Mustang and shuts the door. It smells like his neck, right behind his ear. Amazing.

"So," Ryan says as he starts the car, "word on campus is that you and Hannah had it out in the girl's bathroom today. What happened?"

"Are you kidding me? You mean people actually heard that? Talk about mind-your-own-damn-business at its finest."

"Yeah, I know," he replies, "but what happened? Did she say something to you?"

"It's no big deal, really. She's jealous that we're dating, that's all."

"Jealous?" Ryan shakes his head. "She's just mental."

"Yes, she is sort of mental, but I suppose that's what happens when too much bleach drips into your brain."

"Ouch, nice one." He grins. "She's a hot mess all right. I don't know what I was thinking dating her."

"Oh, you say the sweetest things."

"You crack me up, Julia."

In a couple of minutes, we're pulling into the

driveway of what can only be described as a mansion. It's Southern charm at its finest and has probably been in his stepdad's family a hundred years or more. Are you kidding me? I can't feel my legs.

"So, here's my place," Ryan says as he parks the car.

"It's gorgeous." I'm curious and nauseated at the same time. How is Ryan going to feel if I ever work up the courage to reveal my living situation to him? He can't know, not yet anyway.

"My mom's inside," he says as we get out of the car. "But don't worry, she's cool. She usually leaves me alone when I have friends over."

"Friends?" I wink, and he pokes me in the ribs until it tickles.

"You know what I mean. Come on, let's go."

We step inside the front door, and he heads straight to the kitchen. I try not to stare at the gorgeous furniture, wall-hangings, and the mega-load of childhood photos of Ryan filling the rooms. Some of the photos are actual paintings. It's a lot to take in. I don't think I've ever seen a house this fancy. I stop staring when Ryan seems to notice.

"I know. Sick, right? The paintings of me as a baby, I mean. Like I said, only child."

I smile, trying not to seem too overwhelmed by my surroundings. "So, I would be curious to know the history of this house. I guess it's been in your stepdad's family for years, right?"

"Nope. The folks bought it after they got married. I don't know the house's history, but it's old."

I try to bite my tongue but fail. "You mean you live in *this*, and don't have a clue about its history? How can you not be dying to know its legacy? It's obviously a piece of New Orleans's history somehow. Look at it.

This is no ordinary house. You should check the archives and find out who built it originally, the whole nine yards."

"Okay, Jules, slow down. I get what you're saying. My folks know more about its history than I do. I didn't mean that we don't know anything about it." He laughs. "Typical you ... kickass reporter. You're major. I love it."

We enter the kitchen, and Ryan pulls out a large bowl and a bag of something he sticks directly in the microwave.

"Knock, knock," a female voice says into the room.

Ryan looks in her direction. "Hey, Mom. You need something?"

"No, just wanted to meet your friend." She gives me a once-over.

"Hi. I'm Julia." I feel like a total dork the second I say it.

To call this woman attractive is an understatement. She's the epitome of refinement. Perfect skin, not a hair out of place—even her clothes look better than the mannequins' in the store window at Macy's. No wonder Ryan's a god.

"Well, hi, Julia. I'm Margaret. Ryan's told me a lot about you."

"Really? That's so sweet."

Ryan's grinning like she just pinned a medal on him or something.

She reaches into the refrigerator and retrieves a ginger ale. "So my son tells me you just moved back to the area. How do you like it?"

"I really like school," I blurt out, embarrassment hitting me like a fist to the face. But I backpedal quickly. "What I mean is, Ben Franklin is one of the nicest schools I've attended. The criteria for acceptance is way beyond anywhere I've ever gone."

She smiles and then tugs Ryan down to meet her gaze. "I like this one, son. Hang on to her." She winks and then exits with a, "Enjoy your movie, kids."

"Your mom's cool," I say.

Ryan fiddles with the microwave again. "Yep," he replies. "Hey, you're gonna love this." He presses the timer and start button.

"What is it?"

"You'll see."

A distinct aroma fills the room, and I know immediately it's popcorn. Then another smell hits me. I can't put my finger on the scent at first, but it's familiar. "What kind of popcorn is that?"

"Guess."

After a few more pops, I recognize it. "Don't tell me."

"Yep, bacon-flavored popcorn."

"Eww, gross," I say through laughter. "No way I'm eating that."

Ryan moves close and pulls me into an embrace. "Are you saying you have something against bacon, young lady?"

"No, but my arteries have something against bacon."

He nuzzles my neck with his nose, and I squirm from the tickling. "That's really too bad then. I guess I can't kiss you now."

I pull back and look him in the eyes. "And why is that?"

He winks. "Bacon-flavored dental floss this morning."

"What?"

"Just kidding."

Ryan pulls me into a kiss. His lips are warm, so warm that I almost forget we're in the middle of his kitchen and his mom could walk in any moment. But when the kiss lasts several seconds, I trust his boldness and close my eyes, trying to take in every feeling, every small sensation of his hands on my waist, his breath tickling my face, and his smooth lips on mine.

My mind drifts to this time last year, when I was enrolled in a high school filled with judgmental, superficial kids who would have rather spit on me than have me touch them. I was no better than my mom's job or the shack we lived in, but here I have worth. Part of me feels like I should tell Ryan the truth, let him decide for himself if he still wants me, or just let him go if he thinks he could do better. But I keep my lips pressing to his instead, knowing with every fiber of my being that I could never do better than this. No one can top perfection.

****

Ryan has one hand on the steering wheel and one clasped with mine. I love riding in his car. If anyone would have told me before the move that I would be in this exact spot at this moment, I would have been looking around for the TV cameras like an episode of *Punk'd*.

"Which direction is your house, Julia?"

Time to test the waters a little. If Ryan is ever going to know where I really live, I need to work up to it. "Well, actually, I live in an apartment."

"Oh, that's cool. What street is it on?"

His decent reaction allows me to breathe normal again, but at the moment I still can't tell him a street. I haven't picked my decoy apartment yet, but I have a plan. "Oh, you know what, could you drop me off at the library? I have some homework, and the computers there are better than mine at home."

I have a reason for letting him think I need the library

computers, too. I really don't have a problem doing homework on my computer, but if he thinks I have to use the library, he'll have to figure that we don't have a ton of money. Maybe if he at least realizes that, then I can float more painlessly into the truth later on.

"You could've used my computer, Jules. No big deal, you know."

Wow, he's infinitely sweet. I feel bad for lying, but I know what *could* happen if I reveal everything at once. I can't risk it. "I know, but how much homework would I get done, really?"

"Good point." He smiles. "Okay, the library it is."

After a couple of minutes, I'm standing in front of the library, and Ryan is driving away. It actually makes my insides hurt, lying to the nicest guy I've ever met. I want so much to totally trust him, but I know my past, and I'm not going back there. At Ben Franklin, kids actually respect me. They know I have a kickass blog, a brain in my head … and they know I'm with Ryan. I'm not blowing it. And maybe soon enough I *will* be able to tell him the truth, and then the lies will seem small.

My phone buzzes a text alert. **What you up to? Can you hang out?**

It's Tyler. And I have a spectacular, delicious idea. **Can you meet me at the Ursuline?**

My phone chirps. "Hey, Tyler."

"Are you sick?" he says. "Why do you want to meet there?"

"Just do it. I have something to show you. What are you, a chicken?"

"No, I'm not a chicken. I'm a dude who's scared as hell of that place and not afraid to say so."

"I'll be there in fifteen minutes, Tyler. You better be there too."

I shove my phone in my book bag and dig in the front pocket for bus fare. I'm not sure why I haven't thought of this before. I'll have Tyler walk me home and see how he reacts to my living situation. After all, we go to different schools, and he doesn't know any of my friends at Ben Franklin. *And he doesn't know Ryan.* He's the perfect guinea pig. And if Tyler treats me differently after seeing my strip-club doormat, then I'll know what not to do in the future as far as telling the truth goes. It's brilliant.

****

"I was about to think you weren't coming," I say as Tyler heads in my direction. "I've been standing here twenty minutes."

"Nice to see you, too, Julia. I swear, with that warm reception, I'm not sure why we haven't hung out since our *date*."

"I didn't mean to be harsh. I just really want to show you something. I have some pictures from inside the Ursuline—"

"Yeah, like you *really* minded me being a little late." He nods toward the convent. "I already know you worship this place."

I won't deny that, so I flip open my notebook instead. "Seriously, Tyler, I have to tell you something and I need you to listen."

"Yeah, because I normally stand with my fingers in my ears like this when people start telling me stuff."

I pull his hands down from his ears and shove my notebook in his face. "Listen, the day I met you, I toured the convent, and I made it all the way to the third floor. Now I took some—"

"Shut up. You're lying! No way you got on that third floor."

"Why do you say that?"

Tyler states matter-of-factly, "Because you're still alive."

"Well, I never said I got *on* the third floor, I said I made it *to* the third floor. But, there's a locked door at the top of the staircase, so I couldn't go in. The lock looks really old too. I took some pictures of it. They're at my place. You wanna see 'em?"

"You're serious," Tyler says, facing the Ursuline. "You really snuck up to the third floor of that place?"

"Sure did."

Ty stands in front of me and mock bows. "Damn, girl, I was way off. My dad's not the major one. You're hardcore as hell!"

"Well, as much as I appreciate your admiration, it's not that big of a deal. I'm a Journalism student, you know, and I'm doing a story on the convent. So, will you help me with something?"

He points to the Ursuline. "Yep, as long as I don't have to actually snoop around that place, 'cuz I'm telling you now, ain't gonna happen."

"Wuss." I lightly punch his arm.

"I may be a wuss, but at least I'm a live wuss. So, lead the way to your place, vampire hunter."

We start walking away from the convent, my stomach twisting at the prospect of Tyler learning my secret. But I have to do this, so I fill up my nervous angst with questions. "You believe there are vampires on that third floor, Tyler? Really?"

"I believe that people who snoop around that place end up dead. I don't know if vampires are responsible, but I know people die. That's enough for me to stay the hell away from there. My dad sees some crazy shit, Julia."

"I bet. And I bet he sees some cool stuff, too."

After several minutes of trivia about the convent and discussions on who has the better football team, his school or Franklin—like I really have a clue—we're standing in front of my apartment, my glowing, naked lady in all her glory.

"This is it," I say as nonchalantly as possible. "You coming in or what?"

"You live here?" Tyler blurts. "In a strip club?"

"Yeah, Ty, I hang my clothes up on stripper poles."

Tyler's eyes pop like a spooked fish.

"I live *above* the club, in the third-floor apartment, you derfwad."

"The name-calling hurts, Julia. And it would hurt even more if I actually knew what a derfwad was."

I smile. "Listen, you don't have to come inside if you don't want to. I understand."

"Are you kidding me? This is awesome."

Awesome? Really? He thinks this is awesome? But Tyler's kind of twisted to a fantastic degree. I have to take that under consideration. I mean, would everyone think this is awesome? Would Macey? Ryan? I tell one of the bouncers that Tyler's with me and we go upstairs.

"Mom," I say as we step though the front door. "I have a friend with me. We're going to my bedroom, okay?"

I hear a faint *yes* and we head to my room.

"I can't believe you live above a strip club?" he says again. "So, do you know any of the, um, dancers?"

I stare him straight in the face. "That's disgusting, Tyler Elder. Don't ever ask me that again."

"Sorry," he mumbles, looking defeated. "So, what do you want to show me?"

"Here." I sit in front of my computer. "Like I said, I

made it to the third floor of the Ursuline, and I took some pictures, but this is the one I wanted to ask you about."

Tyler leans over my shoulder and stares at the screen. "I still can't believe you went up there."

I ignore his remark and find the pictures I'm looking for. "I downloaded these from my camera. The third floor is behind a locked door, and it looks ancient. I took a picture of the lock." I show him the picture at one hundred percent to start with.

"That lock *is* ancient, and the keyhole is cool." Tyler leans in even closer.

"I know, right? But look at this." I zoom in on the keyhole as much as my photo software will allow before it's completely distorted. "Do you see that through the keyhole? What does that look like to you? If we can make it out, it might give me some clue about what's up there."

He takes the mouse from me and scrolls the enlarged keyhole himself. "I can't make it out clearly, but I know where we can download some free photo-enhancing software that's kickass. I have it on my laptop. I bet we could see exactly what's in that keyhole with it." He looks at my machine a little closer. "You think your system can handle it?"

"Only one way to find out."

I trade places with Tyler so he can download the software. It feels like Christmas morning. What if the software does allow me to see what's behind that locked door? But a few minutes into the download, Tyler gives up.

"Your computer doesn't have the specs for it, Julia. I'm sorry. But, here, let's email the picture to me. I'll see what I can do with it when I get home, and I'll email you whatever I come up with. Sound good?"

"Yeah, that'll be great. Thanks, Ty."

"No prob." He gives my chair back. "And you know something else, Julia. The police use lock-picking kits all the time. My dad has two or three in his car. With all the old buildings around here, I'll guarantee you they have kits that'll work on old locks like that. Would you be interested if I could snag one for you?"

I know I'm gushing like a little girl, but I don't care. "Oh my God, Tyler, you would do that?"

"Not for just anyone, but I'd do it for you. But you have to promise me you won't get killed in that place, okay? I mean, I felt guilty when I got my friend put in detention last week because of a stupid prank I dared him into. Imagine the therapy I'll need if I get you killed." He flashes that boyish smile.

I concede. "I promise."

A light tapping makes us look at the door in unison.

"Hey, Julia," Mom says. "I have to start getting ready for work in a little while."

Mom's actually being sensitive to my feelings, knowing that I wouldn't want Tyler to see her in her server's uniform. Tyler looks back at the computer as I join Mom in the doorway.

"He's leaving in a few minutes," I whisper.

"Is that him?" Mom peeks over my shoulder. "Is that Ryan? He's cute."

"No." I stifle a laugh. "That's Tyler. He's a regular hottie. Ryan's a total hottie."

"So, he's just a friend?" she whispers close to my ear.

"Yes, and he's helping me with something."

She raises her voice. "Oh, okay. Nice to meet you, Tyler."

He gives a little wave as Mom leaves the doorway. "She's cool," he says. "If that were my mom and dad, they'd be grilling you like a steak. And then they'd grill me after you left. It's tiring."

"Your dad's tough, huh?"

"Uh, yeah. Hello? Homicide detective."

"I know," I say. Then I ask another burning question. "Your dad, he's the reason you won't step foot in the convent, huh? His stories about that place have you terrified."

"Well, doesn't he have you scared now too, Julia? I mean, you said you went on the third floor the day we met… Was that before or after you talked to my dad?"

"Before."

"And have you been inside the convent since?"

"No," I confess. "I haven't."

Tyler smiles. "Well, there you go. I have to split now. Gotta get home before dark. Thanks for the invite, and I'll see what I can do with the picture when I get home."

"Thanks, Ty. I appreciate it."

How could I be so gullible? Tyler's dad obviously keeps him in line through fear. Telling me what he did about the convent is the police department's way of keeping monster-hunters and thrill-seekers out of the Ursuline. If detectives were really killed investigating the murders and that third floor, then why haven't I found even one story about their deaths? Wouldn't the public know about it? Unless someone's hiding it.

There's something else I know about the New Orleans Police Department. It's common knowledge, although I'd never say a peep about it to Tyler. Awkward wouldn't even begin to cover that conversation. But the NOPD has a history of corruption a mile long. The people here don't trust cops, period. Hell, they're scared of the police. I even heard the mayor on the news once saying the public doesn't like the police department because of its injustices of the past. He gave an entire speech about gaining back the citizens' respect. One interviewer compared New Orleans to Gotham City. Well, there can't be a Gotham without a villain. Maybe Tyler's dad is playing the Joker when it comes to my investigation of the Ursuline. I know the NOPD didn't do squat for Aubree. I remember Aunt Beth cursing a detective out when he suggested that maybe Aubree fell into prostitution or simply ran away like most "depraved girls" do.

I pull out my notebook and write down everything Ty said. I glance over my notes again. There has to be a rational explanation for everything, just like Ms. Dunkin says. I type in *New Orleans police officers die at Ursuline* and many variations of the phrasing. After several minutes, still nothing. Who knows? Maybe the mafia used the convent as a cover to take out some fine, upstanding investigators in the NOPD. But more than likely, it's just bogus. Tyler's dad can sucker him, but not me. I'm going back on that third floor when the opportune moment arrives. Fool me once…

Chapter Eight

As the Great Fire of 1788 in New Orleans was devastating the Vieux Carre corner, the Ursuline Convent faced imminent destruction as fierce winds blew the unrelenting fire toward Jackson Square. The nuns and female students were instructed to evacuate the convent, but a nun named Sister Anthony climbed the convent steps instead, holding a small statue of the Virgin Mary, praying, "Our Lady of Prompt Succor, we are lost unless you hasten to our aid!"

Immediately, the wind shifted direction, blowing the flames away from the convent and allowing the fire to be extinguished. The Ursuline Convent was one of the few surviving buildings. Upon witnessing the miracle, a crowd unanimously cried out, "Our Lady of Prompt Succor has saved us!"

After reading twenty or so articles on the salvation of the Ursuline during the massive fire, most credited divine intervention, but I tend to believe that if God had a hand in it, he would've spared the church too. But it burned slap to the ground along with the other eight hundred and fifty-five buildings in the French Quarter that day. So I choose to believe that the weather was the redeemer, be it the cold front on top of the warm front that shifted the winds, or vice versa. Either way, there's a rational explanation for the convent being spared, and not a snip of it has anything to do with vampires.

So if the vampire theory is total crap, then why do people insist that the third-floor houses bloodsuckers in coffins? I type *Coffins in the Ursuline* in the search bar and hit enter. The first article that appears reads, *Ursuline Nuns, Casket Girls, Coffin Girls.*

Paydirt. I read some more.

A group of young, virginal French women arrived in New Orleans with their belongings in coffin-like boxes call casquettes. Expecting to find respectable men to marry but finding criminals instead, the girls were given a home at the Ursuline with the nuns, and their casquettes were stored in the convent attic. When a young woman did marry, her box was retrieved, but always found to be empty. Local legend claims that the young women smuggled vampires into New Orleans with their unique boxes.

Interesting. So that's where the vampire folklore originates. I jot it in my notebook, questions piercing my tired brain like fangs. Why would young women attempting to marry and settle a new colony bring vampires along for the journey? Wouldn't that complicate things to the mega extreme? I mean, after all, wouldn't *they* be the potential victims? Where's the rationale in that? The prey bringing the monsters to their own town? Yeah, vampires in the girls' luggage is a totally ridiculous notion. Still, the third-floor windows *are* shuttered with blessed nails, so what could be hidden up there that merits that degree of security? I'm definitely missing something, and I intend to find it.

"Okay, so here's the deal—"

My butt lifts off the chair when Jesse yells, and I bang my knees on the lip of my desk. "Hey, toad, you scared the crap outta me. Ever heard of knocking?"

"Sor-ree. Your door was open. Didn't think you'd freak out."

Just what I need, another distraction. It's a school night and I still have to study. "It's getting late, Jesse. Tell me what you want and get out."

"Your Charizard card, and I have an offer you can't refuse."

I should've figured it had something to do with Pokémon. This should be good. "Okay, little man, lay it on me."

He takes a deep breath, as though he's been building up the courage to ask for days, and I stifle a laugh. "Okay, so, I have this Dragonair card that's pretty rare. A kid I met at school traded me for a Pikachu. Yeah, that's right, a Pikachu." Jesse shakes his head. "He's twisted or something. Anyway, if I throw in a Dratini card and the five bucks I have saved up, will you give me your Charizard?"

I actually feel bad for the little termite. I have to admit, he's pulling out all the stops this time. But, Charizard's not up for grabs. He should know that by now, but I have to give him props. The boy's persistent.

"Come on, Julia. You know it's a sweet deal."

I shrug. "Sorry, no can do. Charizard's off limits. You should give it up already, Jesse. Keep saving your money, and I'll help you buy one online, okay? I bet we can even find a card just like mine."

"That sucks, and it'll take me forever to save enough."

"I really need to study now," I say, trying more to get his puppy-dog eyes out of my doorway than anything else.

"Hey," Mom says, poking her head in the room. "You two got any laundry to add to the pile? I'm on my way to the machines."

"Doing laundry on your night off?" I pick up a pair of shorts from my floor and toss them to her. "Fun."

"Hey, I'll take volunteers if you're offering."

"Sorry, Mom. Homework."

"Yeah, me too," Jesse says.

Doubtful.

"But let me grab all my dirty boxers." He tugs the

waistband on the pair he's wearing. "These are on day two already."

"Oh, gross." I pinch my nose. "No wonder something smells funny in here. You're such a toad."

"You know," Mom says, "the average number of days a West German goes without washing his underwear is seven."

"Oh, my God, Mom. Don't encourage him."

"No fear, Julia," Jesse replies. "I'd go commando before wearing mine seven days." He heads to his room and Mom laughs.

"He's such a troll," I say, but I can't hide the smile.

"Admit it, you think he's funny." Mom looks at me a moment, obviously not thinking about Jesse anymore. "So, this Ryan guy you're seeing, is it serious?"

I know what she means … the kind of serious she's talking about. Am I the serious-with-this-boy-that-gets-you-pregnant-and-makes-you-lose-your-choices kind of serious? I know she wants desperately to warn me not to make the same mistake she did at my age. But since *I'm* the mistake she made, awkward topic doesn't even begin to cut it. So I let her off the hook while she's barely nibbling.

"We're dating, Mom, and I like him a lot." I look her in the eyes, directly into the question I see burning there. "But I'm smart. I'm not going to do anything that might jeopardize my future, okay? So you can stop worrying."

I know that's what she needed to hear when her shoulders relax and she releases a small breath. "You and that good noggin … not sure why I even thought I had to ask. Well, this laundry's not getting any cleaner with me standing here. Don't stay up too late, okay?"

"I won't. And, hey, I love you, Mom."

She smiles. "Love you too, chica."

It's a shame my mom got pregnant in high school. She deserves better than the hand she's been dealt, could've been more than a woman who serves drinks in a casino—a lot more. And as guilty as I feel for being born too soon in her life, I know my accomplishments make her feel better about herself. That's why I need to crack this Ursuline mystery somehow. Besides possibly finding out what happened to Aubree, it would make Mom beyond proud. Dad should be ashamed for not doing better by her. I mean, how hard is it to hold down a job, really? I just hope he doesn't screw up this time. I plan to stay in New Orleans a while—a long while. I'm not leaving 'til I find Aubree.

I ignore my homework a little longer and tug on a sleep shirt and pajama pants before settling in front of my computer again. I pick up where I left off before Jesse's interruption. I skim another paragraph about the Casket Girls, my thoughts drifting to the tour of the Ursuline and all the times our guide mentioned the female students. I open a folder on my desktop containing pictures of the silver brush and mirror set I'd photographed on the tour. Is it possible that this set was carried into the Ursuline by a Casket Girl? Buried deeply in her coffin box on the treacherous journey to her ultimate disappointment?

I zoom in on the intricate scrollwork on top of the brush. Beautiful, that's for sure, and it had to be expensive. But what's its story, its message to the world? Whom did it belong to, and why was she important enough for her set to be preserved in the glass cases of the convent for tourists to admire for generations to come?

Right before I close out the photo, I notice something in the swirling lines I thought were mere designs. They look like letters. Closer inspection confirms my theory. It's definitely letters—'KA' to be precise. My stomach tingles. *Initials.* I jot the discovery in my notebook. Who is K.A.?

****

My ponytail is a little tight, so I loosen it before pulling it through the back of Jesse's Yankee hat. I hope the cap and my lack of makeup is enough of a disguise to fool tour guide Steve, in case he happens to work on Thursday afternoons. If he recognizes me, he'll toss me out on my butt for sure. But I have to get inside the Ursuline again—see if there's anything else that might tip me off about that third floor, or the Casket Girls. The convent's only open for a few more hours, so I shove my notebook and camera in my backpack and bolt.

In a couple of minutes I'm on the trolley heading in the direction of the convent. I never mind walking, but time's not my friend today, I realize I'm gnawing my bottom lip when I taste blood, a nervous habit I picked up when I was little and terrified about moving to a new place. But the nerves are good— keeps me focused, more determined.

What am I missing? If what's on that third floor really has nothing to do with vampires and everything to do with the girls, then what secret is worth guarding so diligently? Worth killing for? What are those nailed shutters trying to keep in? Or keep out?

The trolley slows to a crawl at the sidewalk adjacent to the Ursuline and I step off. After a fortifying breath, I glance around to see if Steve is anywhere in sight when the last tour group makes its way into the building. So far, so good. No sign of him. I move cautiously past the group and into the Ursuline undetected.

I make a beeline to the glass cases. I need to see the

silver brush and mirror set again and try to determine their significance. Maybe I missed something the other day. Fortunately, I'm the only one interested in the contents of the cases at the moment, so I start snapping pictures and taking notes of the other items too, like an inventory. But honestly, the other trinkets in the cases look so predictable—the crosses, rosaries, and other "churchy" things galore. The brush and mirror set stick out like a muddy pig in a Westminster dog show. I focus on the mirror and brush again, taking closer photos of the initials finely etched in the silver now that I am aware of their existence. K ... A... I need to see if those initials are anywhere else in this place.

After an hour of retracing my first tour of the convent and focusing harder on the things Steve pointed out to be important that day, I'm no closer to answering my questions than I am at achieving access to that third floor. I lean against a cold, stucco wall when my feet start to ache, and I jot a few more things in my notebook. I pull at the brim of my cap when a tour guide ushers some people past me. This was a total bust. I head for the front entrance, remembering that I have another task ahead of me today that needs to be accomplished before dark. Better get to it.

When I pass the steps leading to the second floor on my way out, I can't help but smile. *Oh yeah, I'll be seeing you in my future.* I start shoving my camera in my backpack when something on the wall catches my eye. Why didn't I notice that before? I grab my camera again and head for an ironworks plaque that's jutting from the wall. It looks old, like something straight out of a Camelot movie. It resembles a shield but is way too small to actually offer any sort of protection. What is it?

I can't contain the excitement and snap pictures more

furiously than I should. What does it symbolize? Why is it here? And why wasn't it part of the tour on my first visit?

After taking at least twenty photos from different angles, I drop the camera in my bag and look for any kind of inscription on the plaque that might say what it is. No such luck. There are no words anywhere, not even an explanation of its significance, or the year it represents. I'm tempted to ask a tour guide, but the last thing I need is to draw more attention to myself. Maybe I can find something out about it online tonight. Guess this visit wasn't a total loss after all.

"Hey," a voice says from behind. My breath catches in my throat. Could it be?

"Fancy seeing you again, Julia." He leans into me. "We have to stop meeting like this."

I let out the stalled breath. Thank God for cute history teachers. "Hey, Brady. Good to see you. I thought you were that evil tour guide for a second there."

He laughs. "Eew, well, sorry I startled you. Hey, I read your blog. You're very talented, by the way. I was impressed."

"Thank you." I know I'm smiling like some fan girl, but I don't care. I don't bother telling him that I'd already noticed his comment. Brady actually read my blog. Man, his students are so lucky. Aubree was right. Coolest. Teacher. Ever.

"Hey," I say, "you wouldn't happen to know anything about this plaque, would ya?"

"I do, actually."

Excellent. "So, tell me."

"Honestly," he replies, "it's not really a plaque. It's a coat of arms. It's believed to be from the period of King Louis XV's rule because it has similarities to his actual shield. But the differences leave unanswered questions as well. There are no other documented photos or references to this particular piece, so I'm sure it's a reproduction. No way they'd have the real thing hanging in here unprotected. It's unique, that's for sure. Pretty cool, huh?"

My stomach tingles wildly. This has to mean something! "Yep, very cool."

Brady moves closer to the coat of arms and smiles.

"How do you know so much about it?" I ask.

"Well, instead of The Father, Son, and the Holy Spirit, my parents worshipped Michelangelo, Christopher Columbus, and Napoleon. Guess I was destined to be a history teacher, huh?"

"Well, my folks worship Jim Beam, tax evasion, and useless trivia, so where does that leave me?"

"You're a trip, Julia," he says, but he's grinning.

I sling my backpack on my shoulder "Louis XV.

Better write that down. And thanks for the 411, Brady. I really appreciate it."

He leans in close to my ear and glances upward. "Wanna know another cool tidbit about that third floor?"

"Absolutely."

Brady's eyes look like Mom's when she's about to tell me something juicy. "During Hurricane Katrina, one of those shutters and the window behind it was busted from flying debris. In less than forty-eight hours, the window area was bricked up from the inside. And I mean totally bricked up. In seven more days, the window and shutter were replaced with new ones and the shutter was once again nailed closed. Do you know why it took so long to replace the window and shutter?"

I still can't get past it being bricked from the inside. "Why?"

Brady pulls out his phone and shows me pictures he'd taken of the bricks and the new shutter. "It took a week because they had to wait for the nails to arrive from Rome."

The hairs on my arms stand on end. "The nails that are blessed—"

"By the Pope," he finishes.

I slide the backpack from my shoulder again and pull out my notebook. I write down everything Brady just said, not caring how Nancy Drew-ish I look at the moment.

"Glad you found that useful." Brady glances at the coat of arms. "I remember telling Aubree that story, too. She loved it."

My stomach catches so hard I might fall down. "You and Aubree used to talk about the convent?"

"Sometimes. She thought vampires could be on that third floor. She loved talking about vampires. Well, enjoy the rest of your evening, Julia. See you around."

All I manage is a nod. Aubree used to talk about the convent. Funny, she never mentioned anything about it to me.

****

My steps quicken as I cross the street and head for the apartment building I've been eyeing for a week. Task number two for the afternoon pales in comparison to the productive visit to the convent. This place is halfway between the Ursuline and my actual apartment, so it's perfect: the perfect decoy for Ryan, the perfect location, the perfect lie. Now if I can just enter the building without needing someone to buzz me in, I'm golden. In a few seconds, I'm on the steps leading to the foyer. I hold my breath and tug the handle on the front door. It opens. *Thank God.*

I go inside the small area to check the place out a bit. A woman is seated on a small bench, settling her baby into a stroller. She eyes me at first and then flashes a warm smile. I return it and head for a small staircase in the corner that obviously leads to the upstairs apartments. I retrieve my phone and pretend to call a friend down to meet me. After sizing me up, the woman steps out of the foyer and onto the sidewalk. Guess I'm not very threatening. Yeah, this place will do, at least until I muster the courage to confess to Ryan where I really live. I push the door open again and head for the strip joint.

And yet, as much as my mind justifies the need for a decoy home, I know lying to Ryan is wrong on so many levels. I mean, I'm actually choosing to build a new relationship based on dishonesty. Then another thought cripples me. What will he do if he finds out before I have the chance to come clean? The thought sends panic pains radiating through my limbs and down my center until I'm forced to stop walking and take refuge on a metal bench to manage my chaotic thoughts.

Maybe I should drop this whole fake apartment idea and simply tell Ryan the truth. He's been so amazingly sweet, so beyond anything I thought could ever happen to a girl like me … and there it is. *A girl like me*. I stand, the pains lessening with each deep breath I take to clear my whirling head. I remember the taunts, the teasing that flew at me in every direction in Mobile, and in Memphis, and in Clearwater.

And I'm not going back there, not ever being that girl again. I jot down the street name and number of the apartment building before I forget them. I'll take my chances with the lie. I already know what the truth gets me.

****

Brady couldn't be more right about the coat of arms I photographed this afternoon. I've scrolled through dozens of pics of shields and tapestries and old statues, anything at all to do with Louis XV, and nothing looks exactly like the plaque. And even though having knowledge of something so mysterious is mega cool, it doesn't get me one inch closer to the mystery I'm trying to unravel. And since the Internet isn't yielding the results I need, I know the next best place to turn. One advantage I'm actually benefiting from for being born into the Reynolds clan—no access to a computer for a very long time earned me some mad library skills.

My email alert dings and I open my Inbox. It's from Tyler.

Hang on to your drawers. You will not believe what I found through that keyhole from your picture. This is wicked wild stuff. Open the attachment. That's what's on the other side of that door. Do you have any idea what it is? Call me later.

My hands are shaking when I hit the paperclip icon to open the attachment. I wait for the picture to download for what seems like eons. "Come on." Then it appears.

Oh, my God! What … a bird? And the emblem on its body. What the…? I open the photos I took earlier of the coat of arms. Brady wasn't right after all. There is another instance of the plaque, and it's on a picture of some kind of bird wearing it like a badge of honor. And it's up there. Whatever that artwork signifies, it has everything to do with the contents of that third floor.

My heart's racing and I'm typing so fast my fingers are hitting multiple keys at once. Tyler can't show this to anyone else, especially not his dad. Is it possible that we're looking at an image that only we know exists? Is this what's being protected so heavily? I finish the email to Tyler. He has to keep this a secret until I can figure out what it means. What kind of bird is that? And why is it so royally adorned? I have to know.

Chapter Nine

I gaze down the length of the football field, trying fruitlessly to appear the slightest bit interested in the game. Ryan calls my bluff.

"You don't know the first thing about football, do you, Jules?"

"Well, I know you invited me to come with you, and that's all I need to know. Never been much into contact sports. Sorry."

"That's a real shame." Ryan cups a hand around my hip and slides me even closer to him on the stadium bench. "I happen to like contact sports."

"Get a room," Macey says, rejoining us after her trip to the concession stand. "Okay, so I have three nachos and three Cokes. Help me out here, Julia. I almost tripped and busted my ass on the way back up here."

"You're such a lady," I say and Ryan snickers.

"Hey, I'm a lady. Excuse me for not having six arms. Geeze." Macey leans across me and hands Ryan his food. "I thought you said Chris was coming?"

"He'll be here," Ryan assures her. "He texted me a few minutes ago."

She makes eye contact with me and winks. "Excellent."

Macey's been trying to hook up with one of Ryan's friends since we've been dating, not that I blame her. They're all majorly hot. Not *Ryan* hot, but hot.

"Hey, don't look now," Macey announces, "but that is one disgruntled cheerleader."

She points to Hannah, who's eyeing Ryan and me like a badger in a snake pit, all while keeping the pace of the cheer she's performing. A rare talent, I'm sure.

"What's her problem?" I turn my eyes to Ryan instead

of the razorblade stares from Hannah.

"Jealous much?" Macey shakes her head. "I swear, that chick's demented."

I couldn't help occasionally peeking through my limp hair to see if she was still staring. Why does she care so much? She's the one who cheated on Ryan, but you'd swear it was the other way around.

"Hey, there's Chris," Ryan says, motioning him to sit with us.

"Awesome," Macey says. "Hey, Julia, is my lipstick still good?"

"It's fine. Relax already."

In a few minutes, Macey's talking Chris's ears off. So much for her nerves. It's halftime and Ryan stands to stretch his legs. I notice Hannah and some of the other cheerleaders, including Jasmine and Kimmie, pointing at me and laughing. I glance at Ryan out of the corner of my eye, wondering if he sees them. I know my face is red. Why are they bothering me? Then Macey does something more than a little cringe-worthy.

"Hey, Hannah, your preoccupation with Julia is pathetic. I mean, don't you have a date with a bottle of bleach somewhere? Or with some jock in the field house?"

Chris and Macey break out in raucous laughter, along with a few other kids who are seated close to us. Ryan looks a little uncomfortable, but can't hide the smirk sliding over his lips. But I stay still and silent. In that moment, I wish I wasn't the only exception to the pleasure of seeing Hannah squirm. Instead, I'm glancing about, waiting for someone to step from the shadows and say, *But that's Julia Reynolds. Her mom works in Hooters and her dad's a bum. What are you doing here with her?* That's exactly what had happened at the one and only football game I'd attended my first week in Mobile. I'd made a couple of fast friends and we were at a game when a group of senior guys pointed out my identity, or rather, my mom's occupation. The humiliation followed me the rest of that year. And no matter if Hannah were asking for it, no one deserves to be ridiculed in public. Not even a bitchy ice queen.

I tug Macey's pants leg. "Sit down and stop it, please. Just leave her alone."

"Are you kidding me?" Macey sits. "She's a witch, and you're too nice. She'd stab you in the back in a second given a spiked heel and a clean shot."

"I know, but don't call her out in public like that, okay?"

Macey shrugs. "Whatever."

"What's wrong, Jules?" Ryan places a hand on top of mine. "You okay?"

"Oh, yeah. I just don't feel very well all of a sudden."

"You wanna go?"

"I think I do."

"Then we're outta here."

The traffic isn't as thick since we're leaving at halftime. I feel guilty for making Ryan go, and I'm not really sure what came over me. Things have been so different in New Orleans this time—better. Much better, actually. If Aubree would just show up, say that the cops were right and she had simply run away for a while, things would be perfect. But I know that's not true—will never happen. And being in that situation, one that mirrored a painful memory from Alabama, pulled me back there before I could blink. And I hate going back. Having to go back to painful memories too much. I can't believe I let it get to me like that.

"How you feeling?" Ryan asks when we're almost in

front of the decoy apartment.

"Fine now, thanks. I'm not sure what happened back there. Sorry you're missing the game."

"No biggie, I'm just glad you're okay.

Infinitely sweet.

Ryan pulls up and parks in front of my fake apartment. He gets the door for me and I join him on the sidewalk.

"Is it all right if we stay out here and talk a few minutes?" he asks.

Sure, it's not like I really live here. "Yeah, it's okay."

"There's something I've been wanting to ask you."

This has to be a good something, but my stomach's not buying it. "So ask me."

"Julia, will you go to the Homecoming dance with me?" His eyes hold my stare, waiting for a reaction.

"What?" I can't believe it. "You're asking *me*?"

"Well, of course." He laughs. "I mean, I don't think it would be right to ask anyone besides my girlfriend."

"Your girlfriend?"

He's cloudy through the tears that fill my eyes. I wrap my arms around his neck and hold him there for several seconds. I want this moment to stay suspended here a little longer, to never forget the rush that's holding my breath and causing my heart to pound wildly.

"Yes, I'll go to the dance with you. I'm your girlfriend. I mean, I knew it, but hearing you say it—"

He kisses my nose. "You're my girlfriend, and you're adorable, among other things. Now I better let you get inside before your dad comes down here and stomps on my head. Your dad is up there, right?"

"Uh, yeah."

"Then I better go."

I walk up the steps of my false address and step inside

the foyer. When Ryan's Mustang is out of sight, I exit the building and head in the direction of home. I try to push the guilt to the back of my mind. How can I keep lying to him about my home life when he's putting it all out there for me? Taking risks, asking me to Homecoming. Telling me I'm his girlfriend. It's more than I ever imagined ... like a dream.

But this is my dream, the one I've been chasing since middle school, and it's finally coming true. I'm popular, accepted, and I'm not ready to give it up—not ever ready to lose Ryan. I've never been this lucky in my life. *Lucky.* I pull my fountain pen from my back pocket and read the inscription for the umpteenth time. I'll take its advice willingly, practice discretion a little longer, although I'm sure the discretion it advises has nothing to do with being deceitful, even if it is for the right reasons.

****

"Glad you're home. I was getting worried."

"Hey, girlie."

"Mom, Aunt Beth. Why aren't you at work?" I expected Jesse to be the only one home.

"We're playing hooky tonight," Mom says. "Thought we'd both skip work for once and watch a movie."

"Liar," Aunt Beth says, her sweet eyes glassy and words slurring. "I have to go to the bathroom."

When she's out of the room, I look at Mom. "Is she drunk?"

Mom pulls me close to her face. "Yeah, she's had a few drinks. We both went to work tonight, but I had to leave with her a couple of hours ago. A girl who looked a lot like Aubree walked up to Beth's game table she was dealing for. Freaked Beth out to no end. It was heartbreaking. I didn't want her to be alone tonight."

My chest tightens. "Oh, crap. That's horrible."

"I know," Mom replies. "But you and Jesse don't need to see her like this. Why don't you go to your room, okay? I think Jesse's asleep already."

"Sure," I reply. "God, Mom. I'm sorry."

Her eyes shine. "So am I."

I turn to go to my room and then look at Mom again. "Aubree … do you miss her?"

Mom's eyes let the gathering tears fall. "Every day."

Guilt floods my body like an ocean before I make it to my bedroom door. Being with Ryan tonight pushed Aubree far from my thoughts. Honestly, nothing in New Orleans is like I thought it would be. For so long, all I wanted to do was be back here so I could look for her. I've been so wrapped up in school and in learning what's on that third floor of the convent, she's as lost in my thoughts as she is to the world. What's wrong with me?

I'm at the computer with my blog pulled up within ten seconds. I retrieve a blog post from two years ago titled *Shadow People? Fact or Fiction?* I use the same story and facts I wrote then, but add to the bottom of the article:

Have the Shadow People in New Orleans ever found an actual vampire coven? Have they ever claimed to? Where would this information be publicized? Have you ever heard of a teenager named Aubree Marie Turner? Help me out, people.

I wait for the gazillion bogus comments I know will come, but maybe something in the chaos will give me a clue about Aubree's whereabouts, her disappearance. And in the meantime, I'll keep digging up everything I can about the convent. I still can't believe she used to talk about the Ursuline with Brady. Yeah, I'll figure out its secret and write about it … have credibility out the ying yang. Then I can get Aubree's name out there to even more people.

Bring her home.

****

"So, this is what this place looks like on the inside. Nice … and boring." Tyler drops his backpack in the chair beside me. "I must say, we meet in the most peculiar arenas, my dear."

He's a total goob, and I can't help but laugh. "Yeah, like you've never been in the public library before."

"Do you think I've been without a computer before in my life ever? Not hardly. So, the answer is no, I've never been to the public library."

"That's so sad." I wipe mock tears.

"Now," Tyler continues, "what I want to know is, where's the shy girl in glasses who poses as a bookworm but is really a goddess when the glasses come off, like in movies. I want to meet *her*."

"Well, too bad, player. You're stuck with me. Did you bring your laptop?"

Tyler taps his backpack. "Always."

"Great. Pull up the picture of the bird. I want to see it with the actual program on your computer."

"Not a prob." Tyler pulls his laptop from the bag. "So what's your next move?"

"What do you mean?"

"With the convent and finding out what's up there. You know, your next move."

"I'm not sure yet, but I have some questions floating around that need answering, ergo, the bird. I need to know what it represents and why it's wearing that coat of arms."

"Coat of arms?" Tyler opens his laptop. "You talking about the shield thing it's wearing? How do you know what it is?"

"Because there's one hanging in the Ursuline that looks exactly like it."

"Shut up. That's awesome. You can find out what it is, then. I mean, can't someone in the convent just give you some facts about it?"

"Someone already has, and the thing's as mysterious as that third floor. No description, no date, it's just there. And I couldn't find a single article, photo, nothing on the Internet about it. You know, too many things are a complete puzzle when it comes to that place."

"Yeah, no kidding. So, I guess that's why you're here, for a little bit of good old-fashioned digging?"

"You got it."

Tyler busies himself with the laptop and I flip another page in the Louis XV book that's in front of me, along with a stack of four others. The coat of arms hasn't made an appearance in a single one, and I'm starting to doubt the good-looking history sage. Maybe that plaque has nothing to do with good ole' King Louis after all.

"Okay, here it is," Tyler says when the picture of the bird fills the screen.

"Excellent." I scoot my chair closer to his. "I don't suppose you have any idea what type of bird this might be?"

"Actually, I do." Tyler looks infinitely proud of himself. "Dear heart, I do believe we are looking at an albatross."

"Bird enthusiast much?"

"Not really." Tyler's cheeks go pink. "But I do know a little about them." He points to the screen, leaning and attempting to hide the fact that he's blushing. "See how the wing on the bottom is very long? The albatross is known for that feature, so I looked up these photos of a real albatross to compare. It's a spot-on match, see? The beak's the dead giveaway."

I stare at the pics for a moment. "Oh, my God, you're right, Ty. That's brilliant! It is an albatross."

He leans back in his chair. "You're welcome."

I jot the fact in my notebook. *But why an albatross? What does it mean?*

Tyler closes his laptop. "My work here is done. I hate to bolt, Julia, but I have to meet my dad at the station in a little while. It's my mom's birthday and we're surprising her with dinner."

"Sweet. I really appreciate you stopping here with that info. It's a major help." But I know I have to bring up something else before I let him go. "Hey, Ty, I need to ask you another favor, okay?"

"Lay it on me."

"I was serious about what I said in my email the other night. I really don't want you to tell anyone about all this, okay? I don't want anyone to know what I'm doing as far as investigating the convent."

"So, it's a secret?"

"Sort of. I mean, it'll be a lot easier for me to do this without someone trying to stop me. You can understand that, right? And if someone knew—"

"Like my dad?"

Busted.

"Yes, if someone like your dad knew what I was doing, I may not get to see it through."

Tyler's expression hardens. "And you're positive this is something you really *want* to see through?" His voice is raw and tight. "People have died investigating that place, Julia. I mean, all this fact-finding and clue-gathering is fun, but what if at the end of the day, you're dead? Is it worth it?"

I can't move, struck momentarily by the fear I see in

Tyler's eyes as clear as I see him standing in front of me. He believes what his dad says about that third floor and the investigators. He thinks I really might die if I do this.

"Ty, listen to me." The words sound weak and I have to clear my throat. "I know that two interns died investigating the convent, but New Orleans is a dangerous place. Anything could have happened to them, and a murderer could use the fear of that third floor to his advantage. I know they died because I read it, found that to be a cold hard fact. But when your dad said police detectives died investigating the murders, well, I haven't seen any evidence that supports that. No facts at all. I mean, think about it, when a cop dies, it's all over the news. I can't find anything about it. Nothing. Doesn't that seem strange to you?"

"It's true, Julia. My dad warned you already. If you go snooping around that place and get in trouble, the police will not come and help you. That's because they know how dangerous it is."

"Fine. Then show me the proof."

"Okay," he whispers, "you win." He looks hurt, which is nowhere near my intention. "I'll keep your secret, Julia, but I hope you know what you're doing. Later."

"Bye. Enjoy your mom's birthday dinner."

He waves, but keeps his back to me.

I take in a breath, relieving the tightness in my throat. I wish Tyler would try to see things my way, stop being so intense. When police detectives are murdered, it's front-page news, period. End of story. He has to know that deep down. And if they are dead and it's been kept under wraps, then I'm sure it has more to do with the NOPD's parasitic background than the third floor of a convent, no matter how secretive it's kept. I'll talk to him about it more later, try to reassure him somehow. But I

have to admit, his concern is touching.
****

I'm frozen in my seat, staring at the back of Ryan's head. Sometimes I wish I sold ads for Journalism instead of writing articles just so I could sit with him for the entire class. *Not!* I laugh at my overactive brain. Man, I've got it bad for that boy.

The last couple minutes of class Ms. Dunkin allows free time as usual, and the girl next to me gets up so Ryan can sit. She knows the drill.

"I hope you studied for the Biology test you have next block," Ryan announces when he's within earshot. "I took it first block and it's a killer."

"Don't have to take it. I aced the lab and pop quiz, so Mr. Campbell gave me an automatic A. Matter of fact, I don't even have to show up for class." I breathe on the top of my fingernails and run them across the shoulder of my blouse. "I rock, you know."

"Obviously." He mock bows. "So, Teacher's Pet, where you going for next block, then?"

"Ms. Dunkin said I could stay in here. It's her planning period anyway, so I'm doing a little research on a story I've been working on."

"Soon enough you'll have the entire administration wrapped around that pretty little finger of yours, huh? Guess I better slide over and make room."

I lean in and hide my face against his shoulder. "You say the sweetest things, you know that?"

"I simply speak the truth."

The bell sounds, and I lift my head to look in his eyes. "See you at lunch, okay?"

He raises my hand to his lips and kisses the top of it. "Can't wait. Bye, Jules."

Ryan's the second guy to kiss my hand since moving

here. The NOLA Welcome Center should add that little piece of male southern charm to its brochures. He flings his book bag over one shoulder and heads for the door. I appreciate his honeyed spikes from behind yet again and take a deep, slow breath. I catch myself doing that every time he's leaving a room, like the air is somehow sweeter the final moments we're occupying the same space.

When the room's empty, Ms. Dunkin offers a warm smile and the class computer for my research. "Help yourself, Julia. Hey, I never mind a student working on a potential story."

"Thanks, Ms. Dunkin." I pretend to be engrossed in my research, but the truth is I've been dying to ask her a few questions … pick that brain I love to hear her spout from so freely in class. After a couple of minutes, I muster the courage.

"Hey, Ms. Dunkin, do you mind if I ask you something?"

She closes the book she's reading. "Not at all. What is it, Julia?"

"Well, you talk about finding *the story* all the time, and about how much you love journalism. You're so passionate about it. I can't even begin to tell you how much you've inspired me to be better. So, why are you a teacher? Don't get me wrong, you're amazing at teaching, but wouldn't you be happier working as a reporter? You know, finding that one perfect story that changes everything."

She flashes a ready smile. "The truth is, Julia, I was a print journalist for several years. But journalism has changed, evolved. All of the papers are mostly online now, and that's fine. Truth be told, the best time I ever spent as a reporter was when I was a student. There's something contagious about teenage energy. Young people think they can handle situations that they really can't. No one can, no matter their age. But teens will try, no matter what. And when those attempts actually work out, well, it's pure gold. That's why I teach, to simply be a glimmer in that gold."

She's done it again. It's no wonder she consistently boasts an award-winning Journalism class. She makes gaining momentum as simple as tying a shoe. "How do you do that?"

"Do what?" Ms. Dunkin sticks her nose in her book again. "I have no idea what you're referring to."

"Yeah, yeah." I pull out my notebook and turn back to the computer. I've done so much research on the Ursuline, something has to start adding up sooner or later. I type *Origin of the Albatross* in the search bar and shift through the cookie-cutter definitions with a yawn. Nothing I read has anything to do with why an albatross would be chosen as the creature to bear the mysterious coat of arms. So I reword my search a couple of times, and then a line intrigues me. *The albatross is supposed to have supernatural powers...* I click the link.

   "The albatross is supposed to have supernatural powers, and by some is believed to be the souls of dead sailors. They guarantee a fair wind. So if you kill an albatross, you lose   all chance of a fair wind and will be blown off course to drift aimlessly with no chance of redemption."

If you kill an albatross? My frenzied fingers grab a pen and write furiously in my notebook.

"Did you find something?" Ms. Dunkin asks, peeking from behind her book.

I mumble one word. "Gold."

Chapter Ten

I brush through my hair quickly and check my teeth in the mirror before giving my mouth a final rinse. I had intended to do more research on the albatross last night after homework, but ended up texting Ryan until way too late. So I'm up an hour early before school, nearly bursting at the prospect of finding actual facts rather than relying on mere speculation when it comes to the picture of the mysterious seabird and the elusive coat of arms it bears. I have a hunch about the albatross, though. Time to put my mad skills into action.

My dinosaur of a computer has been loading since I've been in the bathroom—a time-saving trick I've mastered from being a slave to low-tech for so long. I pull up Google and click the cursor in the search bar. The one line that stuck in my head when I read about the albatross in Ms. Dunkin's class yesterday was: *So if you kill an albatross, you lose all chance of a fair wind and will be blown off course to drift aimlessly with no chance of redemption.*

It said the albatross is believed to be the souls of dead sailors. *If you kill an albatross* … that's what I have to focus on. Who would the albatross represent in regard to the convent? The first individuals that come to mind are the students of the Ursuline—the Casket Girls. After all, the nuns and the girls are the topic of the tour—the legacy of the Ursuline. I can only assume that the albatross represents the girls because of their treacherous sea journey to New Orleans. Brady thinks the coat of arms is from the era of Louis XV. And, the albatross in the picture locked away on that third floor is wearing the coat of arms. So what is the connection between Louis XV and the Casket Girls? My stomach tingles as my fingers fly over the keyboard. I think I'm onto something.

I type *King Louis XV and The Casket Girls* into the search bar and hit enter:

When the nuns of the Ursuline arrived in New Orleans in 1727, their goal was to impart dignity and reverence to the reckless hoodlums inhabiting the penal colony. The Sisters set up a school to educate and a hospital to heal, and also provided security and shelter to the middle-class yet well-bred French girls. The filles á la cassette, *or Casket Girls, as they became known because of their coffin-shaped trousseaus carried for the journey, began arriving in 1728 and for several years after for the sole purpose of providing respectable marriage material for the men in the colony. 'Send us virtuous women, Our Beloved,' the men and founders wrote to Mother France. But how cruelly they abused the gift.*

Virtuous women? Our Beloved? Abused the gift? I jot the phrases in my notebook, my heart thumping like a mallet on a bass drum. I sift through dozens more academic-looking articles before my hour runs out. I find a few more facts worth including in my notebook, but nothing as interesting as the first article. I have little doubt now that Louis XV did indeed send the Casket Girls to New Orleans and that the albatross is somehow a symbol of that terrible decision, but I have to find at least one concrete fact to support my theory. And if the king did feel some form of guilt, why would he feel such pity for middle-class young women? Did the elite of that time period ever do that? Ever feel enough pity to create a symbol of a commoner's plight, well-bred or not? I write down my theory and brush away the discovery goose bumps now tickling my arms. I know I'm hitting on something big. The question is, what?

I hurry into the kitchen to grab a quick bite before catching my bus. Jesse's almost out the door, and Mom's nursing a cup of coffee.

Jesse pushes the front door open with his foot and then stops in the doorway. "Hey, Julia, why the hell were you up so early this morning?"

"Language," Mom says, never looking up from her cup.

"I had something to do. Don't worry about it, troll bait."

"Well, you woke me up a whole thirty minutes too early."

"Oh, Earth shattering." I retrieve a spoon from the dishwasher and cut him a look. "Don't you have somewhere to be?"

"Bite me," he says and lets the door slam.

"You're not too big for soap in the mouth," Mom yells at the closed door.

"You've never put soap in our mouths," I remind her.

She smiles. "I know. So, why *did* you get up early this morning?"

"Wow, nosy family."

"Ha! You're calling us nosy? Now that's hilarious." She sips her coffee and yawns.

"You got me there." I pour milk on my cereal and join her at the table. "I'm researching a story for Journalism. You know, the story on the convent."

"Oh, the one with the vampires on the top floor."

"Well, not really. The one that is *rumored* to house vampires. But I'm no more convinced that it's a vampire coven than I am that Jesse is my biological brother. Please tell me he's adopted."

"Sorry."

"Damn."

"Language," we say in unison and then smile.

"I do have some news, Mom, and it's juicy."

She sets her cup down and stares me in the face. "Okay, I'm ready. Spill it."

"Well, Ryan asked me to the Homecoming dance."

"Really? Well, that's awesome, baby. I'm so glad."

"Yeah, I'm super excited."

"When is it?"

"Not for several weeks, and I'm glad I have time because I really don't know what I'm going to do about a dress. I'm gonna have to think about it."

She suddenly looks like a deflated balloon, and I'm sorry I even brought up the part about the dress.

"Well, it'll all work out," she says. "It always does."

I take the last bite of my cereal and place the bowl in the sink. "I better get outta here."

"All right. See you this afternoon."

In a couple of minutes, I'm out the door and walking the few blocks to my bus stop. Part of me is tempted to share my investigation of the convent with Ryan, but I know the headache it could create, so I push the brief lapse in judgment to the back of my mind. I really don't need any hassle, just in case he's the type to worry profoundly about my safety. I mean, I know there's a certain amount of danger, but I'm not stupid. I'll be more careful the next time I get on that third floor. Yeah, I'm not telling Ryan about the Ursuline.

I glance at the time on my phone. The bus is a couple minutes late, as usual. I hate waiting, especially if I have to scramble to make it to class on time. I start reading signs in the businesses across the street—anything to get my mind off the possibility of being late. As I hear the bus approaching, a sign in a jazz club catches my eye: *Come and Hear The Count, a Direct Descendant of*

Jacques St. Germain, The Vampire Scourge of the French Quarter.

Excuse me? Who is this guy?

The bus pulls up and I climb on, my eyes still skimming the sign in the window as I take a seat. I pull out my notebook and quickly write down the name while I can still see the spelling. *Jacques St. Germain. Vampire Scourge?* It has to be hype, a piece of folklore used to put butts in the seats. I'm sure it's nothing, so why is my stomach wrestling my brain?

****

I make my way to Journalism, my brain a fog of questions, all of them about the sign I read at the bus stop this morning. Normally I'd be excited about seeing Ryan this block—and I am happy about that—but I really hope Ms. Dunkin gives us extended computer time today. I have four words ready for my impending Internet sleuthing: Jacques St. Germain Vampire.

I can't help but wonder if Aubree ever heard of him. I wish more than anything I could remember all the folklore and vampire stories she used to tell me. Don't get me wrong, I listened. I worshiped my time spent with her, actually. But it's funny how details escape you when your world stops. Had I known the future, I would have hung on her every word. But I do remember one thing Aubree always said. *Nothing is untraceable, Julia. If you search long and hard enough, clues are left behind. Everyone leaves a little piece of themselves somewhere. Search long and hard enough and you'll find them.*

Ryan's seated when I enter the room, and I give him a pinky wave.

"What's up, Jules?" he says when I pass his desk.

"Not too much." *Lie.* "But the day's a lot better now that I'm seeing you." *Truth.*

I start walking past him to sit before the bell rings, but he grabs my arm and pulls me into his whisper. "I have something to tell you later. Awesome news, actually."

"Sweet." I smile. "Can't wait to hear what it is."

"Everyone, please take your seats," Ms. Dunkin says when the bell sounds. "Today we're going to talk about the proper way to interview. Whether you work for a school newspaper, CNN, the "Nightly News", or the *New York Times*, there is a right way and a wrong way to conduct an interview. Rule number one: Ask all the questions, even if you think the answer is obvious. If you skip a question, you miss an answer ... possibly *the* answer you've been searching for from the beginning. For it is in the obvious that the truth comes out. Never forget that, people. Never skip the easy question or you'll miss the obvious answer."

Midway through class, Ms. Dunkin assigns an article to me on school board approval for a new program to support the arts in public schools. Interesting fodder, but not the story I'm pumped about at the moment. I know I shouldn't be using class time for my own personal story, but at least no one can ever question my dedication. I type the four words that have been pestering my mind all day into the empty space and press enter. I swallow hard when several articles and blogs actually appear regarding the rumored vampire.

Oh. My. God.

In New Orleans in the 1700s, there was a gentleman of superior wealth named Comte Saint Germaine. He was strange and beautiful; a man who was charismatic and so extraordinarily different from the other gentlemen of court. He was so extremely wealthy that he even carried rare gems in his pockets as if they were mere coins. He had an affinity for chemistry and was masterful with the violin and piano. He spoke several languages. Some people said he never aged—the man who knows everything and who never dies. He would throw lavish parties for the elite of society, serve large spreads of food, yet no one ever saw him take a bite. He would instead just sip his wine and enjoy the company of others. It was reported that he died in the late 1700s, though no one ever really witnessed his death or saw his dead body. And some claim to have seen him many years after his recorded death. Some years later, in the early 1900s, a man by the name of Jacques Saint Germain appeared in New Orleans. He matched Comte perfectly, right down to the extravagant riches, and the most fascinating of dinner guests attended his lavish parties as well. Where he came from and his true identity remained a mystery, just like Comte. But one night, Saint Germain got careless. He had a lady of the night staying with him. She was on his balcony when Germain grabbed her and tried to bite her neck. She escaped by falling from the balcony and told the townspeople and the authorities. When the police investigated, Jacques Saint Germain was nowhere to be found. They searched his home and found tablecloths with large blood stains on them and many bottles of wine. When the policemen tasted the wine, they made a shocking discovery. This was not simply wine ... it was wine mixed with human blood.

As chilling as the article turns out to be, it seems more mythical than factual. I browse through a few more St. Germain sites, and they all have the same *feel*. Could St. Germain have been a real vampire terrorizing the streets of New Orleans? The scourge of the French Quarter? I guess it's possible, and I hate thinking he could be on that third floor, simply lying in wait for me when I do make my way into his lair. But I'm still not buying it.

Is a vampire coven the real reason for that sealed third floor? *Maybe*. Or is it folklore and a fear tactic concocted to conceal the real mystery that rests there? *More than likely*. After all, I've been researching the convent, observing the contents and the history. I need stronger evidence to put more stock in vampires smuggled in the trousseaus of well-bred French girls as many would have folks believe. Then, I'm jarred by my own rationale. *Many folks do believe. Aubree believed.*

That logic is enough to make me scroll through a few more articles. I stop at one when I notice a more recent date. 1978. I still need answers on two dead interns that were murdered in 1973. My doubt turns to excitement. Maybe I've found something here.

In 1978, two amateur reporters, twenty-year-old Jeremy Sills and twenty-five-year-old Nathan Griggs, set out to solve the mystery of the Ursuline Convent and the vampires said to occupy the premises. After browsing the convent, they begged a guide to let them in to see the rumored coffins housed on the third floor. The guide fervently denied their entrance. So the young men took it upon themselves to stake out the convent and the mysterious third floor. They waited until nightfall, then scaled a wall and set up a mini-camp, complete with recording equipment and several cameras. Come morning, the street in front of the convent was littered with smashed camera equipment. The bodies of the two amateur reporters were found on the convent steps, their bodies placed in a cross formation atop each other, most of the blood drained from the corpses. Investigators have yet to solve the crime—an unsolved mystery 'til this very day.

Amateur reporters? I jot the details in my notebook, trying to ignore my racing heart and prickly skin. These men were going for the story, like me. *Just like me*. No matter if the killer was a vampire or something entirely different, they're just as dead. This isn't folklore. This is a news article with names, like the female interns who died before them. They were murdered. All of them, murdered. I can't believe I've stumbled across more dead reporters. It's insane. Maybe Detective Elder isn't lying about investigators winding up dead.

"Hey, what ya got there?"

I jump and quickly exit the page when Ryan comes up behind me.

"Nothing. What's up?"

"Whatever you're reading must be intense. Sorry I startled you, Jules."

I clear my throat. "It's okay."

"Listen, I have epic news."

I try focusing on Ryan instead of my shock from a few seconds ago. "That's right, the news. What is it?"

"My parents are going away for the weekend, so I'll have the whole house to myself. I was thinking we could grab a pizza, watch a couple movies, and just kick it Friday night. How's that sound?"

Almost as scary as the dead reporters, but delicious at the same time. "Sounds great. But try to stay away from the shoot'em up, bang 'em up flicks, okay?"

"Deal."

****

Today has been mentally exhausting. I can't believe I'm going to be alone with Ryan this weekend. I mean, I've been alone with him before, just not *alone* alone. It's terrifying, yet I'm so excited I can hardly contain myself. And this morning, finding the vampire references and discovering two more dead reporters. What else is waiting to be found about that convent, and do I really *want* to find it? I can't keep telling myself it's fine to keep digging when it comes to the Ursuline. Sooner or later, I have to admit the danger involved in snooping. Maybe I should back off a little. Ha, Tyler will be so pleased.

I toss a few crackers in a plastic bowl and open the nearly-empty fridge, even though I know we've been out of butter for two days now. I dig in the side tray for the hidden treasure I hope no one has confiscated. Yes, success! I retrieve some strawberry jelly packets I lifted from McDonald's one morning last week and head to my room. I need to research the deaths of the two reporters a little more. What I don't get is why didn't Tyler's dad mention them when I made the trip to the station to ask about the dead interns? Surely he knows about them ... has to. Telling me about two more murders would have been an even better deterrent to keep me out of the convent. It just doesn't add up.

I plop at my desk and check my blog comments first, hoping someone gives me any information at all about Aubree. There's the usual. People pulling up old articles about her disappearance—like I've never seen those before—and giving their own theory on what might've happened to her. Nothing new is jumping out at me, and then I see a comment from Mr. Hottie History Teacher himself. Brady reads my blog regularly now. He wrote:

Love the title of your blog, Julia. A Little Mystery In Between. Cool.

Truth be known, Brady follows my blog to read up on the Aubree comments, too. I have no doubt he wants to know what happened to her—probably piecing together some of the same things I've looked at a hundred times already. It's ironic that he asked about the title. No one ever has. And Aubree had everything to do with it.

One time Aubree was getting ready to go out with friends. Her boyfriend had just broken up with her, and she was acting like she was fine with it. Even at twelve I knew she wasn't fine. I saw two pieces of paper on her dresser and read them.

"What are these?" I'd asked.

"Love letters from Kyle," was her reply.

"Why only two?"

I'll never forget her eyes that day, the way she looked at me. It was like she was about to tell me something hidden, something buried so deep in her heart that it hurt to pull it out.

"I only kept the first one he wrote and the last one," Aubree said that day. "Because after someone breaks your heart, none of the ones in between really matter, do they?"

"Julia!" Mom's voice pulls me from my thoughts. "Come here. I want to show you something."

I pop a cracker in my mouth and talk through the crumbs. "Coming."

When I step back in the kitchen, Mom is holding up a pale-lavender, knee-length gown with a beaded bodice and spaghetti straps, and it's the most gorgeous thing I've ever seen. I can't breathe.

"Well, do you like it?"

I can barely squeeze the words out, my throat tight with tears. "It's beautiful. Where did you get it?"

"After we talked this morning, I called my friend I work with—you know, Bonnie? I remembered her telling me that her little sister was in a wedding in Metairie last week, and that the dress was actually very pretty. She'd said it was a shame it would never be worn again. So, I called her up. I have to share my tips with her for the next two nights, but it's yours. I know it looks a little big, but I can take it in. Isn't it pretty?" She pauses and then adds, "Please say something, Julia."

But I can't say anything. I fall into her instead, wrapping my arms around her neck, and then squeeze out, "Thank you so much, Mom. It's so gorgeous. Thank you, thank you. I can't believe you did this for me."

Mom holds my shoulder and pushes me back to look in my eyes. "Julia, you're a good kid, and you don't ask for much. Hell, you never ask for anything. I want you to know that I'm here for you when you need me, when it counts. This dance is important to you, and you needed a dress. And now you have one."

I hug her so tight I can barely breathe, but I don't care. My mom got me a dress.

"What are you two blubbering about?" Dad says when he comes into the kitchen. He points to the dress. "What's that for?"

"Homecoming," Mom says. "Julia has a date for the Homecoming dance next month."

He stares at Mom, the typical question in his eyes. "Nice, but how much did it cost?"

"Nothing," Mom says, giving a look to remind me not to mention the dipping into her tips part. "It belonged to a sister of a girl from work."

"Even better," he replies. "So, Julia, this guy you're seeing, does his family have money?"

I roll my eyes. "Tacky, Dad."

"Hey, I'm just looking out for your best interest."

"No, you're looking out for *your* best interest." *As usual.*

"Whatever." He grimaces. "Erin, find me something to eat. I'm starving. And, Julia, make no mistake. I'm glad you got that dress. I mean, you're *my* kid. Gotta look good." He winks and retreats into the living room with the newspaper.

Mom hands me the dress and pulls a box of macaroni from the pantry. "Maybe it wouldn't hurt if Ryan had a little money."

****

He's late. I've been waiting outside my fake apartment for ten minutes, so nervous that my hands are shaking and my insides feel all crawly. I'm about to step back into the foyer when I see Ryan's Mustang down the street. I run my hands down the front of my jeans and smooth my blouse. My palms are sweaty, but it can't be helped. I'm not sure I've ever been this nervous.

"Been waiting out here long?" he says as he steps out of the car.

"Not really."

He joins me on the sidewalk and kisses my cheek. "You ready? I hope you like the movies I picked." He's smiling, but there's an uncomfortable edge in his voice. Could he be as nervous as me?

In a couple of minutes, we're headed to his house— his ginormous, empty house.

Ryan briefly peeks in my direction. "You look very pretty, Jules." He glues his eyes to the road again. "I like your hair. It's different."

Aw, he noticed. It took nearly twenty minutes to get the barrette to stay in place in my thin, stringy hair. His attention to detail is totally fab.

"Thanks. You look great, too." And he does. He's wearing a white knit polo and black jeans, understated to sheer perfection. I can tell he just showered. His hair's still a little damp, and I can smell his recently applied deodorant. I love the way a guy smells straight from the shower.

"So," I ask, trying not to sound meek, "what's the

plan for tonight?" God, I sound like an eight-year-old.

His hands are rigid on the steering wheel and his jaw clenches. "I just want to spend some quality time with you, Jules. We can do whatever you want."

After more idle chit-chat and a firm decision to order Chinese takeout, we pull into Ryan's driveway. He opens the car door for me—ever the gentleman—and we enter the house through the back gate to avoid nosy neighbors.

We go to the kitchen and Ryan rifles through a slew of Chinese takeout menus. "Do you have a preference?"

"Nope, just pick one." I hope my eyes don't give away that I've never had Chinese takeout in my life. After a couple of minutes, we decide on a restaurant and some items and Ryan calls in the order.

We kill the first hour on the couch eating fried wontons and cashew chicken while watching a romantic comedy that is more than a little cheesy. I bite another wonton. "I like these. I never thought they'd taste this good." *Oh God, why did I say that?*

Ryan laughs. "You've never had a fried wonton?"

I'm not sure where my bravery's coming from, but I test the waters. "I've never had Chinese food." I feel flames on my face.

"Get outta here!" He leans back and looks me in the eyes. "You've *never* had Chinese food, ever?"

"Well, unless you count the fried rice they call Chinese food in the school cafeteria, then no, I've never had Chinese food, but it's good. I really like it."

Ryan's jawline tightens, and I suddenly feel embarrassed. "You know, you can tell me anything, Julia. It really doesn't matter what it is. You can trust me with anything, okay?"

"Sure," I say, knowing he can't possibly imagine the anythings in my life, and I don't want him to. "Okay."

When the food is consumed and we've talked about every approachable subject, Ryan stretches out on the couch and opens his arms for me to join him. I freeze, hoping I can will my body to lean in, to curl up beside him. I've never been this close to a guy before. But I want to be close to him. Crave it more than air.

When my courage overtakes my reeling brain, I grant Ryan's wish and snuggle next to him, our denim-covered legs tangling like wild vines on an oak. He pushes his face into my hair and inhales.

"Mmmmm, Julia, you smell so good."

I want to say something, but it's hard to form a coherent thought with his face on my cheek and the length of his body flush with mine. I can't get my nerves in check, and Ryan seems to notice my tension. He traces a finger along my collarbone and whispers, "Relax."

I close my eyes, giving in to the warmth of his hands on my skin and the heat surging through my body. When I feel his lips on my neck, I shudder, the sensation like a peal of thunder and the hush of a whisper all at once. My nerves are replaced with gratification. I'm still terrified, but I like the new sensations too much to even consider telling him to stop. And when he pulls me into a tight embrace and strokes my cheek, reassurance in his eyes like a warm blanket, I know I have nothing to worry about. Ryan would never do anything to hurt me.

Soon, his hands are on my stomach and he covers my mouth in a kiss that's a little rougher than usual, but I like it. His fingers crawl up my shirt, but when his thumb slides over my bra, I pull back.

"I'm sorry, Ryan. This is a little too fast for me."

"Oh, God. I'm sorry, Julia," he says. I can't tell if his cheeks are flush from embarrassment or from being so close to me.

"No, don't apologize," I say. "I want this, I really do, but it's just a little too fast, know what I mean?" *I don't want to be pregnant at sixteen like my mom is what I mean. No way I'm saying it, though.*

"It's fine," he says, kissing my nose and pulling me close to him again. "You are just so cute. How's this? Do you like this?"

He covers my lips with his and kisses me slow, his tongue playing with my top lip until I'm breathless. When he stops and looks in my eyes, every inch of me tingles.

"How about we do that instead?"

I take his face in my hands. "Absolutely."

"How late can you stay?" he asks after another hour passes.

I look at the time on my phone. "Not much longer."

"I wish you could stay all night."

"Yeah, I bet. Some of us still have parents at home, remember? Well, a dad at home. My mom's..." Then I stop. I can't believe I just said that, let my guard down that far.

"Your mom's not home? Where is she?"

"Out with friends, and I better make it home before she does." I lift myself off the couch and pretend to look for my purse. I can't look him in the face right now. I can't believe how easily I lie to him. Well, not so easily now. It hurts my soul, and I hate it.

"Okay, I'll take you home." Ryan reaches his arms over his head in a long stretch. "But the deal is, tomorrow night"—he points to the couch—"same spot, same time, same sappy movies, different food. Deal?"

I smile. "It's a deal."

He gets all serious and wraps me into a hug. "I need to tell you something, Julia."

We sit back down, and I can't take my gaze off his face.

"You make me feel so different." Ryan takes a deep breath, but I can barely breathe at all. "I don't know, I've just never cared about a girl like I care about you. I love you, Julia."

I feel the tears before they fall. Every dream I've ever had pales in comparison to this moment. "I love you too."

****

Ryan pulls the Mustang up to the curb in front of Phoneyville, and I step out of the car. He meets me on my side and pulls me into a long kiss.

"I'll see you tomorrow night, around six?" He kisses my nose.

"Can't wait." He better catch me before I reach the moon. I'm pretty sure I'm floating.

"I love you, Julia."

"Love you too."

"Bye."

I walk up to my fake place and step inside the foyer. I stand a little longer than usual, waiting until the last hint of the Mustang is gone. Ryan loves me, and he said I could tell him anything. *Anything.* I step out onto the sidewalk and head in the direction of home, my keys between my fingers for a weapon like my mom taught me soon after Aubree disappeared. Ryan deserves to know the truth, no matter how terrified I am to confess it. I look around at the scenery I've become familiar with on the sidewalk toward home, and tonight I'm walking it one last time. I'm telling him the truth tomorrow. He needs to hear it, and I need to say it: I live above a strip club on Bourbon Street.

Chapter Eleven

"He said he loves you? OMG, Julia! This is huge ... huger than huge! So what did you guys do last night? Anything juicy? This is way major."

I should know by now never to call Macey with news like this. That girl never lets me get a word in when she's crazy excited about something, and she was over the moon when I told her about me and Ryan last night. So I let her talk, and talk. Little does she know she's about to be shocked for an entirely different reason.

"Please tell me you're going back over there tonight. I mean, his parents being out of town and everything. God, it's so perfect."

I sigh. "Macey, listen, I have to tell you something."

"Better than what you just told me? Doubtful."

"Just listen, okay?" I take a deep breath.

Macey's tone softens. "Girl, you sound intense. All right, tell me. I'm listening."

"Well, there's something you don't know about me— about my family. All the times I've told you that you can't come to my house because my dad's sleeping and all, well, that was a lie."

"What do you mean?"

"I've never let you come over because I'm ashamed of where I live."

She's quiet for several seconds, and then she squeaks out, "What, like you're poor or something?"

This is it. "Yeah, like I'm poor, and I live above a strip club on Bourbon Street."

"Get out!" she blurts. "You do not! Is this a joke or something?"

Oh, it's most definitely a joke, but not on her. It's the joke with the punch line that's been aiming at my gut since birth. And I still don't find it the least bit funny.

"I'm not kidding, Macey. We live in an apartment above a strip club, and my dad's a bouncer on the weekends. That's how he got the place. He knows the guy who owns the club. My folks never hold on to jobs very long, and we move around a lot. It's not easy."

She's quiet at first. I know it has to register with her. "Wow, this is heavy, Julia. Does Ryan know?"

"What do you think?"

"Well, you have to tell him."

"I know, and I am. I've only told one other guy, but he doesn't go to our school. No one at school knows. And you can't tell anyone, Macey. Please."

"Don't freak. Your secret's safe with me."

"I'm sorry I didn't tell you when we met. I really wanted us to be friends, and I didn't want you to think I'm a weirdo or something. It's just—"

"It's okay. I get it. And so you know, I'm not that shallow. But if I were in your same position, I wouldn't have said a word to anyone either."

"Gee, thanks." I laugh. "That makes me feel a lot better. Like, it sucks to be you, Julia."

"You know what I mean. And I won't say squat to a soul. But you still have to tell Ryan."

"I know, I know."

Macey rambles and lectures for a few more minutes. I listen, taking my medicine like a big girl. After all, I've been lying to her from the beginning, too. When we finally hang up, I breathe some relief, but not enough to make me feel any better about having to tell Ryan. I mean, Macey was hurt to some degree that I wasn't honest with her. It was easy to tell that. How is Ryan going to feel?

I make my way to the kitchen. It's still early for a

Saturday morning. I'm going to call Ryan, too, but I need a little sustenance first. And a tad more courage.

"What's up, troll?" I say to Jesse's back which is sticking out of the fridge.

"There's not shit to eat in this house, that's what's up. I'm starving."

"Great," I mumble. I dig out some bread. "How about some toast?"

He grimaces. "No butter. Mom said she's going to the store today, but they'll sleep 'til noon. I can't wait that long." He grabs the bread from my hands. "I'll just eat it like this."

"No wait." I look down at my pajama pants and t-shirt, realizing my sleep clothes look better than what most people wear out in this town. "Let me slip on my flip-flops. I have some quarters saved up for an emergency. I'll go to the corner store and get us some butter."

"Cool. Thanks."

I step back in my room, push my feet into shoes, and retrieve the coins and my phone from the dresser. "I'll be back," I say to Jesse and head for the door.

In a few seconds, I'm down the stairs and making my way out the front of the club. I step onto the sidewalk and my breath catches in my throat. I choke on the panic as I look him directly in the face.

Ryan.

He's standing on the street near his car, staring at me … struggling … probably trying to put together a rational thought—a reason why the girl he loves is coming out of a place like this. "Julia, what are you doing? Why?"

I lower my eyes, feeling as exposed as the neon naked lady flashing behind me. It's easier to answer him when I'm looking at the ground. "This is where I live, Ryan. In the third-floor apartment, above the club."

"But I drop you off a few blocks from here…"

I can't bear to see him fumbling and awkward. "You drop me off where I *told* you I live. When you first asked me out, I was too ashamed to tell you that I live here. I was afraid you wouldn't want to go out with me."

"And what about after the first couple of dates, huh?" His voice is raw and tight. "You couldn't trust me then? I have to cross your path in front of this place, like a total stranger? I thought maybe you'd…"

He thought maybe I'd what?

Then it hits me. "Why did we cross paths in a place like this, Ryan? What are *you* doing here?"

His eyes are glassy, and I feel like a wretch, knowing damned well there's nothing wrong with him being out on a public sidewalk.

"See that donut shop over there?" He points across the street. "They have the best cheese danishes in the city. I wanted to surprise you for breakfast." He holds up a white paper bag. "I was on my way to your apartment. Well, to what was *supposed* to be your apartment. Guess I would've looked pretty stupid, huh?" He looks at me, disappointment etched on his face. "Why didn't you just tell me the truth?"

"I was going to tell you today, I swear." I hold up my phone. "You can call Macey right now. I told her the truth about ten minutes ago. I needed to go out and get something for my little brother, but I was going to call you, too, as soon as I got back. I was going to tell you everything before you picked me up tonight."

"Last night, when you said your dad was home…" He looks at the flashing signs behind me. "Your mom, is she a—"

Ryan can't be asking this. This can't be coming from

167

the guy who professed his love for me less than ten hours ago. He's supposed to be different. Why is he judging me, like everyone else?

"Is my mom a what?" I snap back, unable to control my tone as the words tumble out. "A stripper? Is that what you're asking me? You think my mom's a stripper now?"

"Why are you yelling at me, Julia? Huh? I should be the one yelling, but I'm not. You've been lying to me all this time. I don't know." He wrings his hands through his hair. "I don't know what I'm supposed to think."

I can't fight the tears any longer, so I let them fall. "That's right, but I know exactly what you're supposed to think! I know what everyone around me thinks the minute they know I'm poor, and that my dad's a bum, and that my mom serves drinks at the casino. You stand there looking all pained and judgmental, that's what's *supposed* to happen. And now you're thinking I'm trash, right? So go ahead, think! Don't you get it, Ryan? When people see this, they don't see me. I wanted you to see *me*."

"I saw you." Ryan's jaw tightens. "I saw a girl with a jet-black ponytail and striking blue eyes taking on the class know-it-all her very first day in Journalism, armed with nothing but her brain and love of history. I saw the girl who stood up to Hannah Parker and her friends at such a level, I heard about it within ten minutes of it happening simply because it had never been done. I saw the girl who shuddered at my touch, and who cried real tears when I said I loved her. Yeah, I saw you, Julia, or at least I thought I did. I just never thought that girl would lie to me. Why couldn't you trust me? Be honest with me? I would've understood."

I shake my head, the pain in my chest so brutal, I

think I might collapse. "Yeah, like you're understanding now?"

"You lied to me, even though I told you that you could tell me anything."

"And you're judging me, just like everyone else does."

"It's not a judgment, Julia."

"Really? Then what happened to *Jules*, then? Now that you know I live in a strip club, it's Julia. Not worthy of a pet name now?"

"Hey, I'm allowed to not understand why you couldn't tell me the truth, *Julia*. I'm allowed to be hurt. I feel like you're breaking me."

"It's not about me breaking you, Ryan. My God! This is about me trying to go through life after being broken. Don't you see that? I never meant to hurt you."

My head's spinning and I feel sick. I thought things were different here now, but nothing's changed. No matter how much I thought I fit in, thought I was accepted, I'm still the same girl—underestimated, misunderstood, teased, cast aside. And the way he's looking at me now, I've seen that look a hundred times. I hate it, can't stomach that look coming from Ryan. So I throw on the armor that's protected me practically since birth.

"You're allowed to be hurt?" I put my arms up as if showing off a display. "Let me get this straight. You're allowed to be hurt by this? You take me to your mansion. You live in luxury, and you don't even know your home's history. Well, here's my history, Ryan. You're looking at it, and I know every sick detail, right down to the dime-store decorations and half-empty pantry, a hungry little brother waiting for me. I'm sorry, but I don't think you know anything about being hurt. I do, and that's why I was scared to tell you the truth about all this. And it looks like I was right."

Ryan searches my eyes, and I want to crawl into a hole somewhere, be anywhere but here. "Where's that girl I fell in love with, huh? You know, when I dated Hannah, she lied to me any time it benefited her, and I hated it. And there was no honor in her lies. She wasn't protecting anything or anyone, she lied for nothing. You can't just tell me the truth when it's convenient for you, Julia. You have to tell me the truth all the time, no matter what. And I told you last night that you could tell me anything, do you remember that?"

I scramble for any words that might redeem me. My God, he's comparing me to Hannah! Have I fallen to that category, sunk that low? "Yes, I know what you said, Ryan, but—"

"No, not but. I told you that I love you, and that you can trust me with anything. Why didn't you trust me, Julia? Believe me, I know what it feels like to be hurt. And let me ask you another question. When I dropped you off at that other apartment, you waited for me to drive away and you what? Walked home? Is that right?"

I nod. What else can I do, really, but agree? He's exactly right.

"Yeah, and what if something bad would've happened to you on one of those walks home, huh? How do you think that would've made me feel? I guess you never thought about that, though."

Me? Never thinking about the possibility of something bad happening? My God, he has no idea! Oh, that's right. He doesn't have an idea—because I've never told him one thing about Aubree. I simply shrug. What else can I do?

Ryan shakes his head. "You know what, I can't do

this right now. I can't think. I have to get outta here."

No, please, don't go. I love you. But I don't say it. As much as my soul pleads for Ryan not to do this, I'm not begging. I've spent too much of my life as a beggar. I simply watch him get in his car and drive away, my heart screaming from the sudden rips mutilating my chest. I draw in a burning breath. The whole world is on fire, but I will my scorched legs to walk back inside my living hell.

"Hey, where's the butter?" Jesse says as I enter the kitchen.

"I … I didn't make it to the store. I'm sorry." I go to the fridge and retrieve my last two jelly packets. "Here, use these."

"Thanks. Hey, you been crying? What's the matter?"

"Nothing." *Everything.*

I go to my room, closing the door and grabbing a pillow from the bed, shoving it to my mouth and sobbing full out, the way I'd wanted to do on the street. I allow the sounds to pierce the pillow, hard and brash, painful and stabbing. I'm not sad, or angry. I'm devastated, crushed like a dry leaf under his feet.

Ryan says he's hurt because I didn't tell him the truth. Or is he really just mortified because my truth slammed him in the face like a sledgehammer? But in reality, this is not my truth. Matt and Erin Reynolds created this, not me. I have my own brand of truth. I have the passion for investigating, the love of the story. And I'll be damned if I'm giving up on Aubree.

We've been conditioned not to take risks, not real risks—the life-and-death kinds of risks. Investigating the Ursuline is a risk many have avoided, supposedly even law enforcement, but I'm doing it. I have to. After all, it's my story—has always been my story. Deep down, I know the truth, that if I die trying to be more than the girl with screwed-up parents and cheap shoes, it's better than living like this. Better than living without Ryan, without Aubree.

I'm a reporter, that's my truth. It's who I am, what gives me worth. And when I solve the mystery of the Ursuline, everyone will know my name. More importantly, they'll know Aubree's name, too. Newspapers, TV stations, Internet sites, everyone. I'll be a legend. No one will be making fun of me, or my folks, or where I live. Not ever again. And everyone in this whole damned world will be looking for Aubree … finally.

I throw the wet pillow to the floor and glance at my closet door, my Homecoming dress hanging like a reminder of all that was good in my life mere minutes ago before the truth did its damage yet again. I lean into the silky fabric and pull the skirt to my face. The tears fall again, my heart reminding me that it's shredded.

****

My phone chirps a text alert. I open my eyes and assess my whereabouts, the shine of morning glow stinging my eyes with its stupid light. Nothing's changed since the restless night before.

Still my bedroom.

Still above a strip joint.

Still no Aubree.

Still no Ryan.

Still in Hell.

I look at my phone, praying Ryan's name will decorate the display. But it's Tyler. **Meet me at McDonalds. Have something for you. I'm waiting.**

I'm still wearing the same sleep pants and t-shirt as yesterday, but I really don't care. What difference does it make? I slide my feet into shoes and wrap a rubber band around my lifeless hair. I swish some water in my mouth to relieve the dryness, too drained to actually brush my teeth. It doesn't matter anyway. Nothing matters.

It takes thirty minutes to walk to McDonald's. My stomach is gnawing a hole in my backbone. I haven't eaten a bite since Ryan left me yesterday. Maybe I'll die of starvation. Maybe I'll die from heartache. Maybe instead of Tyler and his dad warning me about the risks of investigating the convent, they should have told me to take caution when falling in love. It seems a hell of a lot more dangerous.

Tyler holds up a wrist and glances at a fake watch when he sees me. "What took you so long, Jul—wow, you look like shit. Nice jammies, though."

I cut him a drop-dead look. "Thanks, Ty. How sweet of you to say so."

"No, really, what happened to you? Something's definitely wrong."

"Guys are the worst." I take a deep breath. "The one I was dating…"

And loved more than air, but I don't say it.

"…he found out where I live yesterday and bailed on me."

"What? Well, I'm sorry. That really sucks." But his expression doesn't match his words. He's smiling like his cheeks should hurt. He shouldn't be so happy about my obliterated heart. "But, I could've told you that. Guys are dogs—well, except for me, of course. I don't have *any* problem with where you live."

That manages to pull a smile from me. "Yeah, I bet. Thanks for the support. So, what do you have for me, Ty?"

"Well, first I have food." He slides a breakfast burrito

and a container of OJ in my direction. "And you're not leaving 'til you eat."

I start unwrapping the burrito. "What else you got?"

"Oh, nothing major. Just this." He holds up a small metal tool with a wire on the end. It's not very big but looks like it could be heavy.

"What is it?"

Tyler shakes his head. "Man, you *are* out of it. Well, let's see if this does anything for you." He holds up an ancient-looking key.

I perk up immediately. "Oh, to pick the lock on the third floor?"

"Ding, ding, ding, we have a winner, folks." Tyler slides the items to me. "It's a skeleton key for old keyhole locks, and in case the key doesn't fit for some reason, the other tool is for lock picking. Old locks like that one have a bolt that slides across to actually lock the door. Folks back then who wanted more security put a plate over the bolt with a hole in it, and a very simple key would open it. But most of those locks can be picked easily, too."

"You know a lot about picking locks, Ty. Is there something you're not telling me?"

"Yeah, you got me. I'm a cat burglar during the week and a jewel thief on weekends, so you should be highly impressed that I'm missing out on a million-dollar gig to have breakfast with you in McDonald's."

I roll my eyes.

"I have a basic knowledge of lock picking because of my dad's line of work. That's all. Don't get too excited."

I have a delicious idea. "Tyler, we have to test the skeleton key, see if it works."

"*Au contraire, mon frere*. I told you already, I'm not going near that place. The only reason I brought you this is because I know your stubborn ass is going to keep trying to get on that third floor with or without my help. Might as well make it a little easier for you."

He's such a wuss. "I'm not talking about testing it at the Ursuline. There are tons of old historical homes here, and some are up for sale, abandoned. I'll do a little digging, find out which ones have keyhole locks like in the Ursuline. We'll test it out on one of those. How hard can it be?"

"Ha, famous last words. How hard can it be?" Tyler finishes off his juice. "Oh, and by the way. In case you don't remember, my old man, he's a cop. We could get in trouble, you know."

I sigh. "I'm aware, but sometimes you have to take a few risks. No biggie."

"Girls are so bizarre."

****

Bumming a few bucks from Tyler so I could take the trolley to the library was easy. He practically threw it at me when he thought it could earn him more potential new boyfriend points. Sweet, disillusioned boy. I glance at the skeleton key and lock-picking tool on the table in front of me. I have to admit, he came through. And he doesn't judge me.

I had to come to the library. I can't face going back to the apartment right now, the place that flaunted its disgusting face and made me lose the only guy I've ever loved. Why didn't I tell him one day sooner? One day. One hour. It's amazing how time can change things so quickly. Ten seconds can change something that took a lifetime to build. Ten seconds can move you to New Orleans above a strip club. Ten seconds can force you to face the guy you love and reveal you in a whole new light. Ten seconds can read a positive pregnancy test for a teenaged girl and rob her of her choices in life. Ten seconds can make a sixteen-year-old girl disappear forever. Ten seconds made all of this.

I have to find a way to shut off my spinning brain. Damn Tyler for making me eat. At least the hunger slowed me down, numbed my brain cells to a weary crawl. But I'll channel my energy to my benefit. I'm in the middle of chaos, but I remind myself that it's nothing new for me. The only difference now is my torn-to-bits heart. But healing is a process, and the only part of it I understand is the part where I flash a finger to the world and focus on my future. I focus on the story. *My story.* I'm very aware of this part, the part where I sit down and figure it out. I head to the history section and retrieve the books on Louis XV.

Nothing pops out to me at first. I scan the pages over and over, trying to see if I've missed any important verbiage. Old Louis was a sharp dresser, I'll give him that. There are several pictures of him standing all stoic and regal, and some of him on the throne with his queen beside him. Nothing in the photos reveals any further clues, so I look harder, beyond the images of the people. Maybe there's something on the walls, on the throne itself, anything.

I'm keeping a sharp eye out for the albatross or the coat of arms, even if they're displayed in a backdrop, or on someone's clothes, on a shield, anywhere. *Nothing.* My eyes are tired from the lack of sleep and burning like heated coals in my sockets, but I don't care. What am I missing? It has to be here. Then I notice something I'd ignored before. The book is written in English, but underneath one photo of King Louis XV, in tiny French letters, is this phrase:

Louis XV le bien-aimée de France
et de Navarre

I've been assuming it's just his title—and it probably is—but I bum a piece of paper from the librarian and write it down anyway. No stone left unturned and all that jazz. I return the books to their rightful section and make my way out the door. This was a total bust, just like the rest of my shabby existence.

****

Dad's in full assault mode on Jesse when I hit the front door. *Great.*

"Listen, boy, I need you to help me do this. I don't care if it's Sunday, I don't care if you're tired, this is happening. This stuff can fetch me a lot of money, and it's free for the taking."

"But it's stuff from your work, Dad," Jesse reminds him. "Isn't that stealing? I mean, you don't want to lose your job, do you?"

"It's not stealing, Jesse. It's in the dumpsters, and other men who work there take it all the time. No one there cares, but I need a little manpower behind me. Come on, we're doing this. Me and you, a Sunday just for the guys. And I'll take you somewhere to eat when we're done. What do you say? Hey, it's not what you do that counts, it's what you do with the people you love that counts."

"Stop saying that!" I can't halt my lips from moving. "Stop spouting that phrase every single time you're setting us up for something, Dad. It's exhausting! If you really love us, then just say it." I look at my brother. "Hey, Jesse, I love you." I glare at my dad. "See, was that so hard?"

Jesse stares at me. "Hey, Julia, you okay? You've been weird since yesterday."

"I'm weird every day, Jess! That's the problem. Why can't you be normal, Dad, huh? Stop looking for shortcuts and do your job. No side trips to rummage through dumpsters, or going to the casino to gamble away our grocery money. Just do your job. Then maybe Jesse and I could feel normal, not have to move around so much. And, God, if you want to tell the boy you love him, here's a concept. Just tell him. Believe me, nothing poetic coming off your lips seems real anyway, so stop it already. You're why we're so screwed up, you know."

"Who peed in your cornflakes, girlie?" Dad replies. "And you look like crap." He turns his back to me. "Hey, Jess, we're losing precious time. Get your shoes and let's go."

"Ugh, see what I mean?" I'm so angry, I'm shaking. "I'm so sick of living like this!"

I slam the door when I hit my bedroom, but I don't care. Why would I think he'd ever listen to me anyway? I'm just *the girl*. Damned Neanderthal.

A few deep breaths and curiosity about the Louis XV phrase pulls me back into focus. When my computer's humming and the search engine is ready, I type in the words: *French to English translation* and hit enter. At least a dozen sites appear, so I choose one and type: *Louis XV le bien-Aimée de France et de Navarre.*

I hold my breath. Then, it appears.

Louis XV The Beloved of France and of Navarre.

The Beloved? I stand up and pace, unable to sit. This is what I've been looking for, the proof I've needed! I grab my notebook and flip to the pages about the Casket Girls. I remember the phrasing: *'Send us virtuous women, Our Beloved,' the men and founders wrote to*

Mother France. But how cruelly they abused the gift. The men in New Orleans in the 1700s were asking Louis XV directly! Our Beloved. And he sent the Casket Girls per their request. But how cruelly they abused the gift…

I make more notes, my brain moving faster than my hands can write. The albatross, the coat of arms, they have to be symbols for the girls, the gift of the king that was abused. What happened to the girls?

Chapter Twelve

I'll be the only girl walking into Ben Franklin High today who doesn't have a crush on Ryan Grandle. I'm madly, prophetically in love with him, and he hates me now. Probably will forever. I blew it.

Nothing feels comfortable on my body, not even the most worn knit top I own. The pain that has crushed my chest since Saturday has permeated my brain, my senses, my skin. I can't imagine I'll ever be comfortable again. But I pull on the top and the loosest fitting jeans I own. What choice do I have? Of these facts I'm sure: I'm not fading away, I have to go to school, and I'll see him in Journalism. There'll be no rewriting this script.

But there is a new scene I can pen, and it's as prominent as my aching heart and the nerves rolling in my stomach. I'm going to the Ursuline after school today with one agenda … to make a plan—a plan to reach that third floor and eventually open the locked door that hides my answers.

I push my camera and notebook into my book bag and rummage in my desk for the old fountain pen. I roll it in my fingers to glance at the inscription for the hundredth time. *Discretion is the better part of valor.* And I did practice discretion when it came to my home life, but it blew up in my face like a firecracker with a blunt fuse. So this time, I'm making the rules, willingly putting myself in danger for the one chance to prove I've got the goods. Being a kickass reporter defines me, it's who I am. And I'll never measure up to Ryan, Aubree, or anyone else if I don't finish my story—solve the mystery of the Ursuline, no matter what it takes.

****

My breath catches painfully in my throat when I

glance in Ryan's direction, and he diverts his eyes. I realize in that moment this is the first time he's ever avoided me in Journalism. My mind rewinds to the day at registration, the first time I ever set eyes on him. He was seated on a stool in front of a table filled with newsprint, the most gorgeous male specimen I had ever encountered, and I was the new girl with nothing but potential and enough curiosity to check him out—to etch his face on my soul. And it's still there.

"Will everyone take their seats, please?" Ms. Dunkin says when she steps in front of the class. "We have some things to punch out."

Ryan takes his usual spot and I try not to bore a hole through the back of his head with my stare. He'll have permanent brain damage before the next hour and a half is over.

"Okay, people, listen up," Ms Dunkin says. "I've decided on the feature story we're doing this issue. Everyone give a big hand to Julia and Ryan."

Julia and Ryan. I ignore the sporadic applause, focusing on how glorious our names sound being said together.

Ms. Dunkin continues, "I've decided on one of their story ideas for the special this edition. The subject title is, 'Keeping Tabs: GPS Tracking for U.S. Teens.' We'll poll the student body to get a consensus on this controversial parental tactic. And since it was their idea, Julia and Ryan will be in charge of the project. So, they'll be deciding on the reporters, photographers and lay-out assistants." She looks in our direction. "Good job, guys. Okay, everyone, any questions?"

Some of the students start speaking at once, obviously passionate about their own opinions on the subject, and I do my best to listen. I know I should be excited and flattered that my story idea was picked, but Ryan's too much of a distraction. And he seems completely unfazed, not saying a word to anyone.

When class is finally over, I make my way to Ryan's desk before he barely has time to stand. Thank God Ms. Dunkin picked our topic, otherwise, I'd have no reason to be this bold. Hardcore journalism skills work their magic again.

"Hey, Ryan. Um, I guess we need to choose our team, huh? Maybe we can meet after school or something."

"It was your idea, Julia, not mine. You do it. I have to go now."

I swallow hard, trying to dislodge the lump in my throat as he walks away. It's impossible, and it's killing me. But I don't try to catch up or reason with him. After all, I'm the one who lied. It was me. I'm responsible for this. I wait until he's had enough time to make it to D-Hall, and then I walk out, my body no longer uncomfortable, just hollow.

"So, Julia, where's Ryan?"

Oh God. Hannah. I can't do this, not now.

"I told you the deal," she says. "You wouldn't listen, though."

"Hey!" Kimmie pipes up. "Stop walking. Hannah's talking to you."

I turn and face Hannah and her sidekicks, not really caring what they say. Nothing they can do or spout off about could possibly make me feel worse than I do right here in this moment. How do you deepen empty?

"Like I told you," Hannah says, "the flavor of the month."

"You were right," I reply. *She was wrong.*

"He was just using you."

"I know," I say. *He wasn't.*

Hannah's shocked, as though she was expecting me to lay into her or something. I would have to care at least a smidgen to do that. I couldn't care less.

"Well, I'm glad he didn't string you along, honey." Hannah smirks. "You know, you could've had a little fun in the field house with a football player yourself." She eyes me head-to-toe. "Oh, that's right. You couldn't."

The girls break into wild laughter and walk away. It's Mobile all over again, times ten.

"Hey." Macey joins me. "What did the bitch squad say to you?"

"Nothing."

"Liar. I know about you and Ryan. Are you okay? Why didn't you call me?"

My chest feels like an anvil fell on it. "What do you mean, you know about me and Ryan?"

"That you broke up. Everyone knows. I guess telling him the truth backfired, huh? I'm so sorry, Julia. I didn't know Ryan was that shallow. His loss, for sure."

I can feel the color draining from my face, and I think I might faint. This can't be happening. "You mean, he told everyone where I live?"

"Oh God, no." Macey pulls me against a wall out of the busy hallway. "I didn't mean to make you think that. No one knows your business, Julia. Chris popped in on Ryan Saturday night, asked why you weren't there. Ryan told him there was a problem. That's it. Everyone assumed you guys were broken up. That's it."

I breathe again.

Macey leans close to my ear. "So what exactly happened after you told him? I'm guessing he didn't take it very well."

I inhale another much-needed breath. "I never told him."

Macey grimaces. "I'm confused."

"Listen. After you and I talked, I waited before calling Ryan. I went to get something from the store for my little brother first, and Ryan was standing on the street outside my apartment."

Macey gasps. "Get out! He knew?"

"No. He had just left a donut shop across the street from my place. He was going to surprise me with them at the fake address I gave him. It all came to a head at once, right there on the sidewalk. If I would have called him after I talked to you, none of this would have happened."

"OMG, that is so wild! Talk about shitty luck. Can you imagine if you hadn't seen him and he would have showed up at the other place? Man."

I roll my eyes. Yeah, I can imagine that. I've imagined every scenario since my world ended three days ago.

We start walking to our classes and Macey's still chatting away. "Look, I don't know what Hannah said to you, but no one gives a crap what she says, except her little stalker girls."

"No," I remind her, "*you* don't give a crap what she says."

"True, I don't. And give Ryan time, he'll come around. See you at lunch, Julia-cakes. Hold your head up. It'll be okay."

I know Macey means well, but she's in Macey-World. This is Julia-World, AKA Gypsyville, and in Gypsyville, there are no white picket fences and rainbows.

****

Jesse's Yankee hat is securely in place when I step off the bus and onto the street in front of the Ursuline. It's funny how I feel more at ease here than at school. I never thought the day would end. I shift gears, focusing my energy on the task at hand instead of on Ryan, my classmates, Hannah, my life.

I gaze at the shuttered windows, snapping a couple more pictures before moving inside the convent. *The windows.* That's what started it all. Mention of a secret third floor housing vampires on some random blog, and a snapshot of a crack I'm certain I saw on shuttered windows that are supposed to be totally concealed. Boy what ten seconds can do.

Once inside, I head to the coat of arms first and just stare at it. Now that I've been trying so desperately to discover its secret, standing in front of it is like confirmation that it's real. It does have importance, a life of its own—a point and time in its history that was so poignant, people have died to reveal it. And it repeats itself in this convent, around the neck of an ancient bird hidden on that third floor. My eyes widen, allowing its likeness to pierce my soul. I know it has significance, and I'll show it to the world.

I pass the stairs leading to the second floor and scrutinize the velvet ropes that allowed such easy passage the last time I attempted to ascend them. Tour guide Steve must've ratted me out. The ropes are now attached to built-in hooks that have been secured to the banisters and the wall. Someone would have to go under or jump over the ropes to reach the stairs, or patiently stand and unlatch the ropes from the hook for passage. None of those options will work without drawing attention. But that's okay. Steve-O underestimated me. I know another way.

The alternate route to the third floor requires going outside. Most of the old buildings in New Orleans have outside staircases and fire escapes. I know the Ursuline is no exception. I've done my homework. I head to the doors that lead to the manicured gardens and creepy statues, but I can't resist stopping at the glass case holding K.A.'s silver brush and mirror set. I stare at the scrollwork again, so intricate and detailed. I gaze at the handle of the mirror, imagining a young girl staring at her frightened reflection, unsure of a future in a strange, new world. Does she polish her face to sheer perfection, or dull her delicate beauty to make herself less appealing to the strangers lying in wait? I swipe my prickly arms to release the chill bumps and head outside. The second set of stairs await me.

Pretending to be interested in the activity outdoors is easy. Other people touring the gardens are milling about, pointing and snapping pictures. I pull out my camera to blend in, and pretend to snap a few shots of the immaculate shrubbery and massive statues. I start to walk the expanse of the building, my eyes scoping every crevice to ensure my privacy. I see the stairs.

A uniformed man is lazily motioning tourists to certain parts of the gardens, not paying attention to my activity at all, so I head to the bottom of the metal stairs sticking out from the side of the building. I hold my breath. Now to see what's at the top when I climb them. This decides everything.

When I reach the stairs, I glance around the corner to see if anyone is paying attention. Thank God the stairs are on the side of the Ursuline and not directly in back. It makes discretion a lot easier. I tighten my hands on the banister and climb the stairs quickly, making sure each step is light enough not to be heard. The stairs stop at a door on the second floor. A locked door.

I try not to panic. This is a regular utility door with a bolt lock, not an ancient lock like I was expecting. I snap a picture of the door and the lock, and quickly descend the stairs, my mind spinning with the next aspect of what to do. Maybe Tyler can help me with this lock, too, snag a different lock-picking tool from his dad. I have to figure out my next move.

Finally off the last step and heading toward the gardens again, I will my feet to move slower and catch my breath. The uniformed man from before is standing in a small crowd of people, his arms folded in front of him and his face drooping. He looks tired. Must've had a rough weekend. I'm about to head inside the convent again when I notice something else. The uniformed man has something dangling from his belt loop. Keys.

Never thought I'd get excited to be reminded of the summer my dad taught me and Jesse how to snag keys from his belt loop in hopes we'd be able to lift the landlord's much-sought-after set. Jesse ended up doing the deed. I chickened out—more like flat-out refused. But not this time. My heart's pounding so hard I check my hands to be sure they're steady enough to do what needs to be done. I mumble for courage, "It's for the story, for Aubree." I unzip the front pocket of my book bag and make a beeline for my victim. *Sorry, guy.*

Once in front of the uniformed man and small crowd, I position myself beside him and point to a third-floor window. "Hey, I thought those shutters stayed closed all the time. Do you see that?"

His head jerks up and people start chattering. In five seconds, his keys are off the loop and in my book bag. He looks at me. "I don't see anything."

"Weird." I shrug. "I could have sworn I saw that shutter move. Oh well, sorry."

I retreat to the inside of the convent and take the first real breath since my thievery. Better not stay much longer. I head for the door to the main entrance and notice a small table in the corner. A huge, opened book and pen are the only things on it. I realize right away it's a guestbook. I sign my name, and then a thought hits me. This book has hundreds of pages, and from where I just signed, maybe twenty or so pages remain. I place the pen inside to mark the current page, and then skip back to the dates before Aubree was missing. I focus on the pages when she would have been fifteen and sixteen. Brady talked about the convent with Aubree. Could she have visited here—believed the vampire folklore enough to investigate herself?

I use my finger to scan down the rows of names. After ten or so pages, I can't breathe. It's there, as real as my shaking hands:

Aubree Turner

I rub a finger over her name, knowing that she wrote it, needing to feel close to a piece of her right here in front of me. It's so overwhelming I have to steady myself. I resist the urge to tear the page out just to have Aubree's handwriting, but I know if I actually get caught stealing, I'd never be allowed to come back. Lifting the guard's keys was risky enough. I fumble through my backpack for my camera and snap a picture of her signature. I flip the book back to the page with my name and take a picture of it as well. According to the date of her signature, she was sixteen when she signed it. I'm sixteen, too. The irony jars me. *Oh Aubree. What did you do?*

Within minutes, I'm back on the street and headed for home. Is it possible that Aubree tried to discover what was on that third floor, too? Is there any way in the world that's possible? Nausea and confusion wrack me. I place a hand on the pocket of my backpack to feel the keys. I can't believe I stole them. Everything's in place now. If

Aubree really did investigate this convent, try to find out if her beloved vampires really did exist, and she died in the process, I may be the only person willing to find her. Things just got real...
    ****

I plop my book bag on my bed and turn on the computer as soon as I get home. I'm still recovering from the rush this afternoon—finding out a locked door awaited me on the outside staircase, and snagging the keys to open it, realizing that Aubree might have tried to get on that third floor, too.

There's one more thing I need to take care of today. I have no intentions of standing in front of that door on the third floor of the convent cold turkey. I need to practice with the skeleton key and the lock picking kit, so I need a house. I type: *Historical Homes for Sale in New Orleans* in a search engine and hit enter.

Pretty soon, my screen is filled with potential homes and real estate agents ready to show them. I take my time opening each listing, scanning the ones with photographs, hoping to find any doors that have the kind of lock I'm looking for. After about twenty minutes, I have three prospective homes and the names of some realtors.

When I was still in Mobile and at my most desperate point in high school, I loved pretending I was like some of the other kids I knew. That I was popular, had money, lived in a house. So, once, after I saw a lock box and a For Sale sign on a home I had admired for weeks, I called the realtor on the sign and pretended to be a potential buyer. The lady was nice, but busy, so she gave me the lock box combination and told me to take a peek inside. That was the day I turned the key on a home that would never be mine and my heart onto the possibility that I could make a way for something better if I just took a chance.

I get my phone and dial the number for the first realtor on a home that looks to be filled with doors containing old keyhole locks. This would be a goldmine if I could actually get myself and Tyler inside it. I clear my throat and take a deep breath for bravery. I scramble for a fake name when someone answers.

"Bayou Realty, may I help you?"

"Yes, I would like to speak to Martin Warner, please?"

"May I ask who's calling?" the sweet-sounding voice replies.

"This is Hannah Lindslee." *I crack myself up.*

"One moment, please."

After a few seconds, Mr. Warner answers. "This is Martin."

Show time. "Hi, Martin. My name is Hannah Lindslee. My husband and I are interested in a listing you have for a historical home at 413 Royal Street."

His voice lifts. "Oh, yes, ma'am. I know the home you're referring to—gorgeous place. It even has most of the original hardware and a stained-glass window. Have you been inside the home yet?"

"Unfortunately, no," I reply. "That's why I'm calling. We would like to look at the home ASAP, but my husband has a very busy schedule. What would be a good day for you?" *Never skip the easy question, or you'll miss the obvious answer.*

"Well, Tuesday and Thursday I'm wide open, but Wednesday—"

Bingo. "Oh, Wednesday afternoon is the best time for us. My husband is in classes the other nights of the week. That's too bad. I guess I can call—"

"Oh, no, wait," he says. "There is a lock box on the home. If you'll give me a little personal information, I'll give you the combination. Just remember to lock up the house and put the keys back in the box when you leave. We'll talk again after you have a walk-through."

"Sounds great."

A little fake information and ten seconds later, I have the combination to the lock box on the guinea-pig house. This day almost feels too easy.

I send Tyler a text: **Meet me at 413 Royal St. on Wed. at 4:00. And wear your big boy pants.**

My phone chirps a response: **I'll be there. But I like my clown pants better.**

Chapter Thirteen

I reach for my phone and look down the street again. 4:15. Where is he? If Tyler doesn't show up soon, I'm going it alone. I can't stand here all afternoon waiting for another potential buyer to decide to look at the house, too. We need to practice on the old locks and make a clean getaway. Where is that boy?

After another minute I spot him, his chaotic hair bobbing back-and-forth to whatever tune is funneling through his ear buds this time. He throws me a thumbs-up and a ready smile.

"What took you so long?" I say when he's within earshot.

"Chillax." Tyler yanks the wires from his ears and shoves everything in his pocket. "I got held up after school." He nods toward the house. "So, I'm guessing we're going in there?"

"You would be correct."

We approach the door, and I roll the numbers on the lock box into the proper combination and let out a breath when it opens. I retrieve the keys and unlock the front door.

"Oh my God, this place is awesome," Tyler says as we step inside and a stained-glass window greets us from across the room. "How old do you think that thing is?"

"Not sure." I ignore the window and inspect the first couple of doors I see. "Tyler, come on. We have to try the locks."

"This window is stupid awesome." Tyler pulls out his phone and starts snapping pictures of the painted glass. "And look at the light reflections it makes when the sun hits it at the right angle. It's like an optical illusion or something."

Ritalin couldn't keep that boy's focus in check when something fascinates him. "Well, you need to get optical amnesia."

"What?"

"Forget about what you're looking at and help me find the doors with the old locks."

Tyler makes a face. "Very funny. All right, all right. I'm coming."

Within a minute, we're both in full-out search mode.

"Hey, here's one," Tyler says.

"Great. I've got the skeleton key and the—"

"Uh-oh. We have a problem."

"What?"

He pulls the handle and the bedroom door opens. "It's not locked."

"Are you kidding me?" I actually can't believe I was so clueless. Duh, house is on the market. Of course the doors are all unlocked.

"Okay, not really a problem," Tyler announces. "Just use the skeleton key and lock the door. Then we can practice with the lock-picking tool. No worries."

I close the door and slip the key inside the lock and turn. It doesn't budge. "The skeleton key doesn't work. This can't be happening."

Tyler nudges me out of the way. "Give me that." He takes the key and shoves it in the door. After jiggling it for several seconds, he announces, "You're right. It doesn't fit. Damn."

I shake my head. "No shit, Sherlock. Unbelievable. What do we do now?"

"We do the only thing I *can* do … lock it from the inside—"

"But you're supposed to show me *how* to pick the lock. That's the whole point of you being here. How can you do that if you're locked in the room, huh?"

Tyler winks. "Hey, have a little faith, would ya? Here, gimme that." He takes the lock-picking tool and inserts it in the keyhole, then bends to get a better view of the angle inside the lock. "Here, Julia, give me your hand." He places it on top of his and mimics the motion needed to pick the lock. "That's all you'll do, really. Sometimes you have to push really hard to release the little bar in there, but just work with it. It'll loosen and open eventually. You ready to give it a try?"

"I suppose so."

Tyler hands me the tool. He steps into the room and closes the door. The lock clicks and my heart sinks. I hope I can do this.

"Okay," Tyler's muffled voice prompts through the thick door, "work your magic, oh brave one."

I take a deep breath and insert the tool into the keyhole. At first nothing happens. I'm not feeling the bar or anything that seems like it would pop the lock. "Ty, I suck at this. Wish you were out here showing me."

"Well, I'm not, so get over it. Just wiggle it around. And don't be afraid to use some muscle."

I push the tool harder and it slips under the bar. "Hey, I think I got it!" I try turning to release the bar, but it won't budge. I pull hard on the tool, and it won't move either. *Great.* "Ty, go ahead and unlock the door from the inside."

"Why?"

"Because the pick's stuck."

"Way to go, Julia." Tyler jiggles the knob for several seconds and then cusses. "I can't open it. Listen, you have to get the pick out of the keyhole first. Yank on it or something."

I pull as hard as I can but it's stuck like Super Glue.

Panic tightens my chest. "It's wedged between the little bar thingy. It's too tight. I can't pull it out barehanded. No way. Tyler, what are we gonna do?"

He's quiet for a second then blurts, "Well, I don't know about you, sister, but I'm climbing out a window. Once I'm outta here, we'll figure a way to get the tool out of the lock. Oh, and in case I haven't said it yet, you suck at lock-picking."

"Funny. Now get your ass out here and help me."

Tyler's footsteps let me know he's headed to the window. I clutch a fist over the cold, non-budging chunk of metal again and pull so hard it hurts my hand. I'll never get this out.

"Hell to the no!" Tyler yells. "This is crazy!"

I'm almost afraid to ask. "What?"

"You *have* to get that lock open now, Julia."

"What's the problem?"

"The window's painted shut, that's the problem."

This can't be happening. "Are you freakin' kidding me?"

I can tell Tyler's standing just on the other side of the door again. "I'm not joking. If you don't figure out a way to get that pick unstuck, then I'm breaking a window to get out."

"Or we could call for help," I remind him.

"Call who? 911?" Tyler sounds pissed. "And just who do you think they'll call? The police, and the police equals my dad, remember? No, I'll break a window and we'll split before I ever let my dad know what we're doing in here. So, best-case scenario, figure out a way to open the door, Julia. Please."

"Okay, okay. Let me think a minute."

"Hurry, Julia. It's gonna start getting dark in about an hour. No chance you brought a flashlight, is there?"

Crap. How can I be so unprepared? "Nope, sorry."

"Well, that's just great." Tyler's still mumbling, but I can't make out what he's saying. Probably best that way.

I pull and pry on the tool for a few more minutes, but nothing happens. No way I'm budging it barehanded. "Tyler, let me check on something. Be right back."

"Yeah yeah. I'll be the guy stuck in here ... forever."

I reach the kitchen and start yanking open cabinets and drawers. There has to be something lying around I can use to beat the pick loose from the lock. But after a few seconds, I realize everything's empty. I go from room to room, opening closets and cabinets. Relief finally hits me when I reach a small bathroom. A drop cloth is draped over a sink, and a couple of random tools are scattered on the floor, including a small hammer. "Thank you, thank you, thank you." I head back to Tyler's rescue.

The first strike of the hammer seems to startle Ty. "Hey, what'd you find?"

"A hammer. Just give me a minute." I hit the pick again and it still doesn't budge.

Tyler jiggles the doorknob. "You mean you still don't have that thing loose, and you're hitting it with a hammer? We need to get you to the weight room, girlfriend. You're weak."

"I'm not weak. This hammer looks like it was made for an Oompa Loompa or something. Just shut up and let me do this."

After two more hard licks, the pick slips out of the keyhole and hits the floor. "It's out!"

Tyler unlocks the door and opens it. He mock falls into me. "You saved my life. Now I'm your servant forever. What do you require from me, oh brave one with the tiny hammer?"

I laugh. "You're a dork."

"And you're beautiful. Crappy at lock-picking, but beautiful."

I'm sure I'm blushing, so I turn my back to him. "You don't think I'm beautiful. You're just happy to be out of there."

"Hey, I might be happy to be outta there, but that has nothing to do with the fact that you're beautiful. Two entirely different subjects, just so you know."

"Wait here," I say, changing the one subject I simply can't handle at the moment. "Let me put the hammer back in the bathroom. Need to leave this place like we found it, you know."

Tyler looks defeated. "Okay, whatever."

We go in opposite directions. I take a fortifying breath when I reach the bathroom and put the hammer back on the floor where I found it. The last thing I want to do is hurt Ty. He's so great. He has to know I think he's great, right?

"Hey, you ready to get outta here?" he says, joining me as I step out of the bathroom and into the hallway.

"I guess, but I'm no better off than I was before we got here. I still have no idea how to pick the lock on that third floor. Doesn't make me feel all warm and fuzzy about going up there again."

"Then don't."

"Ty, I have to. I can't solve the mystery without going up there, you know that."

"Then don't."

"Stop saying that. I'm doing it. And hey, maybe the skeleton key will work on that convent door. You never know."

"That's right," Tyler says. "You don't know. What if it doesn't and you have to try to pick that lock, too? Odds are stacked crazy high against you."

"Thanks for the vote of confidence."

"Hey, I'm the guy who was stuck in the room five minutes ago, remember?"

"Ty, listen—"

"No, Julia. You listen. I care about you. I don't want anything bad to happen, that's all."

"Well, if you care so much about me going on that third floor, then why are you helping me? Huh?"

"Because I care about you. Vicious cycle, huh?"

"Yeah, I guess." I know he cares, and it means more to me than he knows. I can't resist the urge, so I touch his face. "Thanks for caring so much, Ty. You're the best friend I've ever had."

"Good, then don't stop me this time." I'm taken off guard when his lips touch mine, and I squirm at first to resist. But the rational part of my brain flies out the window when his hands touch my waist and his chaotic hair brushes my cheek. I need what he's offering … need to feel validated, wanted, cared for. I know I shouldn't kiss him back, but I do. He kisses me deeper when my body responds, and I close my eyes, giving in to the waves now tickling my stomach.

After several seconds, I tug my lips from his. "Tyler, I—"

"I know, don't say anything. It's okay. You ready to get outta here?"

"Yeah."

He takes the key from my hand and guides me in front of him as we walk out the door.

"That stained-glass window really is beautiful," I say, trying to hide the tears now threatening to fall.

"I know." He smiles as he closes the locked door and replaces the key in the lock box. "But this isn't the right house for us. Maybe we should keep looking." He winks and then takes my hand as we step off the porch and onto the sidewalk.

****

I step into the apartment to the smell of Mom cooking, a rarity for sure.

"Hurry up, I'm starving," Jesse says to her.

"It'll be ready soon," she says. She turns to me, "Hey, Julia. You hungry?"

"Very. That smells awesome." I set my book bag on the couch and join her in the kitchen. "Need any help?"

"Nope." She points into the living room in the direction of the TV. "Could you turn that up, please?"

I know the face before I hit the volume button on the remote.

"Hey, did you see that—"

"Shh, be quiet," I say in Jesse's direction, my eyes glued to the TV screen. "Let me hear this."

A voice from the news desk says, "Beloved history teacher from John Dibert Middle School is missing. Brady Swinson was last seen getting into his vehicle in the school parking lot yesterday at three forty-five PM. His wife, Sarah Swinson, said that he never came home and that the last text she received from him was at noon yesterday. Now his phone isn't working. Please look at the photo of Swinson closely. He drives a silver 2011 Kia Spectra, and was last seen wearing a light-blue, button-down shirt and khaki pants. Please call the New Orleans Police Department with any information."

I don't move for several moments, fear gripping me like hands around my throat. Brady … missing?

Mom shakes her head. "That's really a shame. I hope they find him and he's okay, but it doesn't sound good."

"Yeah, that dude's toast."

"Shut up, Jesse!"

"Hey, what's your problem?" he yells back in my face.

I take a deep breath then look at mom. "I know him, okay? I know him."

Mom sets the spoon beside the pot she's been stirring and joins me in the living room. "Oh, Julia, I'm sorry. Had you met him at school or something?"

"Yeah," I reply. No way I'm telling her I met him at the convent, and that he knew Aubree, too.

She cuts I-dare-you-to-say-anything eyes at Jesse before saying, "I'm sure he's okay. They'll find him."

I nod and head to my bedroom, a dozen questions slamming my brain at once. No way the convent can have anything to do with Brady's disappearance, right? I mean, this *is* the homicide capital of the country, although that thought makes my belly churn ferociously. Could someone have robbed him? And I don't really know anything about his personal life. Maybe Brady and his wife were arguing and he simply skipped town. But I feel like I swallowed a rock when the convent enters my head again. Just how close was Brady to revealing the secrets of the Ursuline? How much did he divulge to Aubree? What the hell is really going on?

****

It's hard to focus on my story for school, especially since I didn't sleep a wink last night. I had nightmares about Aubree and Brady. But I push the images from my mind and try concentrating on school. I still can't believe Ms. Dunkin liked my idea enough to make it the special for the next edition. Tomorrow's the day I announce the assignments to the class. Part of me is tempted to come up with some reason to pair up Holly with Ryan, just to piss him off to no end. But I won't do that to the boy.

Damn me for still caring way too much. Damn him for not caring at all.

My computer freezes so I shut it down. It's been hanging up a lot lately, so Tyler's coming by to look at it tomorrow after school. We haven't seen each other since our kiss the other day, and my cheeks feel flush when I think about him being in my bedroom. I wonder if he'll kiss me again. I wonder if I'll let him. I still can't believe I led him on like that. I'd be lying if I said I didn't like Tyler's arms around me, but I'd be lying even more if I said I'm over Ryan. I can't help but wonder if he even thinks about me at all when he's every good thought I have.

Why did Ryan have to judge me, look at me like I disgust him? He says it's because I lied to him, but I know the real deal. He's too good to be in love with a girl who lives above a strip joint. He's always been too good for me. Sad thing is, I knew it from the start. I knew Ryan was unattainable. It just took him a while to realize it, too.

And then there's Tyler—sweet, heart-of-gold Ty. He doesn't judge me when it comes to my living arrangements. I can trust him with anything, no matter what. The boy deserves credit for that. He deserves to be able to kiss me and have me return his affection. I know that as certainly as I know the sun will come up in the morning and I'll still be on Bourbon Street. So why does not being with Ryan make me feel like I can't breathe? Love sucks.

But I can't think about him anymore right now—won't do it. I push away from my desk and stand up to stretch. I pull off my jeans and toss them on the bed, and then I tug on my pajama pants. As soon as I finish my school assignment, I have a little sleuthing of my own to do. I checked out a new Louis XV book from the school library. Okay, not a *new* book, an ancient-as-hell book, but it's new to me. Yeah, I got a date with old Louis again. At least *he* won't break my heart.

In two minutes I'm pushing the power button on my computer, but my attention is broken when I hear the front door open.

"Julia, get in here now!"

Dad? What in the world is wrong with him?

"Coming!"

My mind can't even register who I see when I reach the living room. "What are you doing here?" is all I can say.

"Hello, Julia."

"Um, hey, Detective Elder."

"The officer here says you've been snooping around some convent," Dad says. "He said you can get in a lot of trouble, maybe even killed." He looks at Detective Elder. "Is that right? She could get killed?"

"That's right," the detective agrees. "And I warned Julia a while back about the Ursuline. I told her specifically of the dangers on that third floor, but apparently she's been attempting to get up there anyway. I'm only telling you this for her protection. She needs to stay away from the Ursuline."

"There's nothing wrong with me touring the convent, Detective," I remind him before I can stop myself. "It's open to the public, you know. And I'm a student reporter. I'm doing a story on the convent, that's all." I can't believe Tyler's dad is standing in my living room. My whole body's shaking. What if he knows I have the lock-picking kit and the skeleton key? What if he noticed them missing? And the guard's keys. Oh crap...

"You're right. There's nothing wrong with touring the

convent, but sneaking up the stairs to the second floor that's off limits to tourists and attempting to open a locked door on the third floor is a different matter altogether. You're going to stay away from the convent from now on, Miss Reynolds, or I'll be paying you another visit, and next time I won't be so nice."

Dad steps in before I can answer. "Listen, the girl's only sixteen. And I kinda feel like what you said was a threat. I don't like cops threatening my kid, especially in my own place. She's always been a good kid, never been in any trouble to speak of. And she won't be doing anything to get in trouble from now on. I'll make sure of that. So you can be going now, Officer. Okay?"

"I wasn't threatening her, Mr. Reynolds. I just don't want to get the call that she's been hurt or worse. I'll go now." He looks me dead in the face. "Remember what I said, Julia. We're just worried about you."

"We?" I ask.

"Me and Tyler. My son is the one who told me where you live. He said you're a good friend. He doesn't want anything to happen to you, that's all. Have a good night."

It feels like someone is sitting on my chest and I take a fortifying breath to relieve the pressure. Why? I can't believe it, but it's true. Oh, God. Tyler ratted me out!

Dad sees Detective Elder to the door and then he turns to me. "What in holy hell is this all about? You really been doing something illegal? I thought you had more sense than that, girl."

"Listen, Dad. There's this mystery about the third floor of the Ursuline Convent that's never been solved. There's folklore surrounding it, saying that people who investigate it wind up dead. I'm doing a story about it, that's all." Then I say what I know will put him on my side. "And if I happen to solve the mystery, I could end up rich and famous. Would that be so bad? And Mom knows I've been going there too."

Dad gets a faraway look. "There could really be some money if you do a good story on it?"

"Yeah, you could say that," I reply.

He still looks doubtful. "What about the stuff he said about getting killed if you sneak around that place? Is that true?"

"He's a typical cop using a scare tactic to keep me away from that place. That's all, Dad. No worries."

He shrugs. "Then don't get caught, and be careful."

I head back to my bedroom, my heart pounding like a jackhammer. How could Tyler do this to me? I pull my cell from the desk and send him a text: **My place. Now.**
****

He knows why I'm angry—has to know. How could he rat me out to his dad? There has to be an explanation. I'm standing on the sidewalk outside the club. I can see Tyler standing at the crosswalk, his eyes locking with mine. He reaches me and swallows hard.

"Hey, Julia." His voice cracks.

"Walk with me," I say.

"You taking me to a safe location to hide the body?"

"Don't make jokes, Ty. Why did you tell your dad I'm still investigating the convent? He'll be gunning for me now."

"Do you really have to ask me that? I mean, I'd think it would be obvious."

I stop walking and lean against a streetlamp, my head swirling from his words.

He takes my hands. "I care about you so much, Julia. And when you couldn't get that lock open the other day, I wondered what would happen if you were on that third floor and things didn't go as planned. Anything can happen, and if you're up there alone, the worst can happen. I'm scared of that place, and I'm scared for you. That's why I mentioned it to my dad. I know you think I betrayed you, but I did it because I'm worried for your safety. You have to know that."

I pull my hands free from his. "And you have to understand this. I'm still in love with Ryan. I can't handle this now, Ty. I know you have feelings for me, and I know I kissed you back the other day. Honestly, I have feelings for you too, but I can't just turn off my feelings for Ryan. You have to understand—"

"*I* have to understand? Really, Julia? Well—and I'm being stupid honest here—it's crazy as hell to me. The guy saw where you live and turned his nose up to you and left. He threw you away like trash, and you still love him? Why? Because he loves you so much? Sorry, but I don't get it. And just so you know, I don't trust the guy either."

I laugh. "Ha, you don't even know the guy."

"But I know the type. I'm telling you now, Julia, you can't trust him."

I know it's wrong before I say it, but my words hit him in the face anyway. "What, like I can trust you?"

His eyes widen, then fall. "Point taken. You know what, I'm outta here. And for what it's worth, I *am* sorry, Julia. See you around."

I'm heading back to the apartment when I hear his voice again. "That teacher was snooping around the convent, too. Now he's missing."

I turn and face Tyler.

"My dad's a cop, remember?"

Although he's a little ways down the street now, I can still see the fear in his eyes. But I simply turn my back on him again and walk away.

205

****

Six AM will come early, but I don't care. I can't sleep, not after everything that's happened tonight. I wish I hadn't been so cruel to Tyler, even though I'm still pissed at him for telling his dad. Thank God my dad isn't a candidate for Father of the Year, otherwise my investigating might be a cease-and-desist type of deal altogether. But I know he won't deter me, and I highly doubt the good detective will really try to stop me either. After all, he's the one who made it perfectly clear when I met him that the police won't investigate the convent, or even come to a young girl's rescue if she finds herself in dire straits. Hell, I doubt they've done anything to help find Brady now that they know he toured the convent on a regular basis. Dude should've remembered that before he became all Robocop up in here.

Well, I'm not stopping, especially if finding out what's on that third floor will help find Brady ... find Aubree. I scroll through the search list that pops up when I type *Dead Homicide Detectives in New Orleans* in the search bar. I keep thinking that maybe I've missed something—that anything proving cops have died investigating the convent will suddenly appear. But it's all the same crap I've seen a million times. Yeah, Tyler and his scary dad are full of shit. There isn't one shred of evidence suggesting that any police officers, homicide detectives, or any official of the sort have died at the convent. But there's plenty of rhetoric about crimes and Constitutional violations perpetrated by the NOPD itself. Moving on.

But I do have something more interesting to wrap my brain around. I pick up the book on Louis XV and start flipping through pages. First I turn to every page that has pictures, hoping to see the coat of arms or the albatross.

Nothing. After about twenty minutes, I realize this book is much like the rest I've researched.

Then something catches my eye. There's a section on his family life, and a young girl appears in three of the pictures with the king. My heart skips a beat when I read the words in one of the captions: *Katherine, the king's beloved niece, his heart*. Katherine? Could it be?

I grab my notebook and jot down the name Katherine and then start reading the sections in the book underneath her pictures. I resist the urge to squeal when I hit the jackpot. The magic sentence reads: *Katherine Adélaīde, the king's beloved niece, is seated beside the queen during a royal banquet*. Oh, my God, Katherine is K.A.! A silver brush and mirror set that is only befitting of royalty. But that means the king didn't just send the middle class to wed the rogue men of the penal colony. He sent his niece! He sent the court to marry the criminals. No wonder his guilt was enough to create a coat of arms representing the Casket Girls. But who does it actually belong to? I jot everything in my notebook, my hands shaking from the revelation. What really happened to Katherine?

"Knock knock."

I jump when Mom appears in my doorway. "Oh, hey."

"You know you have school tomorrow." She looks at her watch. "If you go to bed now, you'll get a good four hours."

"I know. It's been a rough night."

"Your dad told me. You okay?"

"A little better now. I found some more information that'll help with my convent story. Getting closer to cracking that mystery wide open."

Mom smiles. "That's my girl, but let me ask you something. I won't have to bail you out of jail when you solve it, will I?"

I laugh. "I don't think so." *But you might have to identify me at the morgue.*

"Well, here. I brought you your favorite."

Mom hands me a bag of fries smothered in ketchup. "Wow. And from Delachaise, too. Outstanding." Their fries are amazing. They cook them in duck fat or something. "Thanks, Mom. I'm starving."

"Well, I know you sleep better on a full stomach. Eat, and then lay down, okay? You need your rest." She looks at me as I take the first bite. "Sweetie, I know you're hurting about Ryan, and worried about your teacher-friend. I hate to see you so sad."

Mom has enough to worry about. I don't need to be added to that list. "No worries, Mom. I'm okay with being sad, really. I'm kinda used to it."

She smiles. "I know how much you miss Aubree."

I don't know what to say, can't say anything really. Discussing Aubree is a rare occasion, too delicate of a subject to toss around in casual conversation.

"You're something else, you know that?" Mom says. "And, FYI, the Dutch prefer their French fries with mayonnaise."

"I love you, Mom."

"Ditto."

Chapter Fourteen

"Okay, people. Settle down. You do understand how a feature story of this magnitude is pulled off, correct?"

"With complete cooperation," we say in unison.

"Very good. Now, Julia, Ryan, I'm letting you two take over from here. Make me proud." Ms. Dunkin sits at her desk and starts fiddling with a stack of papers. I tug on Ryan's sleeve, and he doesn't attempt to hide the drudgery on his face as we stand in front of our Journalism class and begin breaking up the students into teams.

"Can't you even pretend to be involved?" I whisper close to his ear. "You know how important this is to me."

"You did all the legwork, Julia. I've already said I don't mind telling Ms. Dunkin that this story was totally your idea."

Why is he being so stubborn? "Listen, I really wish you would just help me. This is not about what happened between us. This is a Journalism assignment, and like it or not, we're supposed to be partners. It's going to take two leaders, so I'm asking you to help. Please, Ryan."

He sighs, but then he takes the index cards from my hand and starts passing them out to the students.

I clear my throat before announcing, "Now, this is how we're going to poll the student body. We've all been given passes to miss our last block classes—"

Applause and whistles ensue.

"So, group one, you'll take the north side campus. Group two, the south. Group three, the east, and group four, the west. This is a poll, so no elaborate answers just yet. I've written the question on the index cards Ryan is handing out. The teachers know we'll be popping in their classes this afternoon, and I promised them it wouldn't take longer than ten minutes. Three members of your group will pass out the pieces of paper. Please instruct the students to circle yes or no. Your group leader will read what's on the card. Basically, we want to know if students are for or against parents using GPS tracking to keep tabs on them. After you finish your area, report back here and drop your votes into the white box on the back table. That's it."

Holly rolls her eyes. "Well, if that's all we're doing, sounds simple enough to me. I mean, what do you need us for? Anybody can take a poll."

A few giggles emerge and Ryan glances in a different direction. If I didn't know him better, I'd swear he just snickered.

"Seriously, Holly?" I say. "You have to know that polling the students is only the first phase of the project. We'll be taking quotes from some of the students too, and a few of you will help me finish writing the article. This afternoon's numbers will decide the final team with Ryan and me. So if you want to be on it, you better do some good poll-taking, huh?" I glance at Ms. Dunkin. "Oh, and there's that complete cooperation thing, remember?"

Holly shrugs. "Sure, whatever."

The groups separate and huddle in different parts of the classroom, assigning their roles for the task I've given them. Ryan heads for the back table with Ms. Dunkin, and then she wiggles a finger in my direction.

"I like this feature, you two," Ms. Dunkin says when I'm within earshot. You really have a handle on it. Nice organization. Good job."

"Would you expect anything less from me?" Ryan says before I have time to get a letter out, much less a word. Then he winks. "You know I'm joking. We're just honored that you picked *our* idea. Right, Julia?"

I stare at his face. "Right."

She squeezes his shoulder and then smiles at me before returning to her desk.

I move closer to Ryan. "And what exactly was that?"

"Me being involved. Isn't that what you wanted?"

"No, Ryan." I shake my head. "That's not what I wanted."

I walk away before tears are visible. Why is he being so cruel? I know I lied to him, but I've tried more than once to make things right. But just now, that was him. All him.

****

I still can't believe what Ryan did today. How could that boy look me in the eyes with all his *Oh, it's your feature, Julia, and I'll tell Ms. Dunkin, blah blah blah ...* and then just take credit for it, too? And right in front of my face. He thinks Hannah's mental? Hah! He should recognize the symptoms. I'm convinced he has a little psychosis going on, too. Well, if he thinks I need him to pull off a big story, I'll show him. I'll show 'em all.

I've put it off long enough. It's happening. I'm going to the convent, and I'm getting on that third floor. I have to know once and for all what's up there. It's the only way I can finish my story and make my findings known to the world. Instant media attention, instant fame, instant popularity, instant whole world looking for Aubree— that's what I'll face when the deed is done. And my mom will be so proud she'll have bruises from pinching herself. I tell myself those facts over and over, attempting to still the nervous waves rippling my stomach and kicking in my brain like a cleat. Those thoughts make it easier to face whatever is waiting for me in that convent. And if Brady's disappearance has anything to do with that place, then helping him is worth any danger I might face. I know the possibility of Aubree ever being located alive is slim to none, but it might not be too late for Brady.

And who knows? Maybe Ryan will regret dropping me in his recycle bin like a corrupted file once he learns how far my kickass journalism skills really go. And this story has nothing to do with him, implied or otherwise. Yeah, it's happening. I'm getting on that third floor … this Saturday.

I scan my notebook, sorting through the clues I've gathered. Organizing my exact moves is a must. I'll only get one chance, and I can't blow it—won't blow it. Not this time. I reach in my desk drawer and pull out the skeleton key and lock-picking kit. I hope the key works in that third-floor door. Otherwise I'll be left trying to pick the lock. That would be a disaster, considering how well I did the only other time I've attempted it. Hell, I don't even know if I'm capable of picking a lock. A knock at the front door interrupts my thoughts. Who in the world can that be? I hope Mom paid the gas bill. I'm kinda fond of hot water.

"Julia, can you get that?" Mom shouts from her room.

"Sure."

"If it's Selena Gomez, tell her I'll be right there," Jesse says when I pass his bedroom.

"Ha, you wish." But I laugh. Good to know he's a dreamer.

"I'm coming," I say when another round of knocks peal through the living room. I turn the knob and stare for a couple of seconds, surprise not nearly defining what I'm feeling. "Ryan?"

"Hey, Julia. Can I come in?"

Not even shock feels like this. "But, how did you get

up here?"

He pauses for a breath. "Oh, um, I talked to one of the bouncers. He really seemed to like my car. I told him you and I are dating and he said I could come right up. Is that cool?"

"Let me guess. Black hair, medium build but muscular?"

"Yeah, that's him."

"Congratulations, you've met my dad." I shake my head. "And you told him we're dating? Really? But I thought we were broken up." I fold my arms across my chest. "Go ahead, Ryan, tell me why you're really here."

"We have a dance to go to next week, remember?"

"You still want to go to Homecoming?"

He takes my hand and squeezes it. "Of course I do. I know I was a jerk at school today, but I really do want to make things right between us, Jules. Please, can I just come in so we can talk?"

I open the door wider and he steps inside. I can tell he's trying not to be too obvious as he sizes up the place, but at this point I really don't care. I'm beyond exposed. Now I just want answers. "We can talk in my room."

I close the door when we're in my bedroom and Ryan stands in front of the closet door, staring at my Homecoming dress. "Beautiful. I can't wait to see you in it."

"Why are you here?" I ask again. It's all I can manage to say, the only answer I really need.

"Because I'm in love with you. That's why I'm here."

I'm not sure my lips will move if I try to talk. He's in love with me? Still? "What?"

"I love you, Julia. I was really hurt that you felt like you couldn't trust me enough to tell me where you live, and I had to work through it in my own way. But as hurt as I was, I never stopped loving you. You have to believe that."

My raging curiosity gets the better of me. "Then why were you so cold to me today? That was truly sucktastic, you know—"

"Because I have stuff going on in my life, too, Jules. Everyone does. But I did a lot of thinking. And as much as I tried to stay angry with you, the more I realized that when you care about someone, you have to love the whole person and then decide what value they hold in your life. Honestly, sometimes I think you'd be better off without me. You're special, and you deserve—"

He looks at his hands, the floor, everywhere except my eyes.

"We both deserve to be happy," I say. "I'm just so glad you're here. After today, I thought we were finished for sure."

"Do you still love me, Julia?"

Part of me wants to fall into his arms, tell him he's the only reason my heart beats at all. But that's not entirely true. I know deep down we have issues, differences. And those differences might be too big to overcome. I scream for my rational side to be quiet, but it's not listening. We need to take it slow this time. And then there's Tyler. God, I do have feelings for Tyler, as much as I hate admitting it. Ryan needs to know the truth … about everything.

"I do love you, Ryan, but—"

He pulls me to his chest, his lips covering mine so quickly that it hurts a little. His kiss is wild at first, like my breath alone is his only source of life. When my own need for air forces me to withdraw, he cups my face and slows his motions, his thumbs stroking my cheeks. His lips move from my mouth to my chin, then to my neck. I nuzzle closer, needing his touch, his acceptance.

"Ryan, we really should—"

He stops. "Oh, I'm sorry. We're in your bedroom. Someone could walk in, huh? I've just missed you so much."

"Ryan, please don't misunderstand, but a lot has happened. This is a little too fast for me. If we're going to make this work, we need a fresh start. Know what I mean?"

He looks defeated, but I can tell he agrees. "Sure, whatever you need."

I take his hand. "So, you've met my dad. I want you to meet the rest of my family."

"Okay, cool."

We step into the hall, and I knock on Mom's bedroom door. "Mom, are you dressed for work yet?"

"Yeah, do you need something?"

"Could you come out here, please?"

She steps into the hallway and looks completely taken off guard. "Julia, I told you I was already dressed for work."

"I know, and it's fine. Mom, this is Ryan."

Her eyes widen. "What are you doing, Julia?"

"What I should've done a long time ago."

"Oh." She tugs on her skirt a little. "Ah, nice to meet you, Ryan. I'm Erin."

"Nice to meet you, too," he says, obviously trying not to stare at my mom's pushed-up boobs and legs that won't quit.

"Mom works nights. She's a server at the casino."

Ryan simply nods.

Mom clears her throat. "Well, ah, I really need to go. I'll miss the trolley. Your dad knows you have company, right?"

I roll my eyes. "Who do you think let him in?"

"Oh, okay. Well, I'm glad you two are speaking again. You're welcome anytime, young man." Mom leans into me and whispers, "It was nice to meet your boyfriend, and I'm proud of you for introducing us."

I hug her. "Thanks for that, Mom."

As she heads for the front door, I look at Ryan. "You okay with that knowledge?"

"Yeah, it's fine. And I see where you get your good looks."

"Don't even go there."

He laughs.

"Hey, who are you?" Jesse says, heading for the kitchen when he notices Ryan.

"Ryan, this is my brother, Jesse."

"How's it going?" Ryan says.

Jesse stares at Ryan for a second. "It's going all right, I guess. Hey, Julia, I bought the chips in there, so y'all don't eat 'em, okay?"

Why does he forever have to be a troll? "No one wants your stupid chips." I take Ryan's hand and lead him back to my bedroom. "Sorry about him. I'm pretty sure he was switched at birth or something … or maybe I was."

I really have no desire to have the conversation, but it has to happen now. If this relationship is going to exist at all, I have to tell him everything.

"Ryan, there's a reason for my interest in the Ursuline Convent. You see, the whole reason I started blogging about unsolved mysteries is because my cousin, Aubree Turner, is a missing person. When I lived in New Orleans almost four years ago, she lived here, too. She was sixteen then, and one day she just never came home. I know the Ursuline is the most famous unsolved mystery in this city. If I can reveal its secrets, I'd be famous. Then, the whole world would know my cousin's name. I have to find her, and the convent might be the only way."

Ryan's face twists as he turns away from me. He's still, almost frozen. "Damn, this is heavy."

"I know," I say, "but you see why I have to solve it?"

He turns and looks me dead in the eyes. "I understand a lot better now, but I still think it's too dangerous."

No amount of me trying to make him understand will ever be enough. I know that, but at least he knows the truth. "I understand your feelings." It's all I can say.

"Good," Ryan says. "So, what do we do now? Want to grab a bite to eat or something?"

"There's more," I say.

He looks serious. "Okay, I'm listening."

"I have this friend. His name's Tyler. I met him before you and I first started talking. I'm sorry I never told you about him, but I didn't want you to meet because he goes to a different school. See, he's a safe friend to have. And as badly as I hate to admit it, I kind of used him. I told him the truth about my home life from the very beginning. I wanted to know what his reaction would be. I know that sounds horrible—"

"And exactly what *was* his reaction?"

I wonder why that matters. "He was cool with it."

Ryan's obvious anxiety pushes him further from my face. "So he was cool with it, but you still didn't trust me to be cool with it?"

I'm not sugarcoating it. Truth is just that, truth

"That's right. I was still scared you'd reject me. And the last thing I wanted was for the kids at school to know where I live. I was being honest with you that morning out on the street, though. I had just told Macey my living arrangements, and I was going to tell you the truth that same day too. I just never got the chance."

Ryan turns his back to me again and takes a deep breath. "Okay, you know what? None of that really matters now." His eyes are tender when he faces me again. "If we're going to start over, then let's just put all that behind us. Now that I know the truth, maybe I can meet Tyler. I bet he's cool—"

"I kissed him."

Ryan looks like someone just kicked him in the gonads. "What? You kissed him? When? Before all this happened?"

"Oh God, no! It was just the other day. He's been helping me with the convent story, and we got in a tight spot. There was this adrenaline rush, and it just happened. And I've been so crushed about me and you, Ryan. You have to know I'd never do anything like that if I thought we were still together. That's why I'm telling you now. I'm just being honest with you."

The tenderness I saw in his eyes mere seconds ago is gone. He's all business now. "So, it just happened? You don't have feelings for him, do you?"

"Of course I have feelings for him. He's practically the best friend I have … well, had."

Ryan settles a little. "What do you mean, *had*?"

"I'm upset with him about something that happened the other day. Like I said, he's been helping me with my story, and let's just say he broke a confidence. It pissed me off."

My skin feels prickly and my chest is tighter than an overblown balloon. I've cried more tears for this boy than I care to think about. I want our relationship to work. So I have to trust him with this and pray he'll understand.

"Yeah, well," he says. "The convent story is never

going to end well. You can't solve it, Julia. I've already told you that."

Ryan has the same look he had in class today when he took credit for my idea. It's cocky and smirky, like he thinks I'm incapable of solving anything. It's the look he gets when he sees Hannah, and the one he had a few seconds ago when I told him about kissing Tyler. I hate that look.

"It doesn't matter what you've told me," I say. "I think I can solve it."

Ryan takes a deep breath. "You're telling me that you think you know what's on the third floor of the Ursuline? That's what you're saying? How is that possible? People who've lived here their whole lives don't have a clue what's up there, and they actually know better than to try and figure it out."

Know better? Everyone keeps saying the same thing. This entire city's scared shitless. Well, not me. I'm a journalist, a kickass journalist. How soon a boy forgets.

"It's just crazy, Julia," he adds when I'm quiet. "We did a feature on the convent last year. I'm telling you now, it's seriously dangerous to try to scope out that third floor. Just crazy."

I know my face is red, but I don't care. "Crazy? And just what's so crazy about it? You said I was major, the real deal when it comes to reporting. So, what? Has your perception of me changed for some reason? I'm a journalist, Ryan. I go for the story. And just so you know, this is *the story*."

"You could get hurt, or worse. I know the history surrounding that place, what people say happens to folks who poke around too much. They freakin' die. You could *die*, Jules."

"Are you telling me you really believe that, Ryan?"

"I'm not sure if I believe it entirely, but I don't think it's worth the risk. Do you?"

I shake my head. "You just don't understand."

"Then make me understand."

My voice is barely above a whisper. "I can't fail, not at this." I know the tears are visible, but I don't care. "Maybe it's not worth the risk for you, but it is for me. I loved— No, I *love* Aubree. She's all I have."

"That's not true," he says. "You have me—"

"And you have everything, Ryan. Girls fall all over you. Hell, all the guys at school want to be you. You have a gorgeous home, stable parents who love you more than all their wealth combined. When the world looks at you, it sees potential, an amazing young man with opportunities. Do you know what the world sees when it looks at me? The girl who's moved so much she's never had any real friends. The girl with messed-up parents and a reputation she never brought on herself. It sees a victim of circumstance who doesn't want to be a victim forever. It sees the girl who lives above a strip club so she must be trash. The world sees failure."

"That's not what the world sees when it looks at you, Julia—"

"That's what you saw! Otherwise you wouldn't have had so much to work through before coming here tonight. You can deny it if you want, but I know the whole truth. A part of you had to decide whether or not I'm good enough for you."

He takes my hands in his. "You have that backward. I've never wondered whether or not you're good enough for me. I wonder if I'm good enough for you. You're unlike anyone I've ever met. You're special, Julia. I know it, and deep down, you know it too."

"And I know the only thing that makes me special is

my brain and my ability. That's all I have. That convent is my story, and no matter the risks, I'm going to tell it. I'm not giving up, and I won't fail. I'm bringing Aubree home, one way or another. If you love me like you say you do, you'll understand."

"Julia, you don't have to put yourself in mortal danger for your cousin. I know you think you don't have a choice, but you do. I'll talk to my parents, see if they have any resources that might be helpful. You're not alone. Just remember that, okay? I'm asking you not to go on that third floor." He presses his lips to my forehead. "Okay?" he says again.

"Okay," I whisper. And I will remember his words, just like I remember that day on the street when he climbed into his Mustang and drove away. No, I'm not turning back. My answers are on that third floor, and I'm taking control once and for all, I'm sticking to the plan.

Chapter Fifteen

I bite my lip as I read through my theory again.

King Louis XV sent the Casket Girls to New Orleans at the request of the heathen men begging for women to marry. Knowing that he sent his very heart, his beloved niece, Katherine, it's probable that he sent other girls of the court, too. But the undesirable men of the penal colony abused the young women. This angered Louis, as evidenced by the albatross artwork. The bird symbolizes the horrific plight of the girls and the terrible misjudgment of the king. The albatross on the third floor is wearing a coat of arms. Is the coat of arms for the girls, or someone else? What is the ancient king protecting on that floor, and who exactly is doing his bidding? Whatever he's hiding, it's important enough for the room to be protected by windows secured with thousands of blessed nails, important enough for a vampire legend, complete with coffins, to frighten away potential truth seekers. And possibly ... important enough to kill anyone who enters that room.

"What is the king hiding? I'm missing something ... something major."

Not sure why I talk to myself when I'm working through clues, but it helps somehow. I hope my notes are self-explanatory, just in case someone picks up my notebook. If for some insane reason the general population is right and I don't make it out of that convent alive, they'll know one thing for sure—that I'm the chick who came closer than anyone else to uncovering the secrets of the Ursuline. And they'll damn sure know Aubree's name, too.

Rational thinking tells me I should be more afraid. God knows I've been warned. Detective Elder ... Tyler

… Ryan … they all seem to think I'm one cushion shy of the therapist's couch for wanting to go on that third floor.

But they don't know me.

I used to be afraid, like when I was five and the landlord at our place in Huntsville showed up with police to evict us. Or when I was nine and Mom made me tuck two little packs of crackers and cheese down my shirt at the grocery store so Jesse and I could eat that night. Or when I was at the high school in Mobile and Bridget Miller announced to the entire class that I was wearing a shirt she'd donated to Goodwill. She'd recognized it by the tiny ink stain on the bottom hem.

But in every situation, I closed my eyes and took deep breaths, removing myself from the chaos, the panic, the mocking laughter. Yeah, wearing mental armor is something I've gotten really good at. And I'm still not convinced that I'll simply drop dead from being on that third floor. I just need to add a little weaponry to the game plan for extra security. I'm not the first journalist to put myself in harm's way for the story. I'll just have to be crazy alert. I close my notebook. Yeah, crazy…

My bed is a mangled pile of blankets. I never made it before leaving for school this morning. As much as I hate climbing into an unmade bed at night, I'm not about to do the deed at six in the evening. I tug on the sheets a little before sitting down, attempting to give the bed the appearance of order. My phone chirps. **I know you hate me but I need to see you.**

Tyler. My thumbs do their business. **Okay. Where?**

Me, hate Ty? No way. I want to tell him that I'm not as pissed with him as before, and I will. But sometimes you just have to let a guy suffer. **Meet me at the police station. You need to meet someone. Please…**

Meet someone? An offer I can't refuse. **Be there**

soon.

This better be good.

****

Tyler's sitting in his dad's office when I enter the station. His usual wild hair is teased up and high on one side. He looks like a member of Flock of Seagulls or something.

"Wow," I say when I'm in earshot. "The eighties called. It wants its hair back."

"That bad, huh? I thought I'd try something new."

"Well, mission accomplished. And, hey, there's no shame in going back to the drawing board, you know."

He smiles and then takes a second to smooth his hair down. "Listen, Julia, I'm sorry I got the old man involved. I really was just worried about you. And I'm sorry about all the other crap I said, too. Ryan's a lucky guy to have a girl like you all hot for him."

I stifle a laugh from the attempted compliment. "Thanks, Ty. You're forgiven, but if you ever rat me out again, your hair will stick up naturally from the knots I'll put on your head."

He grimaces. "Harsh."

"So, who do I need to meet?"

His face lights up as he takes my hand and pulls me to the doorway of the office. He points to a grungy-looking old woman seated on a bench in the middle of the station. She looks like a voodoo priestess, complete with a brightly colored muumuu and headdress. She has rows of wooden beads mingled with other trinkets around her neck, and if I'm correct, a dried-up chicken's foot on it, too. Gross.

"That's Elize," Ty says. "She's a little twisted, I'll admit, but she's a full-fledged psychic, not like those wannabes that hang out in Jackson Square. No joke. That lady sees things."

I'm more than intrigued. *Oh, God ... Aubree!* "Cool Show-n-Tell," I say instead, trying to be subtle when all I really want to do is ask her about my cousin. "So she sees things, huh? What things?"

"Once when my dad was working on a homicide case, he brought Elize in and asked her to hold the hand of a murdered girl's mother to see if Elize could connect with the girl's spirit. When the dead girl was found, it was determined that her body had been moved to that location after she was killed. Anyway, when Elize held hands with the girl's mother, she made the comment, 'The purple flowers are all around.' So my dad had investigators search a field of wild irises two miles from where the girl's body had been discovered. And, sure enough, they found a pink hair ribbon, torn fabric from the girl's shirt, and blood. In other words, the exact spot where the murder happened. Other clues in that spot led to the identity and conviction of the girl's killer. Elize totally nailed it. Freaky, right?"

"That's awesome," I say. "I need to interview her. Damn, I need my notebook—"

Tyler shakes his head. "No, Miss Reporter, you don't need to interview her. You need to let her hold *your* hand."

A chill hits me. "My hand? For what?"

Tyler swallows hard. "Because she can see the future."

"Get outta here." I laugh. *Now that I don't believe!* "No way that chick sees the future. Hey, if that's the case, tell her I need the lottery numbers for next week."

He looks frustrated. "No, Julia, it doesn't work like that. She can't just spit out the actual numbers. She would have to hold the hand of the future winner and tell them they were going to win. Get it?"

"Yeah, I get it. But why do you want her to hold my—" Then it hits me. "Oh, I see. You want her to tell me not to go to the third floor of the convent, huh?"

"Something like that."

"I'm going, Tyler. You need to just accept it. I don't need some voodoo lady to hold my hand—"

"What would it hurt? If you're hardheaded enough to go through with it anyway, maybe she'll tell you something that can help you succeed, know what I mean? Listen, I just want to know what she has to say. And my dad will be back with the guy she's here for soon. If we're going to talk to her, we need to do it now. Please, Julia ... for me."

"All right. I'll do it." *For you ... but mostly for Aubree...*

We approach Elize. Two compliments and a boyish grin later, my shaking hands are in hers and she's staring at me.

"So," I say, "you're a psychic? That's incredible."

"I'm an oracle," she responds. "Nothing I do is of my own ability. I am a vessel in which the spirits communicate. Nothing more."

"That's amazing—"

"Hush," she says. "Just be still now." She closes her eyes.

After a minute or so, Elize opens her eyes and they lock with mine again.

Tyler seems like he's about to burst. "Well, did you see anything?"

"Quiet, boy!" she says, drawing the attention of others in the station. Her grip tightens on my hands. "You are the one. You will silence their cries."

She pulls her hands from mine and walks away.

"What the hell?" Tyler says. "Come back. What the hell does that mean?"

My knees are weak and my hands are trembling. I don't attempt to stand yet, but simply let her words soak in. *You will silence their cries.* Whose cries? The Casket Girls? The people who have died trying to uncover the mystery of the Ursuline? Aubree? Brady? Both? Whose? A smile lifts the corners of my mouth. Elize has sealed my fate, bless her heart. I'll silence their cries. *Me.*

"Well, that was a total bust," Tyler says. "She's crazy, you know. She just spouted a load of shi—"

"No, she knew exactly what she was saying. See, I tried to tell you. I'm going on that third floor, Ty." I wink. "It's my destiny."

"This isn't a joke, Julia! You know what, come here."

In a few seconds we're back in his dad's office looking at Tyler's laptop. "See that? You're looking at photos of pages from a folder in this station. Read it."

"Lieutenant Daniel Baker was killed in the line of duty on May 20, 1973, while investigating two homicides at the Ursuline Convent. His remains were discovered when he failed to report back to the station on the following day—"

"See. My dad was right. Cops have died investigating that place. Keep reading. There's more."

My head's spinning. "Where'd you get this?"

"I talked to my dad about the dead investigators. I told him I felt the same way you did. Basically said I didn't believe it ever happened because there was no evidence. I pissed him off so bad he finally admitted that a folder existed that proved it. So I snuck into a back office of file cabinets last week and found the folder. Dad's been right all along. The officers sent to the convent to investigate are dead as dirt. You told me once to show you the proof. Well, here it is."

I read further. Another investigator in 1978. Killed in the line of duty. Ursuline Convent. I've been searching for evidence of dead investigators for weeks, and now that it's right in front of my face, I feel sick.

"See, Julia? You can't do this. It's just too dangerous."

There's no way I can tell him that I'm still not convinced these deaths didn't happen because of police corruption somehow. The convent would be the perfect scapegoat for anyone trying to take out a crocked cop, even the NOPD itself.

But I can see the fear in his eyes when I take his face in my hands. "Ty, I know you're scared about all this, and you'll never know how much it means to me. Hell, I can't believe you snuck in a back room to find evidence for me. But I have to finish my story. I appreciate what you did with Elize, too—"

"She was supposed to tell you not to do it! I had a feeling that showing you what I found about the dead officers might not do it, but I thought talking to her would seal the deal. I thought she'd tell you it was dangerous, not some 'silence their cries' crap. What does that even mean?"

I take a deep breath. "I don't know, but I have to find out. Do you understand?"

"No, I don't understand." He sighs. "So, when are you planning your funeral exactly? Next week? Next month? And I don't look good in black, just so you know."

I hate to lie, but I can't chance telling him my plans for Saturday. I hide a hand behind my back and cross my fingers. "Not anytime soon, so don't worry."

He furrows a brow. "Yeah, right. Hey, listen. When

you do it, if you get in trouble on that third floor … call me. I'll be there."

"But I thought you said you'd never step a foot near that third floor."

"Julia, if you need me, I'll be there. I'd do anything for you."

Looking at him in this moment, I believe it. He *would* do anything for me. Already has. My insides tingle and I want to be next to him, the urge so strong I can't resist. "Thanks, Ty." It's all I can squeak out. I pull him into a hug and bury my face in his shirt.

I do need him, and he's here.

****

The psychic's words loop in my head when I leave the police station. *You will silence their cries.* Whose cries? I find a bench on the sidewalk and pull out my notebook. I scan though my theory again, Ms. Dunkin's words taking over my thoughts. *Ask the easy questions.* I bite my lip, then mumble, "Who was a vital part of New Orleans history upon settling the colony?" *The Casket Girls.* "Who was sent by Louis XV according to the clues I've gathered?" *His beloved niece Katherine and young women of the court.*

Oh, my God! They were the *real* Casket Girls, not the middle- and lower-class young women as history would have us believe. And the king loved his niece. That's evidenced by the photo of her at his knee when she was a child. He sent her and her maids of court to be the noble, virginal women to settle his new colony, but that was not the case. History makes no secret of the pain they endured upon reaching the new world. King Louis sent them here with a promise of hope, marriages, better lives in a new colony—the virtuous women sent to answer the lonely pleas of marriageable men. But that's a far cry from the actual welcome they encountered. The Sisters of the Ursuline did their best to save the girls, but not all were rescued from the villainous husbands awaiting them. Maybe Katherine wasn't rescued? And if Louis discovered this, what would be his recourse then? He'd sent his own niece to her death.

I shove my notebook in my backpack and head toward the trolley station. I know where I have to go. I just hope Brady was as close as I am to telling the Ursuline's secret—and I hope his wife will talk to me.

Chapter Sixteen

I take a deep breath when I'm standing on the porch. Brady's house looks like the fairy tale, complete with a white picket fence. It didn't take long to find his address. A quick trip to the library and a few minutes on one of the computers, and presto. I will my hand into a fist and knock three times.

Within a minute, the door opens and I back up a little.

"May I help you?" a woman says. She looks like she'd be pretty without the dark circles and puffy eyes.

"Mrs. Swinson?" I say.

"Yes."

"I'm Julia Reynolds. I know this is going to sound crazy, but I know Brady. I met him at the Ursuline Convent. We both love the mystery surrounding that place and we've talked about it a lot. I was wondering "

She grabs my arm and pulls me inside before I have time to protest.

"Do you think something happened to him in that place?" She stares at me, her eyes like scattered moonlight in a rain puddle. She adds, "When I mentioned to the police that he was interested in the convent, they dismissed me like the very mention of it was criminal. They said they'll keep looking for Brady, but not there. I'm just so scared for him. Do you have any idea where he might be?"

The hairs on my arms feel prickly and I rub the goose bumps away. "I have no idea where he is. I'm sorry."

Her gaze lowers for a moment, and I see tears when she looks at me again. "Then why are you here?"

"Because … if your husband's disappearance has anything to do with that convent, then I might be the only person who can find him. But I need your help."

She's resolute even before the words come out, "Then you have it. My name's Sarah, by the way."

Sheer giddiness fills me and I hope it's not obvious. The fact that I might get my hands on new information about the convent is beyond wicked awesome. "That's great, Sarah. Now, what I need to know is, did Brady keep any kind of record of his visits to the Ursuline?"

She gets a faraway look. "I'm so rude," she says, wiping a stray tear from her cheek. "Come into the living room and I'll get us something to drink."

I do as I'm told and sit on the couch as she steps into the kitchen. Why did she dodge my question? My elation from earlier turns to panic. I have to know if Brady has records of his findings regarding the Ursuline.

She's back in a couple of minutes with two glasses of ice tea and I set mine on a coaster on the coffee table before saying anything.

"It's sweet tea—hope that's okay."

"It's perfect," I assure her. I take a sip then again ask the only question burning a hole through my brain. "So, do you know if Brady has any records of his visits to the Ursuline?"

A sob tears from her throat and she buries her face in her hands. "He has a journal," she says through the tears, "and some stuff in a folder on his computer. I've read it over and over in the last couple of days, but none of it makes any sense to me. I doubt it will to you either."

For a moment, I forget about my story and focus on Sarah. Anyone with eyes can see how much she loves her husband, how desperate she is to find him. She looks like I did after Aubree went missing. I want to tell her that I know how she feels. But instead, I cup her hands in mine. "Sarah, I'm so sorry about Brady. Has he ever done anything like this before?"

She pulls a napkin from her pocket and dabs her eyes. "You mean disappear? No, never. That's just it. I know something terrible has happened. I still have hope that he'll be found alive, but I know deep down he wouldn't just leave. Something's keeping him from me."

Sarah attempts to look me in the eyes, but her stare falls to the floor instead. I try to will my mouth to work, but there are no words, so I wait and listen instead. It just feels wrong to say anything now, like her longing for Brady takes up every free breath in the room.

"I never let him see me cry," she says when she finally looks up.

"What?" I say.

"Brady. I never let him see me cry." She moves to a long table against the wall and picks up a picture of the two of them. She slides a finger along Brady's image and closes her eyes. "Once when we were dating, he told me that some girl he used to date was a crier. He said she would cry over nothing ... over anything ... over everything. I never forgot that, so I've never really cried in front of him." She sets the photo down and places her hands on the table like she'll fall without the extra support.

"But now," she adds, "all I do is cry. I feel like someone has cut my spirit from my bones and flung it into fire. I burn. Hurt. Ache. Die. Whoever did this ... made my Brady disappear ... has killed me from the inside out. I can't sleep. Can't breathe. And I'll never stop crying."

My eyes are watery, but tears don't fall. No way I'm letting them fall. The last thing Sarah needs to know is that her confession is the saddest thing anyone's ever said to me. I understand the emptiness she's feeling, can relate it to my time away from Aubree, to my childhood ridicule and insecurities, to life above a strip joint. To the time Ryan was angry with me. But deep down, I know this is different. She thinks the man she loves more than herself is dead ... and she might be right.

I'd do anything to bring him back to her.

"Listen," I say, "just show me his journal. I've been investigating that convent for a while. Maybe his notes will make sense to me."

She nods and walks toward the hallway. "Be right back."

I'm on my feet before I can help myself, and standing next to the picture of the happy couple. Before meeting Sarah, I wasn't sure if Brady's disappearance had anything at all to do with the convent, but now I'm not so sure. What if he did reach that third floor and opened that locked door ... and now he's dead? And if that's the case, then where's his body? Wouldn't it be displayed on the grounds—or the convent steps—like some kind of warning? Like the others?

"Here it is," she says, pulling me from my thoughts. "Most of his notes about that place are in here."

She hands me a brown leather book and I tuck it under my arm. "Sarah, you said he has a folder on his computer too, right?"

"Yes."

"Would you mind showing it to me? I don't want to overlook anything."

"Sure," she says. "It's in his office. Follow me."

She opens a door in the middle of the hallway. The office looks like Brady, a mixture of mahogany shelves and historical artifacts, lined with books older than my grandparents, each with leather spines that are more interesting than anything in our school library. It smells musky, but clean—a throwback in time with a

Steampunk allure.

"His laptop's on the desk. Go ahead. Help yourself."

I feel like I'm doing something majorly wrong when I sit in Brady's chair and click the folder labeled *Ursuline* on his laptop. My hand bumps an empty Diet Mountain Dew bottle and it falls over. Sarah stands it up before I can react.

"He was drinking it the night before he disappeared," she says. "It's funny, I used to gripe when he left empty bottles lying around, but now I can't bring myself to throw it away."

There are no words, so I nod and focus on the contents on the folder instead. Most everything I scan over looks like my notes. I hope his journal's more insightful. Then, something pops out from the familiar details. Two little words.

Blood Defenders.

Who in the world are the Blood Defenders? I open Google and type in every combination of Blood Defenders and King Louis XV and Casket Girls, but all the usual references and sites I've seen a hundred times appear. Nothing new.

Damn.

But since I'm online and Sarah isn't looking over my shoulder like a troll, I take a few seconds to email Brady's Ursuline folder to myself. I glance at the time on the computer. Almost nine. I text Dad to let him know I'll be home in the next thirty minutes.

"Sarah," I say after closing out everything, "it's getting late and I have school tomorrow. Would you mind if I take Brady's journal with me? I promise I'll take good care of it. And I'll write down my address and cell number for you."

"That's fine," she says, wiping a tear that I'm sure is

stinging her chapped cheek. "Thank you for trying, Julia. It means a lot."

I'm hugging her before I realize it, but she relaxes into my embrace like we've known each other for years. I just hope I can give her what she's looking for … give us both what we're looking for.

****

Muted laughter from the street below wakes me. It's funny how I've grown immune to the muffled music from the club, but laughter or shouts from the street still manage to jar me awake. I glance at my phone. Four AM. Perfect. I pull the covers up to my chin, trying to remember everything in the folder from Brady's computer. I'd read through the contents of the folder twice, and had looked at just about every reference to "Blood Defender" I could find—including at least a dozen cheesy B movies with that reference—when Dad told me to get my ass to bed. I roll over and attempt to find a cool spot on my pillow, but I know there's no way I'm going back to sleep. Good thing sleuthing in the wee hours excites me almost as much as Ryan.

Nature calls, so I tiptoe to the bathroom, careful not to wake Dad or Jesse. Thankfully Mom's not home yet. She sleeps like me … lighter than Cool Whip. But those two sleep like grizzlies in winter, but I know Dad would be pissed that I'm awake. The last thing I need is him ticked at me.

I run my tongue across newly-brushed teeth, glad to be free of morning breath, and climb back in bed. I settle on top of the covers and prop Brady's journal on my knees. I run a finger along the soft, leather binding, feeling almost too guilty to open it. Looking at his notes on the computer was one thing, but this is his handwriting—his private thoughts and theories. The last thing I want to do is violate him even more, but I know this may be the only way I can help him. "I'm sorry, Brady," I mumble, and open it.

At first glance, his journal is very similar to mine, except for the side notes that look all "teacherly." But what I read next breaks my heart. It's a personal note, like some random thought just entered his stream of consciousness. It's written outside the lines:

I want to make my parents proud—make Sarah proud. I want to be part of history, not just teach it. I want all this digging to count for something.

The next three words are circled.

Make it count.

I set Brady's journal on the bed and wrap my arms around my knees, leaning tightly into them to settle my churning stomach. I've just burst through his front door unannounced, just walked in on him showering, just barged through his bedroom door when he's not finished dressing. I've invaded his space—exposed his private hopes and dreams. And they're the same as mine.

My notebook's on the desk and I lean over far enough to grab it, almost slipping off the edge of the bed. I'm not sure why I need it—feel like somehow it's okay to keep reading Brady's intimate notes if mine are near his, too. After holding the stacked journals together for several seconds, I open Brady's again and keep reading. Nothing jumps out at me until this:

I've scoured every inch of the accessible floor of this convent, but something I've been withholding has made my investigating weak until now ... until I discovered it was me.

What is Brady talking about? I run through the catalog in my mind—through everything I know about the convent, every theory I've constructed. I'm not sure why, but that phrase is different, and I know it means something. Maybe Brady really did try to get on that third floor—decided not to withhold himself anymore. And now he's dead because of it.

I let the thoughts that I've suppressed since first stumbling upon this mystery flood my brain. Maybe this is too dangerous after all. Maybe it's really not worth dying for. My death really wouldn't get anyone any closer to finding Aubree.

Maybe I can't do this.

"Knock knock."

I nearly fall off the bed when Mom pokes her head in my door.

"Oh, hey," I say.

"Why you up at this ungodly hour?" she asks. "Homework or something?"

"Not exactly," I reply. "How was work?"

"It was work, you know. Sucky, but thanks for asking. You want some eggs if I make 'em?"

"Sure." I drop the journal on my bed and join Mom in the doorway. "You know I can't say no to your eggs. Just let me shower first."

I walk into the bathroom like a robot—a zombie. It's not until the too-hot water hits me in the face that I realize I'm already in the shower. As determined as I've been during every step of my investigation, why am I so scared now? Because deep down I feel like Aubree's dead, that Brady's dead—and snooping around the convent is to blame.

Before he went missing, everything about the Ursuline wasn't quite real, not quite true. Part of me always thought the dead, curious thrill-seekers were really more imagination than fact—folklore injected at the opportune moment to cover the deeds of common killers. But meeting Sarah and seeing her pain, the way her eyes looked when she talked about Brady, I can't ignore it any longer. Do I really want to do that to my mom? To Ryan? To Tyler? If that convent is to blame for Brady's disappearance, and possibly Aubree's, then the same thing could happen to me. For the first time since trying to break this story, it feels too real now. It goes beyond obtaining more blog followers. And I'm scared.

My skin's a deep pink when I turn off the hot water. I step out of the shower and wrap a towel tightly around my middle. I know I've uncovered enough facts to make my Ursuline story stand out more than all the others I've read. What I've figured out about that place is seriously epic. I know Ms. Dunkin would be majorly impressed. Maybe I should just write my story and forget about trying to get on that third floor. It would be the smart thing to do.

I can smell the eggs when I sit down at the kitchen table. Truth be known, Mom's eggs never have enough salt, and she makes them a little watery, but I love it when she cooks for me. It means we actually have groceries, and that she's trying.

Mom scoops some eggs on a plate and sets it in front of me. "You know, the cuckoo bird lays its eggs in other birds' nests."

I smile. "I actually did know that, Mom. I learned about it in school."

"Wild, huh?" She points to the remote on the table in front of me. "Switch on the TV, please. I wanna watch the news."

Jesse walks in and serves up his own eggs before Mom has a chance to offer him any. "I could've slept another ten minutes, but I smelled the food. I'm starving."

"There's plenty," Mom says. "Eat up."

"Shh, listen," I say when I recognize Brady on the news broadcast. I turn the volume up.

"What you're about to see is surveillance video from a street camera outside of a business on Bourbon Street," the newswoman says. "The man on the footage is Brady Swinson, a history teacher who is now considered a missing person. According to the time of the footage, it is believed that the teacher went missing soon after this was shot. This may be the last known images of Mr. Swinson. Please take a close look at the footage. If you have any information about these images, please contact the New Orleans Police Department."

The video is shown three times, and my weak knees won't allow me to stand. A scream lodges in my throat, but my paralyzing fear doesn't release it. Brady's face is clear on the footage, but so is another. Why the hell is James there?

Chapter Seventeen

"What do you mean you're not going to school today?"

Mom's usually cool with my decisions, but I know how important school is to her when it comes to me. If I don't say the exact right thing, she'll never go for it.

"Well, I'm waiting," she adds.

"Okay, listen," I say. "I have a story I'm working on, and I need to do one last bit of research before turning it in. I need to go to the convent, and it's going to take me a while to find what I'm looking for. If I don't finish it, I'll get a bad grade. I'm not behind on anything in my other classes, so it really won't hurt for me to miss one day. But if I don't do this, I might not make an A in Journalism." And now for the cherry on top. "You know if I don't get an A, you can kiss any chance at a scholarship goodbye. They go pretty far back on high school transcripts now."

She lets out a breath. "All right, just be careful. And if your brother finds out I let you skip school, he'll rag me to no end."

"I won't tell him. Thanks, Mom."

"And be careful, Julia. Lots of crazies out there."

Tell me about it.

I head to my bedroom to gather what I'll need for the day. I hate lying to my mother, but I'll need her on my side in case I get caught by a truancy officer. I doubt seeing James on that surveillance video was coincidence. I have to find out why that *sweet old man* just happened to be standing not four feet from Brady in what might be the last images of him alive.

The journals, my camera, and the eight dollars I got from an ad on my blog are in my backpack. I grab the fountain pen James gave me and read the inscription for the hundredth time. *Discretion is the better part of valour.* Maybe he should've practiced what he preached.

I text Ryan that I won't be at school today. My first thought is to say I'm sick, but instead I simply say I have something to do. I'm proud of myself for being honest with him, even though I hope he won't ask for more details. I'm relieved to receive the reply, **I'll call after school**. I shove the phone in my pocket, and head for the door.

****

Every table at the street café is filled with people. The morning is unseasonably warm and very sunny, and the locals are taking advantage of it. Street musicians are playing a jazzy tune, and an older couple starts dancing. The guy at the table next to me is slapping his knee to the beat, but I just sip my iced tea and keep my eyes on the passersby. I wish a million times over that I had asked James his last name that day. I've been sitting here at the place we met for almost two hours, and still no sign of him. I'm not sure why I thought he might show up here, but having absolutely nothing to go on doesn't leave me many options. But I guess I have to face it sooner or later. He's a needle in a haystack.

Everything about the day we met keeps running through my head—the way he was dressed, his proper speech, his questions about my home life and the strip club. Oh, my God! James had a gold pin on his pocket ... a pin with a bird on it!

"No way," I mumble. I open my journal to the notes about the albatross wearing the coat of arms. That pin on James's pocket could have been an albatross, too! How could I be so stupid—not realize it until now?

"Would you like more sweet tea, ma'am?" the

waitress asks before filling my glass again. "Or something to eat maybe?"

"No thank you," I say, leaving a couple of dollars on the table for my drink. No sign of James, but I know where I need to go. He had something to do with Brady's disappearance. I can feel it. And every sign points to the Ursuline.

****

"Well, aren't you quite the enthusiast?" the woman in the Ursuline gift shop calls to me as I pass the shop's entrance in front of the convent grounds. "I've ran out of fingers to count the times you've been here, and might near run out of toes too."

Enthusiast? No. Maybe it started out that way—the girl with the raging curiosity, searching for a story to put her cousin's name out there, gain her acceptance in a cruel, judgmental world. My strong mind for solving mysteries has been a constant, like the sunrise or the stars. And it's never let me down …'til now. I've never felt so defeated. I have to find James.

I smile my pleasantries, hoping the shop woman won't engage me in conversation. No such luck.

"Do come inside, dear," she says. "As many times as you've been here, I don't think you've as much as browsed the shop. Why not take a peek at a few things?"

Great. But I know it's impossible to refuse without coming off as rude. Still, I didn't skip school, wait forever in an outdoor café for a no-show, and then climb on a trolley and get stuck sitting next to a guy who smelled like moldy cheese just to buy a few trinkets in a gift shop. I need to see the coat of arms again, need to see if anything else in that convent might point to James's true identity.

"I'm Mildred," the woman says as I step through the

shop's door. "And you are?"

"Julia," I reply.

"Nice to meet you, Julia." The elderly lady is well-dressed and attractive, her silver hair in a loose bun with small ringlets framing her heart-shaped face. She's dressed in slacks and a dark blazer, a row of pearls draping her neck.

"Likewise." I glance at the various Ursuline souvenirs, not really focusing on anything in particular. Nothing in here is any help from a research standpoint anyway. It's mostly stuff like crucifixes, rosaries, Beanie Babies, rubber bracelets, and so on. And it's not like I could even afford a collectible pencil if I wanted one. I have exactly three dollars left after the sweet tea and trolley ride.

"See anything you like?" Mildred asks.

"To be honest, I'm broke and kind of in a hurry." I throw her a half-smile and move toward the door again.

"Understood," she says, "but don't go so fast that you miss something worth seeing." She joins me near the exit. "Here, I want you to have this. Anyone who's visited the convent as many times as you deserves a keepsake." She hands me a bookmark with a sketch of the Ursuline on it.

"Thank you," I say. "I like it."

"You're welcome, and enjoy your visit."

I tuck the bookmark into the side of my backpack and head toward the convent. No matter how many times I come here, I can't help but stare at the third-floor windows and their tightly nailed shutters. And it still gives me goose bumps.

Within minutes, I'm inside the Ursuline and standing in front of the coat of arms. I don't bother looking over my shoulder for the annoying tour guide or security. I'm looking instead for *something*, anything that'll help me figure out what happened to Brady, and how in the hell James is involved.

After staring at the coat of arms for several minutes, I close my eyes and think about Ms. Dunkin's personal mantra. *Ask the easy questions.* Everything I know about history reminds me that a coat of arms always has a symbol of a family lineage. Brady and I both knew that the lineage of this shield-type coat of arms resembles no arms of King Louis's house, or any royal house of that day. So, it's unique—obviously designed for a specific group. So, whoever this represents has to be identified somewhere in its framework. I scan the piece line by line, detail by detail. Three things jump out at me, and I mumble as I work them out, focusing only on those details:

"A crown for a king, a knight's helmet, and a chest plate that looks like ... like ... a heart." Why a heart? Then it registers. "The king's heart," I mumble. *Katherine.* The Casket Girls.

I take a few pictures, zooming in on the crown, helmet, and heart-shaped chest plate as best as possible. Questioning any of the tour guides would be a total bust. They're so tight-lipped about the truth when it comes to this place I'm surprised my image isn't hanging in here like a wanted poster. But I know someone who might not be so secretive. Let's hope Mildred knows more about this place than just how to sell a few refrigerator magnets.

She's all smiles when I walk back into the gift shop. "Well, hello again. Change your mind about the browsing?"

I fiddle with my camera and find the images of the coat of arms before returning Mildred's smile. "Not really. I actually have a question for you, if you're willing to answer it."

"If I can," she replies.

"How much do you really know about the convent?"

She loops a finger under the strand of pearls on her neck and gently tugs. "Well, as much as anyone I suppose. I've lived in New Orleans for thirty plus years, and worked in this shop nearly fifteen. What do you need to know?"

"Anything about that third floor," I say. "Do you have any idea what's up there?"

"Ha!" She releases the pearls and joins me in the center of the room. "If I knew that, I'd be rich! Or dead."

"And you really believe that?" I say before thinking about how it sounds. Of course she believes it. I believe it, too, now more than ever. But I need to hear Mildred's take on that third floor, need to know if she has any information I haven't dug up yet. Hell, fifteen years at this place should count for something.

"It's easy to believe something when it's true," she says matter-of-factly. "Belief in something that has no proof is a different animal altogether."

I'm shoving the camera in her face before she has time to finish her sentence. "This coat of arms, it's hanging in the convent. Do you have any idea who it represents?"

"King Louis, perhaps? He *was* the one responsible for sending the Casket Girls to New Orleans, after all. Thank God the good nuns saved some of them from the harsh conditions they were thrown into, poor things."

I try not to let my frustration show. "It's not his seal. Nothing on it represents his lineage."

"Wow," she says. "You really know your history. Trying to solve the mystery of that third floor, huh? I thought so. No one visits as much as you without that same agenda."

It never occurred to me that Mildred might be familiar with some of the others who've tried to solve the Ursuline mystery. The thought makes my stomach tingle, but I ignore the funny feeling and keep her talking while she's willing.

"So, you know others who've investigated the third floor?"

"Sure," she replies. "And most just let the curiosity bug die out after a while. But then one or two keep searching until something terrible happens."

My breath catches. "You know someone who had something terrible happen to them?"

Her eyes fix on me and I don't move, don't focus on anything but her mouth and the words I know will come. "Why, you know him, too, child. And I'm guessing he's the real reason you're here. The history teacher."

"You know what happened to Brady?" I blurt, not caring about the other lady who just walked into the shop. "Tell me where he is!"

"I'll be with you in a moment," she says to the other customer. Mildred takes me by the arm and pulls me toward the door. "I have no idea what happened to him," she says when we're outside, "but I do know that he was spending a lot of time here. And two days before his disappearance, he asked me about that same shield you just showed me. You shouldn't be poking around that third floor, or you might end up like your friend."

"So you believe Brady's dead because of that third floor?"

"It doesn't matter what I believe," Mildred says, leaning close to my ear. "Belief and faith are matters of the spirit. Whether you withhold yourself or indulge in the faith is strictly up to you. Good day, Julia."

I take a couple of steps back, her words slamming me like a fist. They're so familiar I'm reeling. I sit on the nearest bench in the courtyard and pull Brady's journal from my backpack. I read his words aloud. *"Something I've been withholding has made my investigating weak until now ... until I discovered it was me."*

Faith. I stand and gather my things and then head for the street in front of the convent. I've scoured that place for weeks, but I've yet to investigate the building next to it. Faith is a matter of the spirit, withholding myself. Well, St. Mary's Church is right beside the convent, and I'm not withholding myself anymore. I head toward the entrance.

Much like the Ursuline, tourists are milling about the church, stopping every few feet to take pictures or read descriptions of religious items scattered throughout the sanctuary. The church is breathtakingly beautiful, and for a few seconds, I simply stand in awe and take it in. Elaborate paintings on the ceiling show Heaven's blue skies and cottony clouds with angels hovering like direct messengers of God. Massive stained-glass windows and gold statues line the walls. I can't resist the urge to take a few pictures, so I indulge. But I'm not here for the beauty. I need to find out why James was standing near

Brady in that surveillance video. What did Brady know that made him disappear? And why the hell did Mildred all but point me straight to St. Mary's?

Everything looks "churchy" and immaculate, like nothing this perfect could possibly hold deadly secrets. My stomach growls and I check the time on my phone. One-thirty. I'm starving, but I ignore my screaming belly. After reading every plaque on the statues and inscriptions on the altar, nothing seems connected to the third floor. My eyes scan every inch of the massive stained-glass windows, hoping just one will have the image of an albatross or possibly the coat of arms. Nothing. Maybe St. Mary's is simply for praying. Or maybe I misread Brady's cryptic message altogether.

I move to a small area near a side door that I haven't explored yet when I see it—a framed writ or degree of some kind. It's just hanging there, like some forgotten, insignificant document. I take several pictures and then attempt to read it. But it's in French. So I scour every letter, every symbol until two words stick out from the rest. *Sang Défenseurs.* Défenseurs? I remember something I read in Brady's journal and my heart races. Could it be? It's times like these I wish I had a data plan for my phone, but I do the next best thing. I pull out my phone and text Tyler. **Hey, do a French to English translation of this word please. Sang Défenseurs.**

It feels like forever before my phone sounds a text alert. I hold my breath and check the message. **Blood Defenders.**

I push back the wall of fear now gripping me. My mind rushes like a violent wave, the clues in my head joining like puzzle pieces. The gaps start filling so easily that I try to hold back, simply to allow my soul some time to process the information, but fail. I glance at the writ again, and send Tyler a final text containing the four words written after Sang Défenseurs: **Translate this. Pour garder les os.**

He replies right away. **To guard the bones.**

"Guard the bones," I mumble. "And the king's blunder." I step back into the sanctuary and sit on one of the polished, perfect pews. I pull out my journal, tears filling my eyes before I can stop them. I actually did it. I know what's on that third floor, and the realization overwhelms me. I think about the people who have died trying to gain the knowledge now swimming in my head, and my hands shake so hard I can barely write. But I do write the words, have to get it all on paper. Writing it down makes it real, makes it official.

King Louis XV   answered the pleas of the men in New Orleans by sending young women of court to settle the penal colony, his niece, Katherine, included. But the young women were mistreated by the men and some died. This betrayal angered the king. How could he be so trusting?

So he cursed the city by sending a band of men, the Blood Defenders, to guard the forbidden third floor of the Ursuline Convent that holds the coffins containing the bones of the Casket Girls, and his beloved Katherine. This band of men are defined by a coat of arms containing their purpose: a crown for a king whose blunder they keep secret to this day, a knight's helmet symbolizing the honor-sworn men who guard the bones even after the hierarchy has ended, and a heart symbolizing the sacredness of the innocent young women of France who suffered because of a king's poor judgment. Blessed nails protect the windows from onlookers, and as one last curse on the heathen colony, the king's men spread the vampire folklore, and any thrill seekers who disobey the order to keep off that third floor are killed, and their blood spilled as a reminder to keep out. The Casket Girls did indeed bring the vampires to the Ursuline, but not in their coffin-like trousseaus as folklore dictates, but by their mistreatment and violent ends. By a king's curse and vengeance.

I close my journal, shove it in my backpack, and glance around the church. My sudden revelation makes me feel more vulnerable than I ever have. James is a Sang Défenseur. Of that fact, I'm sure. He killed Brady. And possibly my Aubree. I know what I have to do. I just hope to God he'll listen.

Chapter Eighteen

"Detective Elder, please! You have to listen to me! This is not about snooping around a convent anymore. I know exactly what's on that third floor. I met a man named James when I first moved here, and he's one of these Blood Defenders. And I know he killed Brady. Brady's on that third floor dead somewhere, and we have to find him!" Telling him about Aubree would make me sound even crazier, so I don't. Not yet.

Tyler's dad pushes my journal across his desk. "You were warned repeatedly about that place, Julia. And so was Brady Swinson. I'm sorry he's missing, but we're not going on that third floor."

How can he be so narrow-minded? I'm handing the man fame on a silver platter, and he's looking at me like I have leprosy. "Don't you want to be the officer who finally hangs the rules and blows the lid off that place, once and for all?"

The detective looks me dead in the eyes. "Julia, do you actually think you're the only person to come through that door with a theory about that place? Huh?"

"No," I say, "but I'm the only one who's right."

He sighs. "I admire your savvy, but go home. This conversation is over. And, Julia, I better not see you around that convent again."

"But Brady is up there, Detective Elder! I know it. Please, I need your help. I can't do this alone."

"That's right. You can't. Go home, Julia. If your friend is dead, then getting us killed right along with him won't do him any favors, now will it? The sooner you forget about the Ursuline and stay as far away as you can from that place, the better off you'll be."

I've never felt so utterly and completely alone. I've

failed. Failed Aubree. Failed Brady. Failed Sarah. I'm too disgusted to look at Detective Elder when I slide my journal into my backpack and leave his office. The realization hits me before I reach the sidewalk in front of the station. Now forced to grasp the reality of the situation, one thing is brutally certain. I can't do this. Without the police to back me up, it's useless. Going on that third floor spells certain death. I can't stop the tears, so I don't. I cry for Aubree and Brady, for the Casket Girls, and for all the innocents who've died too soon. I pass the trolley terminal and just keep walking. I walk until I see the Ursuline again.

"You win," I mumble. "You effing win." I burn the image of the building in my brain for the last time, and head in the direction of home.

****

"I was getting worried," Mom says as I walk through the door. "Did you finish your story?"

"Yeah," I say. "It's finished."

"Good," she says. "I'm proud of you for working so hard."

The words I can't truthfully say run through my head. *I'll never really finish my story. I'm too afraid of the consequences. I have too much to live for to risk my life like Brady did.*

"So, I have to leave for work in about thirty minutes, and Dad's already at the club," Mom says.

"I know." I set my backpack down. "I saw him when I came in."

"And Jesse's spending the night with a friend. I guess you have the place to yourself tonight."

My stomach makes a sound that would wake the dead. I haven't eaten all day, and my head's killing me. I open the fridge. "I'm starving. Did you make dinner?"

"No," Mom says. "And it's slim pickings in there, too. I'm sorry, baby."

My phone makes its text sound and I pick it up. *Ryan.* Perfect timing. **Missed you today. Wanna grab a bite?**

Very perfect timing. **Place to myself tonight. Would you pick up some Chinese food? Dying for an egg roll.**

It only takes a few seconds for his reply: **Be there in 45 mins**.

I pop a piece of bread in the toaster anyway. If I don't eat a little something now, my head will explode. "Mom, Ryan's coming over with Chinese food. Is that okay?"

"Yep. You two enjoy your night," she replies.

I scarf down the toast and jump in the shower, barely rinsing all the shampoo suds from my hair before climbing out and drying off. I try focusing on Ryan and spending time with him. The sooner I forget about today, the better. How will I ever face Sarah when I return Brady's journal and tell her I can't do it—can't go on that third floor? I bury the thought in the back of my mind and drop my towel when I reach the bedroom. I tug into a pair of skinny jeans and a red long-sleeved t-shirt. I towel dry my hair a little more, and then take my Homecoming dress down from the peg on my closet door. I carry it to the parental units' room, lay it out on their bed and close the door. I don't want Ryan to see it again before I wear it to the dance next week.

I freshen my makeup and pull my hair into a loose ponytail. When Aubree's smiling face reaches my eyes, I lay the frame holding her photo down on my desk. I don't deserve her smile … not a coward like me. I have just enough time to straighten my room a little when I hear a knock on the front door.

"Hey," Ryan says when I open it. "You look … wow."

"Tired, I'm sure," I say.

"Beautiful is what I was going to say."

I'm sure my cheeks are pink, but I don't try to hide how his words affect me. "Here," I say instead, "let me have that." I take the bag of Chinese food he's holding and we go into the kitchen.

"I missed you at school today. Journalism was brutal. Ms. Dunkin set up a mock news station and let us practice being anchors—"

"Oh, man! I missed that?" I say. "Figures."

"Well, you didn't miss much. Most of us sounded completely ridiculous. You would've rocked it, though."

I pull an egg roll from the bag and take a bite. "I know."

Ryan laughs. "Broadcasting snob." He gets his own egg roll and starts eating.

He's wearing a ribbed V-neck t-shirt that complements his muscular chest in all the right ways, and I hope he doesn't notice me staring. He's so fine, it almost makes me dizzy. But I'm thankful for the euphoria. I need a distraction like air right now.

"So," Ryan asks, "whatever you had to do today, did everything turn out all right?"

"Could've been better." It's all I'm saying about it. I hope to God he just lets it drop.

"Well then, I'll just have to make sure you have a better night."

I'm not sure how long we just sit in the kitchen after we finish our food. Ryan keeps looking at me, like he's trying to remember every inch of my face, every line, every crease. I know I blush at first, but then simply enjoy his eyes, allowing them to scan over me like I'm a sculpture he's admiring. He raises a hand to my cheek and slides a finger across. My heart's beating so fast, I wonder if he can feel it.

"You're so beautiful," he says.

"So are you." *And he is.*

He leans in, his lips finding mine in a slow, soft kiss. He pushes his fingers through the sides of my hair, loosening my ponytail until it dips low on my shoulders.

"I like it down," he says, noting his handiwork.

I remove the rubber band, allowing my hair to fall freely. He knits his fingers through it, tugging me into his chest, his lips covering mine again. I close my eyes and quicken the kiss, needing to feel his warmth, reminding myself of the reason I can't go back to that convent.

He backs up to look at me again, his eyes like a hungry babe. "So, wanna go to a movie or something?"

I laugh. "Funny guy. You're joking, right?"

"Absolutely."

"I say we go to my bedroom and chill. Sounds perfect, am I right?"

"Totally." He starts gathering the empty food containers when we stand.

"You don't have to clean up," I say. "I can get that later."

"It's no big deal."

"Just leave it." I take his hand and we step into the hallway. I close Jesse's door, hopefully before Ryan catches a glimpse of the toxic waste zone. I swear that kid could live in a dumpster if it had a pillow and a bag of chips.

"Jesse's such a troll," I say when I notice the grin on Ryan's lips. "I think my parents found him under a rock or something."

"So I guess they found you in heaven with the other angels then, huh?"

"Oh God, you are so lame."

"Oh, really? I'll show you lame." He starts tickling me.

"Stop!" I squeal.

"All right, all right." He stops and I take a breath. "You're so touchy," he adds.

I'm still laughing when we walk in my bedroom and it feels good to be happy, to be normal. We sit on the bed.

He glances around the room. "No TV, huh? Too bad. There's a football game on I wanted to watch." He winks.

"Funny guy, but I know a sport that's much better than football."

I pull his lips to mine and kiss him the way I wanted to when we were apart. I grasp his cheeks with both hands, needing to feel his closeness. Ryan takes my hand and places it on his chest, his heartbeat like a distant, urgent drum under my palm. He trails a finger along the top of my arm and I shiver.

After a few minutes, he reclines on the bed and I nuzzle my face into his chest. I don't think I've felt this relaxed, this safe, in weeks.

"Let's just stay like this forever," I say as Ryan wraps both arms around my middle and hugs me even closer to his body.

He tugs my hand to his lips, covering it with soft kisses. "Deal."

I stay tightly in his arms, a little embarrassed from the street noise that doesn't seem to bother him. When I finally shift and sit up a little, Ryan notices Mildred's bookmark from the Ursuline on my desk.

"From the convent, huh?"

"Yeah," I say, hoping he'll drop the subject altogether.

Then he notices something else.

The journals.

He leans over to pick up Brady's—the fancy leather binding obviously catching his eye.

"What's this?" he asks.

"Please don't touch it. It's not mine." Why didn't I put Brady's journal away? I feel like an idiot. *Please don't ask. Please don't ask.*

"Then who does it belong to?"

Damn. So much for normal.

I don't want to lie to him. We're starting over, and if I want things to work with Ryan, I have to be honest with him. I take a deep breath and say a silent prayer he'll understand.

"Have you seen the missing history teacher on the news?" I hate the way he's looking at me, but I keep my eyes locked with his anyway. "His name's Brady."

Ryan looks like I just punched him. "I know," he says, "but what's this book got to do with him?"

"It's his journal. His wife gave it to me. Brady and I are friends."

Ryan jerks up and steps into the middle of the room. "What do you mean you're friends? He's a grown-ass man, Julia!"

Is he really insinuating what I think he is? "For God's sake, Ryan! I know that! I met Brady at the Ursuline Convent. He was investigating it too before he went missing, and he reads my blog. We have the same interests, that's all. What's the matter with you?"

"And why do you have his journal?" he says, his voice tight.

"Because I wanted to know if his investigating the convent had anything to do with his disappearance. I want to know if maybe he figured out what I have about that place."

Ryan looks me dead in the eyes. "And has he?"

He wants the truth, then so be it. "Possibly. He was really close … but I have it all figured out."

Ryan doesn't look at me. "Are you saying you know what's up there?"

"Yes, I believe I do."

The way he looks scares me. I know he told me to stop poking around the Ursuline, but I never promised him I'd stop investigating, only that I would heed his warning. No way he's accusing me of lying again.

"All right then," he says instead, looking like a deflated balloon. "So what now? You gonna blog about it or something?" He sits on the bed again and I nestle close beside him.

"Yes, absolutely. But you'll be happy to know I'm not going on that third floor like I originally planned. I think you're right. It's just too dangerous."

Ryan wraps his arms around me, pushing me tighter into his chest. "I'm glad, but I wish you'd made that realization sooner—would've saved you a lot of time and effort."

I'm not sure what to say, so I don't attempt any words. I concentrate instead on his arms around me and his slow, even breaths. After a few seconds, I stand again and gather the journals. I put Brady's in my backpack and mine in the desk drawer.

Ryan showers my neck with kisses when I rejoin him on the bed.

"I'm sorry I didn't tell you about Brady's journal and everything—"

"Don't worry about it," he says. "I don't wanna talk right now."

His fingers thread my hair again, and his lips move from my cheek, to my lips, to my neck. I block out every thought and concentrate on nothing but Ryan and the way my stomach tingles when he touches me.

"What was that?" Ryan says just as I hear it, too. *Damn.* Someone's at the door.

"Oh God, what now?" I say. "Be right back."

Ryan cups his hands behind his head and reclines on a pillow. "I'll be here."

It takes a few minutes for me to shoo away my mom's friend who should have enough common sense to know she's working on a Friday night anyway. I hurry back to my room in time to see Ryan standing and pushing his cell phone back in his pocket.

"I'm so sorry, Julia, but I have to go," he says when I'm within earshot. "My mom's car broke down and she can't reach my stepdad. Guess I have to be the hero."

Ugh. I want to beg him to stay, tell him I'm sorry this night hasn't gone as planned. But I know his mom needs him, so I wrap my arms around him instead.

"How 'bout a rain check?"

I look into his eyes. "Deal."

We walk to the door. Ryan turns to me before stepping out, lifts the top of my hand to his lips, and graces it with a tender kiss. "Until we meet again, my love."

A wave of chills hits me and I simply nod as Ryan walks away. I guess considering everything, the night wasn't a total bust. I remember the leftover Chinese food and toss a couple eggrolls on a plate before heading back to my room. I wish he didn't have to leave. That boy slays me in all the right ways.

Ryan not being here gives me time to think. I hate thinking, feeling guilty about turning my back on Brady. That's what I'm doing, letting the fear I know is all too real now keep me from finding out if that third floor really is the reason he's missing. I know when I blog about the convent I'll definitely get more followers, possibly find out more about Aubree's disappearance. But what about Brady? Why can't I just forget about it?

I get on the computer and read a few random celebrity stories. I almost text Macey, then remember she has a date with Chris tonight. I still have an overwhelming urge to read Brady's journal, but I simply chalk it up to old habits dying hard and resist. I pick up the Ursuline bookmark still resting on my desk. "You need to be put away, too," I mumble, and start to shove it in my desk drawer when I notice something. Between the clear plastic casing and cardstock, there's an indenture, like something else is tucked inside. *What the...?*

The cardstock slides out easily, revealing a small, folded piece of paper. My hands shake like I'm in a freezer as I unfold it. And I stop breathing when I read the only two words now hitting me in the face.

He's Alive.

"Oh, my God! Oh, my God!" It's all I can say. Brady's alive ... and Mildred knows it. That's why she gave me the bookmark. "Oh, God."

I'm pacing, but I can't stop. He's alive? And if Mildred has knowledge of it, then his disappearance is all about that convent, that third floor. But why is Brady alive when the other investigators are dead? All of them.

My first reaction is to call Tyler, demand his dad hear me out when I show him the bookmark and its secret message. But I know he'd never listen to me. I shiver when the resoluteness hits me. This has always been about me—has always been my story. And if Brady's alive, then I'm his only chance at a rescue. I couldn't save Aubree, but I am fated to save him, to silence Sarah's cries. I have to go on that third floor.

****

When the last two words are typed in my blog post, I step away from the computer and grab my journal. It's ironic, but before I chickened out, tomorrow was the day I had initially planned to get onto that third floor again anyway. Irony is a twisted sister, but that's okay. Sleep is impossible. Tomorrow is it. Everything I've discovered will be exposed. If Brady *is* alive, then I'll find him. I know the Casket Girls are hidden up there, too, buried like phantoms in unmarked graves. Aubree's body could be up there with them for all I know. She loved the paranormal, was brave to a fault. Vampires would have lured her to that place, no doubt.

My mind races through the plan for getting safely on that third floor. I've done it once, I can do it again. But this time, I'm getting through that locked door. A few hours ago when Ryan was here, all I wanted to do was forget. But now, all I want to do is remember, remember what they lived through, what they died for. I can't let Brady die, too. I have to be brave … and I have an ace in the hole to guarantee my safety, if I stick to the plan.

I'm going to the convent in broad daylight tomorrow. It feels less threatening, going on a Saturday with tourists present. It seems safer somehow, even though I know the sense of security is probably false. I make my way to my parents' empty bedroom. I need something from Dad that'll make my security less false. My heart's thumping to the beat of the music from the club below. I open the top dresser drawer when I'm in their room and pull out the extra stun gun Dad keeps in case one quits on him. I hold it away from my body and press the buttons on the sides. I jump when the charge crackles. I hope to God this is the only time I have to use it.

When I'm back in my room, I put the stun gun in the

pocket of the jeans I'm wearing tomorrow and sit at my desk. There's something I need to finish, even though I've been putting it off all night. I pick up the pen again and read back over the letter to my parents. As much as I try blocking out the possibility that something could happen to me, I know the threat is very real. And my folks deserve some final words, especially Mom.

Dear Mom & Dad,

Sorry my stubborn streak is a mile long, but stubbornness can be a good thing. I went to the convent today. I have to finish my story. Mom, I know you told me to be careful, and I will be, but I wasn't totally honest about the danger I'm facing. Tyler's dad was telling the truth. People have died trying to solve this mystery, and now Brady is in trouble. I plan to make it home safely, but just in case I don't, please read the folder labeled 'Ursuline' on my computer. I've worked so hard on this, and I want to make you proud. You see, I think Aubree's disappearance had everything to do with that place. That's why I'm doing this. We need to bring her home, once and for all. Dad, you've always said I was hard, right down to the core. Guess you were right. And I'm sure there will be a lot of money in interviews and such after my findings are read. Use it to stay in New Orleans. Jesse deserves a permanent home, and so do you. I love you both.

Your fearless daughter,

Julia

I fold the letter and write *Mom & Dad* on the outside. Everything's in place now. I turn off my desk lamp and climb in bed. I'll rest my body even if my mind's still racing. No way I'll sleep tonight. Everything's riding on tomorrow. By the next sunset, I'll be famous … the young woman who solved the mystery of the Ursuline and saved a man's life. *Or the dead girl.* Either way, my family will finally get closure. And so will Sarah. I smile at the thought and close my eyes.

****

My notebook, camera, the lock-picking kit, and the guard keys are securely stowed away in my backpack, along with a few other necessary items. I shove a small hammer I snagged from Jesse into a side pocket of the bag, too, just in case I have the same luck with the lock as last time. My phone's in my right pants pocket for easy access, and I check my left pocket for the stun gun. I take a deep breath and glance around the room. Everything's falling into place.

Dad's snoring loud enough to wake the neighbors when I step into their bedroom. I open Mom's trinket drawer and place the letter on top. She'll find it eventually, but not soon enough to stop me from doing this. Hopefully, I'll be home to retrieve it later when I'm successful, but when I close the drawer, I watch it disappear from view like it's the last time I'll see it. I watch Mom sleeping, but divert my eyes before I think too much. "I love you," I mumble and then close the door behind me.

From the sound of it, Jesse's shuffling around. I'm glad he's back early. There's one more thing I need to do. I reach in my desk drawer and pull out his prize and then head to his room.

"What's new, toad?" I say when I'm in his doorway.

"Actually, something priceless," he replies. "Look at this." He hands me a newspaper. "Look at the name of that radio station in Texas. Correct me if I'm wrong, but doesn't that say KOTX in Texas? How would you pronounce that exactly?"

I laugh. "Oh, my God, that would be 'kotex', I guess."

"Yep, and that's gross."

"And you're a funny little troll. Trying to give Mom a run for her money, huh?"

He grimaces. "Hey, don't judge me, girlie. By the way, do you need something?"

"Just this." I extend a hand and give him my Charizard card.

"Whoa, back up. What're you doing?"

"You can have it. I don't need it."

"But it's your favorite. You're playing a trick on me, right?"

"No tricks, I just don't need it, that's all. I don't play Pokémon anymore, and you do. Enjoy it, and don't say I never gave you anything. See you around, tough guy."

I head for the door and Jesse catches me by the hand. "Hey, you okay, Julia? Something feels off."

"Things have never been more on, Jesse." I smile. "Yeah, it's definitely on."

I head for my room before he asks any more questions. I sling my backpack on my shoulder and turn out my light. Then I remember something else—my fountain pen. "Glad I didn't forget you," I mumble as I tuck it into my shirt pocket. Discretion is the better part of valor. Well, not today. Today it's do or die.

Chapter Nineteen

I step off the curb and onto the street in front of the Ursuline. I stare at the third-floor windows for a few seconds, scanning the shutters for any sign of movement. Nothing. It's as quiet as death. I tighten the grip on my backpack, pull my sunglasses over my eyes, and head for the main entrance.

Once inside, I scope the room for my favorite tour guide. He's nowhere to be seen, thank God. The last thing I need is for ol' Steve-O to stop me before I even get started. But I do notice a group of people I'll use to my advantage: middle schoolers, complete with matching red t-shirts that say *Alba Middle School*. Cute. Yeah, when their guide takes them to the gardens, it's show time.

I'm not sure why I feel as though I have to, but I make my way to the glass cases and stare at Katherine's brush and mirror set for a couple of minutes. Deep down, I know this is as much for her as it is for Aubree and Brady. I'm doing this for all the Casket Girls who were frightened, mistreated strangers in a distant land at the mercy of their surroundings. I'm being their voice, Brady's voice, my voice. We'll all be heard today.

The guide announces to the kids that it's time to tour the gardens. Excellent. "This is it," I mumble to Katherine's earthly treasures and make my way outside. Now to pick my partner in crime. It doesn't take long to spot the perfect pawn. I pull my sunglasses up to rest on my head, smear on a little more lip gloss, and make my way to a young man who's slapping another kid on the shoulder and laughing.

"Excuse me," I say to the young man. "Is this your first time to the convent?"

"Yeah." He stares me up and down. "Hey, I'm Tripp."

"Cool." I act as interested as possible. "Well, Tripp, you guys do know the legend of that third floor, right?"

"Sure," he replies. "We all do. Why?"

Sweet. "Well, do you know what would be classic?" I pull a small mirror from my backpack and hand it to him. "Everyone in this courtyard will freak if you aim that mirror at one of the shutters. You know, make it look like a light's coming from it. Just be discreet. It won't take long for someone to notice and start—"

"Oh, yeah, yeah. I get it," he says. "Awesome. I'm doing it."

I smile. "Nice to meet you, Tripp. You guys enjoy New Orleans."

I ease as close to the back staircase as I can without being noticed and wait. I scope the grounds for security guards. There are two guards and just the one guide. Soon the light is flickering on one of the shutters. Atta boy, Tripp. And sure enough, minor chaos erupts. When the guide and both guards are distracted, I sprint to the metal staircase and climb. At the top of the stairs, I square my body in front of the door and take a deep breath. No one's behind me, and I can't be seen from the gardens now. I take another fortifying breath and reach in my backpack for the guard's keys.

I go through ten keys before finding the one that actually clicks in the lock when I turn it. I open the heavy metal door just wide enough for my body and backpack to squeeze through, and then close it behind me. Once inside, I lay the keys on the floor in front of the door. No way I'm getting caught with them when all this is over. I know the third-floor stairwell is way on the other end. But the second floor's eerily silent. No one should be in the offices on Saturday anyway. I make my way to the stairs quietly but quickly. Within seconds, I'm standing in front of them. My legs are frozen and my stomach's churning. *Just breathe.*

The blackness of the narrow staircase reminds me to grab my flashlight and the lock-picking kit before taking the first step. I focus my mind with the mechanics, trying to block out the terror teasing my brain. This is the third-floor passageway. The second time I've tested fate. And I'm actually doing it this time. A rush of adrenaline hits me as I shine the light ahead. I see the ancient locked door and climb the first few steps.

All of my senses are heightened, the effect of being on full alert. The ringing in my ears is deafening. When I'm standing in front of the old door, I set my backpack down and prop the flashlight on it to shine on the lock. I look down at the bottom of the stairs to ensure I'm alone and then grasp the skeleton key. I hold my breath, slide the key into the lock, and turn. It doesn't budge at first, so I use both hands and dig my heels tighter into the floor for more muscle. When it moves slightly, my knees go weak. I think it's working. I back up a little to brace myself for another hard twist of the key, but I back up too far and bump my backpack.

"Dammit."

The flashlight tumbles off the bag and starts rolling down the stairs.

I want to panic, but there's no time. I head for the darkened steps but stop when I realize the flashlight's not rolling anymore. It's resting on a step about halfway down. Scenes from cheesy horror flicks flood my racing brain. This is the same kind of shit that happens to the girl right before the killer strikes. But this ain't a movie and I'm not that girl. So I take a deep breath, slide my hand along the wall to steady my footing on the dark stairs, and slowly inch toward the light.

I fix my eyes on the flashlight, ignoring the urge to glance over my shoulder. I'm not giving in to a reflex. Rational thinking concludes that no one's behind me. It's impossible. My back is turned on a locked door, so I need to stop freaking out. Just two more steps. I bend and grasp the flashlight when I reach it, fear gripping my chest. I don't want to, but I need to know. I shine the light to the bottom of the stairs and let out a breath when I discover I'm still alone.

My hands are shaking so hard I can barely prop the light up again when I'm back in front of the door. The key is still protruding from the lock, so I tighten my hands around it and twist with all the strength I can muster. The lock finally clicks and I take a much-needed breath. I turn the brass handle and the door opens a crack. I retrieve the key and shove it in my backpack, and then pull out the stun gun before stepping inside. "You can do this," I mumble, and step through the door.

Coffins.

I glance around in every direction. It's hard to take in what I'm seeing. There are just so many! I was right about this third floor being the final resting place for the Casket Girls. Their coffins in literally dozens line the walls like trophies. And on top of each coffin rests a flower.

I glance in front of me, behind me. I'm alone. *Very alone.* I notice the albatross picture on the wall and push the stun gun into my pocket. I grab my camera and start snapping shots of the albatross, the coffins. Then, something else catches my eye. There are tiny coffins too, the trousseaus of the Casket Girls, no doubt. Closer inspection makes the hairs stand up on my arms. Each casket is encrusted with a golden seal of the albatross wearing the coat of arms. I smooth a hand over one of the tiny boxes. I have to know what's inside ... who's inside. Then I see it.

Two caskets are obviously more grand than the others, so I make my way to the golden boxes—one adult-size and one tiny one—forgetting about everything but what's in front of me. My fingers touch the seal of the larger one and I know the distinct letters before I see them. K.A. This is Katherine's box. Katherine's—

I feel a hand cover my mouth and scream through the tightened fingers. I scramble for the stun gun, but it's too late. Everything goes black.

****

My armpits are aching. It's the first clear thought I accomplish as I struggle through the haze in my brain, desperately trying to focus. I know I'm seated in a chair and then realize my hands won't move. They're tied above my head to a rope suspended from the ceiling directly above me. I panic and tug the binds around my hands, but they're too tight. I can't free them. My head's pounding and my breaths burn. Where is he? Oh God, I'm going to die.

"James!" I yell, forcing the name from my aching throat. "Where ... are ... you?"

"So, you're finally awake, Miss Julia. Good."

I try to squeak more words from my swollen throat. "You ... bastard ... where's Brady?"

"That's the chloroform. Don't fret. The effects will wear off soon enough, my dear."

His back's to me, but I see him. I taste tears. "James, why...? You don't ... have to ... do this."

"Oh, but I think I do, Miss Julia." He points something in my direction. *My notebook.*

"I've been doing some light reading while you were,

um, sleeping. It seems to me as though you understand plenty." James turns another page. "To say I'm impressed is an understatement. You're one sharp cookie—you and the fine history teacher. It's actually a shame, the way this is going to play out."

"You're a Blood Defender," I say. "I understand, but you don't have to kill me and Brady. We can just pretend we were never here."

James pulls up a chair and slams it down on the floor in front of me before sitting. "Never here? And just why *are* you here? I warned you, Julia. I told you not to be too curious. Remember, discretion is—"

"The better part of valor," I finish for him.

"That's right. So why are *you* here, Miss Julia? To save your friend? No. You're here because you had to solve your mystery. And you did that very effectively, my dear. For so long I was a missing puzzle piece, one of three remaining defenders of the innocent bones of France." He smiles. "But you figured me out, huh?"

"The innocent bones," I repeat. I look at all the coffins, the tiny ones filling my view again. Tears sting my cheeks. "I will silence their cries." I take in a breath. "Oh, my God, those tiny caskets … they're babies!" I struggle with the horror James has hit me in the face with. "Those coffins hold babies belonging to the Casket Girls. And you're their keeper, too."

"That's right," he says. "I am a Sang Défenseur, commissioned by King Louis XV." He points to the coat of arms on the neck of the albatross on the wall. "That is the shield of my brothers, a secret band of men throughout the course of these two hundred years with one purpose—to protect the honor of King Louis XV without fail."

"Commissioned by the king," I say. "Honor sworn."

"That's right." James gets a faraway look. "The king's last words as he lay dying: *Aprés moi, le deluge*, or, after me, the disaster. He always carried the guilt with him for the fate he'd sealed for the innocents he sent here to the penal colony. He'd not foreseen the treachery that befell the young women, their miserable mistreatment by the savage men they were sent to marry. Even his beloved niece, Katherine, was sent and abused. And when he attempted a rescue, he was greeted with dead women and babies who did not survive the cruelty, destroyed innocence placed before him like a curse. It was a constant reminder of his blunder. The death of his beloved Katherine and her offspring was too much for him to endure.

"His answer to the heathen men who'd once asked him for purity? To punish the city with a curse of his own. So he placed the coffins containing the young women of court, as well as the infant bones, back on a boat with a writ and a secret band of men, the Sang Défenseurs, or Blood Defenders. He ordered that the coffins be sealed in the third floor of this convent, the nuns sworn to carry out his orders to seal all windows, shutter them, pound them each with a thousand blessed nails and vow to never allow human eyes to view the contents of this room—save a select few. The Sang Défenseurs, protectors of the innocent bones of France.

"We were to be the enforcers of a new curse, the blood of the guilty to pay for the blood of the innocent. We allowed the curiosity that we knew would come to be their downfall, killing any seekers of the contents of this room and draining their blood, depositing them on the convent steps come sunrise. We allowed the city to believe that only a creature of the night could evoke such destruction. And so the myth took hold, and the vampires were blamed." He looks me dead in the eyes. "But these truths you know, Miss Julia. I had to explain it fully to your Brady, but not you. Yes, one sharp cookie, indeed."

He's right. These truths I know, and now I'm going to die for it. But not until I find Brady. I think of my parents, and Ryan, and Tyler. Then I think of Aubree. My dad always says it's what you do with the people you love that counts. Well, I happen to think that it's what you do *to* the people you love that counts. And I'm not doing this to them. Not today. "Brady, we're not dying in this room," I mutter. Then I speak to James. "I had to solve the mystery. My cousin, Aubree, she went missing a few years back. The police never looked for her very long, so I figured if I solved the mystery of the Ursuline, more people would know me … know her name. Help me look for her."

"Indeed." It's all he says.

I just have to keep James talking, give myself time to figure out how I'm going to get out of here. I scan the room for my backpack. I see it by the door. But then I see something else, something that kicks me square in the gut. My stun gun, cell phone, and the small hammer I packed are sitting on a side table. James knows my game.

"What exactly happened to the babies?" I ask, saying anything to keep him talking.

James turns his back to me. "And why should I answer any of your questions, young lady?"

"Because I answered yours on the street that day."

He smiles. "Bravo, Miss Julia. And I must say that you do deserve to know all the answers before you die. After all, no one's ever accomplished what you have when it comes to the convent. Not the vampire-hunters, reporters, law enforcement, Brady. Or even your Aubree."

His words smash me in the face like a hammer. *Aubree...* "What about Aubree?" I scream, rage filling my soul like fire. "What did you do to her?"

"What I do to anyone who reaches this floor. I killed her."

I twist and kick forward, pain piercing my soul like a sword. "She was just a girl! How could you? You're a monster!"

"No, Miss Julia. I'm not a monster. I am a man of honor, duty. Her curiosity was her undoing, not me."

Confusion fills me. "But her body wasn't found. Her blood not drained like the others—"

"She almost got away and I had to kill her quickly. I couldn't drain her blood, so she was simply *disposed of.*"

I want to spit in his face, but I know I still have to save Brady, myself. I take several deep breaths instead. Aubree's sweet face keeps flooding my thoughts, and I use it to gather strength. Simply deposed of? No, not in this lifetime.

"So, where's Brady?" I ask.

"There." James points to a room a couple of doors down from where I'm tied up.

"Is he dead?"

"No, but he will be now that we have you."

"How did you—?" Then it hits me. "Oh, he told you he knew someone else who had this place figured out, huh? You were trying to get my name out of him, or hope I'd come for him?"

James laughs. "Yes, something like that."

I ignore the quivers in my lips and ask again. "So, what happened to the babies?"

"Ungodly men with no care or concern for the wives they were so graciously given, that's what happened to them. The young women suffered such horrible abuse that some of the babies were stillborn. Others were mistreated themselves and weren't strong enough to survive. And yet others died on the voyage back to France when the king rescued the women and children. Their deaths would have never occurred had that rescue not been needed. By the end of the king's fateful decision to answer the heathens' pleas, there were forty-two dead babes in all."

"And the girls used their trousseaus as coffins?"

James looks away before answering. "Yes."

"Why?"

"Because their children deserved to be honored by Mother France, and those boxes were all they had. So now you know."

Ms. Dunkin's logic screams in my head. Never skip the easy question or you'll miss the obvious answer. I muster up my most pitiful sounding voice. "James, when we met on the street, you were so nice to me. Are you really going to kill me?"

"I don't want to kill you, Julia. I never did. That's why I gave you such sound advice, remember?"

"Then don't hurt me or Brady. He has a young wife who loves him. He's an honorable man. You've already taken my young cousin. Killing me too will devastate my family. We can just leave. I promise we'll never come back, or ever breathe a word about what's up here. It'll be like none of this ever happened, I promise."

James looks at me for the first time in several minutes. "Now you know that's not possible."

"Why? All you're really doing is defending the honor of the girls, the babies, the king. Well, no one respects them more than me and Brady. I swear."

James looks at me like I'm scum. "You know nothing about honor. You speak of honor to a man who holds true an oath of a hierarchy that has been dissolved for two hundred years? Don't mock me, girl. Honor is my blood." He heads for a door toward the back of the room then adds, "I have to make a call." Then he's gone.

I go to work trying to free my hands. The ropes are so tight, I break the skin on my wrists trying to pull them loose, but I don't care. They're burning like fire, but I tug harder. I have to get free. "Brady! Are you in there?" I hear sounds, like he's trying to answer but something's on his mouth. I work harder on the ropes.

"Help me! I'm on the third floor! Someone please help me!" I scream so loud and so long, my throat's raw. The echoes of my voice mock me as they drift through the room. God, why did I ever come to this place?

"No one's going to hear you," James says when he comes back. "You're just tiring yourself for nothing."

I have to buy more time, appeal to the softer side of him I saw on the street that day. "Those flowers on the girls' coffins, what are they?"

"Lilies," James says.

"You put them there?"

"Yes, and I replace them with fresh ones every two days," he replies.

"Why?"

James sighs before speaking, like the words pain him. "Lilies are a symbol of purity, innocence. The girls were lilies who were once surrounded in sunlight, bright and glowing. But they were sent into shadow, made broken and alone." His eyes cut through me. "That is why I do it, Julia. For the lilies who fell into shadow. Now, no more questions."

I have to make him see me as one of them, like the lilies he guards. "Please, let me go," I plead. "You can't kill me. I'm just a little girl, too. I want to see my mama again. Please let me go home."

Every scenario is running through my head. My hands are bound, but my legs are free. He's an old man for God's sake. When he gets close enough, I can kick him. If I kick him hard enough and he lands close to the chair, I can stomp on his head until he's dead. If I do that, even if I can't get free, Ryan and Tyler will know where I am if I don't make it home. They'll look for me here. I have to strike at the opportune moment. I'm not dying in this convent like Aubree. I'm saving Brady.

James glances at my hands, obviously noticing my attempts to free myself. "Are you thirsty?"

I'm confused. He's offering me a drink? This is my chance. "Yes, very."

James nods. "I know you don't understand any of this, Julia, but we tried to warn you."

"We?" My voice catches in my throat. "Did you say *we*?"

The door opens and I gasp. My stomach clenches and I feel dizzy. How did he? I'm safe now, but how…?

"Ryan! He's a murderer! Watch out!"

"Julia," he says, his motions not desperate but deliberate.

It takes several moments to register. I can't allow my heart to accept what's playing out on this cursed floor. He can't be … not my Ryan. But I know it's true. There's no other explanation for his appearance. Ryan's not here to save me. Somehow, he's part of it.

By the lines on his face, I can tell he's been crying. "I begged you not to do this, Julia." Ryan looks me up and down. "Why couldn't you just listen, huh?"

"Oh, my God! No, no, no … this can't be happening! No, Ryan! Please, get me out of here! You can't be part of this… He killed Aubree. Please!"

Ryan looks at James. "Father, will you give us a moment, please?"

Father?

"Certainly." James leaves the room and Ryan sits in the chair in front of me.

I can't stop the sobs escaping my throat, don't want to stop them. "Why is this happening? Please tell me this isn't happening." I can barely breathe. "He's your father?" I lock my swollen eyes with his. "But how?"

Ryan's voice is low and solemn. "My father is a Sang Défenseur, as his father before him. When the king initially selected the men, they were chosen for their nobility. In order for the line to continue, the king's writ included a clause that future defenders would be heirs of the Défenseurs and the Casket Girls. I was sired in France. James is my father, and my mother is a descendant of a Casket Girl. I am the product of an honor system you couldn't begin to understand, Julia."

"But I met your parents—"

"You met my mother and my stepfather. Although, he's not really my stepfather. He's my guardian, a keeper of the code. I've been in New Orleans for ten years. I'm being raised in the same home as my father and his father before him."

"Oh, my God. But we go to the same school, have the same friends…"

"Because I get to have somewhat of a normal life until I'm twenty-one, Julia. After that, I take over for my father here. That's the way it works. Three defenders at a time is what it takes now. There's my father, Thad, and William. Thad is the one who caught Brady. My father was simply tracking him. Damn his curiosity." He looks at me hard. "Damn yours, too."

The tears burn my face, but I can't stop them. All this

time I've loved him, and he's been using me? He guilted me into believing I was the reason for our break-up, made me feel like the biggest liar on the planet. And his whole life is a lie.

"So when you acted all hurt because I lied about where I lived, that was just crap? What was I, Ryan? Some kind of game to you? Some kind of conquest?" Then it hits me, the day he summoned me to the back table in class, the questions. *My notebook.* "Oh, my God! You saw my notes about the Ursuline in my notebook that day. You didn't really want to date me. You wanted to watch me!"

"Only at first," he mumbles.

I can't hold the sobs in. "How could you do this to me? I loved you!"

"I'm the reason you're still alive! Don't you know if it wasn't for me, my father would have made short order of you the first time you came nosing around up here? You owe your life to me, Julia!"

I stare at him, resisting the urge to spit in his face. "I don't owe you anything."

"I know you're scared, but you have to believe that I love you. I'll admit that I asked you out to keep tabs on you, but I fell in love with you, Julia. I did."

"You love me? And how twisted is that, Ryan? You said it yourself. Your future is in this convent. There can be no future with me. So why did you even give me the time of day?"

He looks like a lost little boy. "Because I wanted something beautiful to be mine, even if I could only have it for a month. A year. Two years. I wanted something real. You were different from any girl I'd ever met. I know it was selfish, but I wanted you to love me. Our love would have been enough for a lifetime for me, Julia.

That's why I needed you to be honest. I needed you to trust me with everything. You were going to be the memory I would cherish forever."

"And yet you were lying to me the whole time. You always knew where I lived, didn't you, Ryan? After all, you were the one who alerted Daddy Dearest of my *curiosity*, huh—that day you read my notebook? You knew exactly where I lived because I told him long before I met you."

"Yes, I knew. I told him about your plans to write a story about the convent, to expose it to the world—and he told me every time he saw you coming and going from that strip joint when he was there, even when you tried to tell me you lived at that other apartment."

"When he was at the strip club?" *What is Ryan talking about?* "I thought he saw me from the coffee shop just down the street that day?"

He takes a deep breath like his shoulders can't relax without it. "Part of our duty is to frequent certain establishments. The city has to believe that creatures of the night inhabit this forbidden third floor—"

The realization hits me like a brick to the face. "My God, he went in the club to carry on the vampire legend, didn't he? Talk to the drunks and losers and convince them of creepy crawlies in the night. That's why he was curious about me. Wow, what a nice occupation you have to look forward to, Ryan. Trapping poor, unsuspecting souls with their own curiosity so you can slaughter them."

Ryan looks at me with tired eyes. "You're wrong. The legend is to frighten them enough to keep their curiosity in check. Keeping people away, that's the true goal."

"And it's sick!" I yell.

"I hold the world as it is," Ryan says, "a stage where

every man must play his part. Mine is a sad one, but I accept it. I did know where you lived, Julia, but I was always hoping you'd come clean about it. It would have meant everything to me."

I struggle against the binds that have my arms throbbing and my wrists hot and bleeding. "So you're going to just let him kill me then, like he did my cousin when she started poking around? Or will you do it yourself? Let me have the honor of being your first victim?"

"I can't change what is already set in motion, Jules—"

"Don't call me that. Don't ever call me that again. I never should've told you about my story, about Aubree. Confiding in you was a mistake."

He brushes a tear from my face, and I cower from his touch.

His eyes are desperate. "Don't be afraid of me. I don't have a choice, Julia. This is my charge in life."

"It doesn't have to be! We all have choices in life, Ryan. You could let me go right now. Let Brady go—" I suddenly feel sick. "Oh, my God! You put that note in my bookmark last night too, didn't you? When I left the room to answer the door? That's why you left so early? You got me up here to save Brady!"

"Yes," he admits, "but you weren't supposed to find it so quickly. I was going to try to figure something out before you—"

"Before I what? Came up here to save an innocent man? Listen to me. The king's curse is wrong. Killing innocent people isn't doing justice to the bones of those babies or their mothers. All you'll ever be doing is murdering innocents, just like those heathen men all those years ago."

I close my eyes, the psychic's words piercing my

mind like a blade. *You will silence their cries.*

"Those bones are crying, Ryan. They want the killing to stop. And if the world knew what was really up here, those souls would be honored properly, not desecrated by vampire folklore, senseless murders, and lies. You can be the one brave man who'll lift the curse of a shamed king. Hasn't this gone on long enough? You control your destiny, Ryan. You, no one else. Those souls would be free, Brady and I would be free ... and so would you."

He looks at my wrists. "You're bleeding. I'm sorry these ropes are so tight. Let me help a little." I feel the tension let out some as he mumbles, "There's no trust, no faith, no honesty in men; all perjured, all foresworn, all naught, all dissemblers."

"Even you, Ryan? Was Shakespeare talking about you?"

He shakes his head and smiles. "I love you, Jules," he whispers close to my face and then pushes back in the chair and stands. "Father," he calls. "It's time."

"No, Ryan!" I plead. "You can't let him do this! Please! Didn't you hear anything I just said?"

James clasps a hand on Ryan's shoulder when he joins him. He hands him my notebook. "Here, my boy. A souvenir." Ryan takes it without looking back at me.

"You can't kill me!" I yell. "If you do, then your secret will never be safe."

They both look at me.

"I wrote a blog post about everything that's on this third floor. If you kill me, it'll upload at midnight anyway. I'm the only one who can delete it, and I will if you let me and Brady go. I have thousands of followers. It'll go viral, I promise you that."

James breaks out in raucous laughter. "You underestimate us to that degree, young lady." He claps a hand on Ryan's shoulder. "Tell her your hobby, my boy."

Ryan clears his throat. "I'm a hacker. We knew you'd set up a blog post as leverage. I took your blog down thirty minutes before I got here." He doesn't look at me, just turns his back and heads for the room Brady's in.

I blink away the hot tears filling my eyes. How could he do this to me? I loved him … still love him. I'm going to die.

"You go take care of the history teacher," James says to Ryan, his eyes wild and crazed.

"But I'm not yet a true Defender," he replies.

"Honor knows no age, my boy. Thad and William will not return until dark. You must be the one."

"Please don't do this," I plead to Ryan.

"I'm sorry, Julia," is all he says.

"You dirty coward!" I scream, tears burning my cheeks again.

It's not going down like this. I won't allow it. Damn Ryan Grandle and damn his deranged father. I wiggle my hands and realize that Ryan did loosen my binds a little. If I keep James talking, I might be able to get free.

"My son really likes you," James says. "I wish you would've just listened to him."

"And I wish you didn't have some sick honor code that allows you to be a murderer, but that's not the case, now is it?"

James comes toward me. "I like you too, Julia, but that last remark makes this a little easier." He pulls out a knife and slices my shoulder blade.

The pain bursts like mini-explosions and I cry and scream uncontrollably. "You monster, get away from me!"

"I know that hurt, my dear. But your death will be

quick and less painful, I promise."

"Then why cut me?" I ask when I realize my right hand is almost free. Just a little bit more.

"It's to drain your blood, of course. I'll have to do that before you die. Unlike your Aubree, your body *will* be displayed for all to see."

Damn him for saying her name! I'll make sure he never says it again. When James turns his back, I give my right hand another hard tug, and it's out. I try to free my left hand too before he notices, but there's no time. Instead, I reach in my shirt pocket and pull out the fountain pen—the only thing in my possession that even remotely resembles a weapon. I clasp my free hand into the other and hide the pen between them so he's not suspicious.

James places a cup to my lips. "Now drink. You said you were thirsty earlier."

"What is it?"

"Something that'll make you sleepy. Believe me, it's in your best interest to drink."

I look him straight in the eyes. "No, you drink, you bastard. I'm not thirsty anymore."

He grins. "Listen, you can drink or I can use the chloroform, but I really don't feel like tussling with you anymore. Now drink."

When he leans like he's going to force the liquid down my throat, I yank my right hand down in one swift motion and jam the fountain pen into his neck all the way to the inscription. He falls in a heap as I tug my other hand free.

"Father!" Ryan calls from Brady's room. "What's going on in there?"

I head for the table with my belongings and tuck the stun gun into my palm and my phone in my pocket. I look at the infamous windows and step in front of one. With all the strength I can gather, I kick the window. Glass shatters and my foot doesn't stop until I've taken out two slats from the shutter. I imagine the surprised people in the gardens below who just witnessed my small destruction. Ryan runs into the room, still clutching my notebook. He glances at James and then back to me and the shattered window. I can hear Brady trying to yell from the other room, thank God.

"Julia, what have you done?" Ryan says.

"Saved my life, and Brady's, too. A coward like you couldn't kill him that quickly, huh?" I look at Katherine's coffin and her tiny trousseau. I think of Aubree. "I saved us all."

He steps toward me and I pull the stun gun from behind my back. I zap him on his chest before he realizes what's happening, and he joins James on the floor. I slip my notebook from his still-twitching hand and head for the door as fast as my wobbly legs will carry me.

I don't stop running until I reach the velvet ropes on the first floor. I'm feeling dizzy and the wound on my shoulder's still bleeding. I lift my phone and find Tyler's name. Nothing sounds more beautiful than his voice when he answers.

"Hey, Ty," I respond. "At the convent. I ... I need you."

When the security guard reaches me I say, "There's two injured kidnappers on the third floor, and a man needs help. They kidnapped him. He's the missing school teacher everyone's been looking for." When the guard says something into his walkie-talkie, I give in to the stars in front of my eyes.

Chapter Twenty

Every breath is a struggle, as if I can't take in enough air to ease the terror still lodged in my chest. I'm still thirsty. A detective sent a lady to get me some water, but she's not back yet. Where's my mom? I really want my mom. Why am I still here? The cops have asked me about a million questions at once, and I've answered them all, except one dude said I wasn't coherent before. I'm coherent. I'm rational. I'm scared as hell, and I don't want to be in this police station anymore. I want the freakin' questions to stop, and I want to go home. Now.

"How's that shoulder?" the cop from before says. He takes a seat in front of me and touches the gauze pad taped on my wound. "It probably doesn't feel too great, but thank God it's not real deep, huh? And let me see those wrists again."

"All right," I say. My throat's dry and my arms are still aching from being suspended above my head for several hours. "When can I go home?"

"Your parents are on their way. When the EMTs at the convent cleared you to come in for questioning, they still thought it wouldn't hurt for you to be checked out thoroughly. You may end up needing a few stitches in your shoulder. So your folks are taking you to the hospital first, then hopefully home. I will say, I don't like the looks of these rope burns, though." He shakes his head. "But you know what? You're a very lucky girl."

A very lucky girl. I'm not sure if I'm so tired I'm delirious, or if his description of me is so far off the mark that I can't control it, but I laugh hysterically. He looks at me like I'm deranged and picks up his cell again to see how far my parents are from the station.

The lady returns with my water and I drink it like I

haven't had liquid for weeks. I don't think I've ever been this drained physically. Emotionally. Mentally. A male detective who's already asked me a gazillion questions rejoins me and touches my knee.

"Julia, I'd really like to get your full statement now, while everything's fresh in your mind, okay? We'll start with the older gentleman again, James. How's that sound?" He turns on a recorder and smiles.

"You want my full statement on James?" I take a breath. "Well, where do I start? I met James on the street a while back. Just some random meeting, you know how that goes. He was nice and kind, and he actually gave me the pen I ended up sticking in his neck. Did I tell you that before? He gave it to me to remind me not to poke my nose where it doesn't belong. Would've been easier for him to just say, *Hey look, girl, if you try to get on the third floor of that convent, I'm going to kill you, like I did your cousin.*" I throw in my hysterical laugh for good measure before asking, "Don't you think that would've been the way to go?"

The officer gives me a deer-in-the-headlights look and nods.

I abruptly end my laughter and stare in his eyes. "But do you know what that bastard did instead? He chloroformed me, tied me up, cut me, and wanted to kill me … and told me straight out that he murdered Aubree. How could he do that to an innocent girl? It's just so … it's so…"

I let the tears fall and the officer looks at me like I'm the most pitiful sight he's seen all week.

I sigh. "It's so hard to explain … so hard to talk about. And I'm just so tired … but I saved Brady. How cool is that?"

He smiles. "Very cool. You know what? I think that'll

do it for now. Your folks can bring you in tomorrow after you've had some sleep. Feel better, Julia." He finally leaves me alone.

I'm glad I scared him off. The truth is, I'd rather be deemed in shock or crazy than have to answer another question about Ryan. It's cruel and unusual punishment, reminding me every six seconds that the guy I was in love with was willing to leave the room and allow his sicko father to slaughter me like some kind of sacrificial lamb. There's not enough therapy in the world to sort that out. All I really need is my mom. Where is she?

The room is as chaotic as my thoughts. And although it's only been minutes and not hours since I was on that third floor, the media is already waiting outside. I guess it's not every day that a two-hundred-year-old mystery is solved—by a kid. Tyler's dad walks through the door.

"How you holdin' up, little missy?"

I'm not sure why, but I fall into his arms and cry. Probably because he's an older version of Tyler as far as looks go and the first familiar face I've seen since thinking I would never see anyone I care about again.

"You're safe now," he consoles. "Everything's going to be okay. Tyler's on his way."

"Excuse me, sir," another officer says to Detective Elder. "He's alive. They think he'll pull through."

I tug away from Ty's dad and look him in the eyes. "Was he talking about James?"

"Yes. You all right?"

"Yeah, I think I'm actually glad. He should have to face up to what he's done, killing Aubree and kidnapping Brady... And I don't want to ever be like him. A murderer, I mean."

"What you did was in self-defense, Julia. You'd never be deemed a murderer by any standard. Stubborn to the core, yes. A murderer, no." He winks.

I smile. I'm glad Ty's dad has his sense of humor. I never would have imagined it. But I need that smile, need to feel normal again.

My dad's voice booms through the station and I stand up.

"Where's my daughter?" Dad shouts. "What the hell kind of place you running here when you allow a girl to be kidnapped in a tourist attraction by some psychopath? I'll own this whole damn town before this is over."

"Julia!" Mom shouts, and I fall into her arms when I reach her. "I was so scared. Are you okay? Did they hurt you? Let me see your shoulder. Oh my God, look at your hands!" She's talking a mile a minute, but I don't care. I'm just happy to hear her voice.

"I'm fine, Mom. I love you."

"I love you too, sweet girl. When I read this, I fell to pieces." She pulls out the note I left and sobs. "I can't ever lose you, do you understand me? Not ever."

"He killed Aubree," I say.

"I know," she says, pulling me into her chest. "I know it, baby. I'm so sorry."

Dad joins us, confusion lining his face. "Hey, girlie, you okay? Don't ever scare me like that again, you hear?"

"I hear ya," I say, moving from Mom to him.

He looks at the gauze on my shoulder and scowls. Then he takes my wrists and turns them over in his hands, examining the rope burns. "Whose ass am I kicking for this?"

"No need. I stabbed him already."

"That's my girl." He pulls me into a hug, and I feel the relief in his chest when he lets out a slow breath. "I was so scared. I couldn't even think about some man touching you, hurting you. I'll kill him. Now let's get the hell outta here. I'm getting you to the hospital."

Tyler bursts through the door before we make it into the station's lobby. "Oh, my God, Julia! Are you okay?"

I am now. "Hey, Ty."

"I should've been with you. You should've never gone up there alone. If anything had happened to you—"

"I'm fine, Ty. Everything's fine now. I'm just so glad to see you."

He touches my shoulder and glances at my hands. His eyes are glassy. "How bad are you hurt?"

Mom chimes in, "We're on our way to the hospital now to find out. You're welcome to come with us, Tyler."

"Absolutely," he replies.

We make our way to the door of the station when three cops bolt through it with a handcuffed Ryan. I lose my breath.

"Hey, what the hell are you doing here with him now?" an officer yells. "I told you not to process him until the young lady was gone."

Ryan locks desperate eyes on me before I can look away. "Julia, tell them! Tell them how I loosened those ropes, how I didn't kill Brady. That's the only reason you escaped, and you know it. Tell them the truth, Julia, please. I love you! I knew you'd get away!"

But I simply remain silent. No way I'm wasting another breath on him.

The officers pull Ryan along as he yells, "Every man can change his destiny, Julia. You taught me that. I changed ours. You have to believe me!"

Tyler steps into my line of vision as Ryan is hauled out of the room. "Come on, Julia. Forget about that loser. Your folks and I are ready to get you to the hospital, okay?"

We start out again and I remember something else. "Oh! Where's my notebook?" I look at Mom. "I need my notebook. I'm not leaving without it."

Mom glances around the room. "Who has my daughter's notebook?"

A smiling officer steps forward and hands it to me. "I still can't believe how you figured out that convent, Miss Reynolds. You know what, young lady? You're going to be famous."

I simply nod. We make our way out the door and into a sea of reporters, my dad's colorful language erupting again. But I can't fault them. They're just going for the story.

Chapter Twenty-One

Part of me still can't believe that James was the killer, one of dozens of killers over a course of two hundred plus years, protecting nothing but an ideal—the guilty conscience of a king's poor judgment that cursed a city for centuries, leaving no one the wiser of His Majesty's intrigues.

James was a secret assassin, lying in wait for the next poor soul to fall victim to their own curiosity. He was a slave to duty, a slave to a crown, a slave to an honor system so outdated that modern-day understanding of it is nearly unfathomable. My own flesh and blood was a victim of his twisted honor. The remains of my cousin, Aubree Marie Turner, were found buried deep in the swamplands in the exact location James described to the police. She was one of several dead found there ... all gone because of the "Blood Defenders." Gone, but not forgotten.

But this killer had the ability to make me think he had a softer side, a side that stopped a poor girl on the street just to ask why she frequented an adult establishment, and then sympathized when he realized she'd been given few options in life. He gave her words of wisdom, words of encouragement, and a trinket so bewitching it became the very thing that gave her courage enough to stop the curse he was charged to enforce.

"You have to understand the whole person and then decide what value they hold in your life." Ryan Grandle said those words to me. I'd like to say that James holds no part of me now, but that's not true. He's a murderer who kept me for hours—a man spouting honor and duty to justify the horror I faced. The horror others didn't survive. The horrors my cousin didn't survive. But here I

am—the one who got away.

And yet, that's not entirely true. James was also the person who reached out to me—the new girl in a dangerous city with little hope for the future except her sharp wit and raging curiosity. He saw my soul within three minutes and spoke with words that didn't talk above me, but through me. He saw me. Just me. And that's the part he holds. And when this nightmare is really over, I just hope I get my fountain pen back. I'd like to keep it.

I rest my hands on the keyboard and read over the last few words. This story is for my school newspaper. I think it's only fair that my paper gets the scoop before the rest of the world hears from me. Besides, every other serious journalist is in France scoping out anyone who can tell them the deal with the Défenseurs and James, Thad, William … and Ryan. This story is hotter than Louisiana in August, but all I really care about is giving it to Ms. Dunkin. Then it's going on my blog. But, on a personal level, I still can't bring myself to write about my true feelings for Ryan. That wound is taking its time healing, but the heart doesn't stitch up like the sutures in my shoulder. When I close my eyes, I still feel his lips on my mouth and his breath on my face. And on some crazy level, I miss him. But I'll survive.

I look at the photo of Aubree and smile. Proving to the world that she wasn't simply a runaway, knowing James will answer for her murder feels like justice, finally. I know I'll miss her every day, but she's not *missing* anymore. It was the one thing I always knew I *could* do. Find her. And I did it. I would have gone to the ends of the Earth if I had to, do anything to keep our promises we made so long ago. And I think somehow she knows that, too. My Aubree…

The therapist I'm seeing says I should be keeping a journal to help sort out my feelings, but I'm taking it a step further. For so long I was afraid for anyone at school to know anything about my folks or where I live. Well, now they all know that I saved Brady. Brady and Sarah have been all over the news, Brady wiping Sarah's tears that he'd never seen before. It's the most romantic gesture this city has seen in a while. I'm just glad she won't have to cry forever—glad Brady's home and doing well. But they're all going to know Aubree's story, too, my story—the real story—and they're going to hear it straight from me. And it actually feels good. I'd being lying if I said I'm not nervous about it, but it's okay. Everything's going to be okay now.

"Hey, shouldn't you be getting dressed?" Mom says when she joins me in my room. "Tyler will be here soon."

"I am. I'm just putting the finishing touches on my story."

She smiles. "You and your story. I can guarantee you're the only girl at Ben Franklin who's doing school work right now. Better get moving, baby girl. It's getting late."

I notice the time. "Oh, I'm sorry I got so caught up. I'll hurry—"

"Hey," she says. "Don't ever be sorry. I'm proud of you. Aubree would be proud of you, too."

"Thanks, Mom."

She taps my shoulder to nudge me out of my desk chair. "Now get dressed."
****

"You look like a princess," Mom says when I step into the living room.

"Really?" I smooth the wisps of lavender chiffon and

adjust the beaded headband and ringlets of curls tickling my cheek.

She smiles. "I can't wait 'til Tyler sees you."

"Yeah, he's gonna freak," Jesse adds. "You look … like a girl."

I roll my eyes. "Thanks, troll."

He winks. "Anytime."

I stand in front of the living-room mirror, checking the still-healing gash on my shoulder. The wound shows with this dress, but it can't be helped. I touched it up with makeup and powder, but I'm afraid it's still visible. Mom joins me when she notices my concern.

"It's fine, baby. Don't touch it."

"I'm just glad you had gloves to cover my wrists. And I like the gloves anyway. Would have worn them with or without burns to disguise. But this…" I touch my shoulder again.

"No one will pay it any attention, okay? I promise."

I sigh. "Okay." But I'm sure I'll get plenty of attention tonight. I haven't been back to school in a week, not since everything that happened at the convent … since Ryan was arrested and put in juvey.

Dad steps from the kitchen, armed with a camera. "So, when's he showing up?"

I glance at my phone display. "Should be here any minute."

"Well, let me take one of you by yourself first," he says. "Can't be showing off my little girl with some bozo standing next to her. It'll mess up the shot."

"Matt, please," Mom says, but she's smiling—hasn't stopped smiling since seeing me all Barbied up.

Dad positions me in front of our small dinner table and the vase of plastic flowers Mom added as her latest decorating attempt. I smile, but he stops.

"You know what? Something's missing."

I'm confused. "What do you mean?"

He looks in Mom's direction. "Erin, didn't I forget something?"

"I think you did." She retrieves a long velvet box from a kitchen drawer and my breath catches in my throat. What did they do?

Dad steps in front of me and I try not to cry. "I wanted you to have something for your first dance. You know, from your mama and me. So I stopped at a pawn shop on the way home from work yesterday. That place has some nice stuff. They're real, too. I checked." He motions for Mom to stand beside him then hands me the box.

I lift the velvet lid and reveal a small strand of pearls. I gulp to relieve the lump in my throat. It's the first piece of real jewelry I've ever owned.

"Dad, I—"

"Don't say anything," he says. "You'll get all girlie and ruin that bang-up paint job you did on your face." He smiles. "You deserve it, and you're my kid. Can't have you showing up for no dance looking less than gorgeous."

I can't resist. "You think I'm gorgeous?"

"Sure do. I've always thought you were a looker. You get that from me."

I fall into his chest and hug him like he's going off to war. I feel his arms respond, tightening around me like he means it. He whispers, "I was scared we'd lost you the other day. You gotta know something … I love you, girlie. I mean, Julia."

I give him a peck on the cheek. "Girlie's okay."

"He's here!" Jesse calls when Tyler's taxi pulls up outside.

Mom promptly hugs me and gives me a once-over,

making sure our love fest hasn't ruined my presentation. Dad snaps a quick picture, and Jesse opens the door for Ty before he has the chance to knock. Thank God the boy recused me from going to Homecoming alone. I owe him big time.

"Hi, everyone," Tyler says when he steps through the doorway, clear plastic box in hand.

I wasn't prepared for the shock of his raw, spectacular beauty. I've never seen him dressed up before. I'd always thought he was cute in jeans and a simple t-shirt, hair flying in every direction. But this ... this is a whole different animal. A guy like this needs full-on bodyguards just to keep adoring females at bay. God, why hadn't I ever noticed this before? My sweet Tyler.

"Wow, Julia," he announces, "you look beautiful. I mean ... wow."

I glance at my gawking family. "Thank you. So do you."

"Oh, here, this is for you," he says, handing me the box.

It's a wrist corsage with small white roses and purple and lavender ribbons. "I love it, thank you."

He takes the flowers from my hand when I open the box and then grimaces. "Oh crap. I forgot about your wrists."

"It'll be fine, I promise," I say.

He slides the corsage on my wrist very carefully. "That's doesn't hurt, does it?"

"It's good, Ty. Thank you. I love it."

"You're welcome. Should we go now?"

"Definitely."

Tyler helps me into the cab, careful not to smash my dress. In a few seconds, we're driving in the direction of my school's gymnasium.

"So, you ready for this?" he asks, placing a hand on my knee and giving it a light squeeze.

"Sure. I'm actually excited about it," I admit. "Thanks for agreeing to take me after—" But I stop. "Well, because I've never been to a Homecoming dance before."

"Well, no one would know it by the way you look. Julia, I just can't tell you how beautiful you are tonight."

"Oh, you can." I laugh. "I never mind hearing it."

"Yeah, but I mean, just seeing you, all dressed up like this ... and happy."

"I know what you mean," I reply. "And I am happy. I don't want to think about anything. I just want to enjoy tonight ... like a dream."

"Yeah, a dream," he says, his lips tightening and eyes narrowing. "Hey," he says to the taxi driver, "can you pull over a minute?"

"What's wrong?" I'm suddenly nervous. "Did I say something—?"

"Just come here a minute." He takes my hands and helps me out of the car. "This won't take long," he says to the driver.

"No problem," the driver replies. "It's your dime."

"I have to tell you something, and I don't want taxi man over there to hear," Tyler says when we're standing on the side of the road. "It's kinda private. I just want you to know that I've been so scared ... having nightmares about those men holding you in that convent. Every time I think about it, I get so pissed, so angry. I just want to beat Ryan's face in, that bastard. I can't believe he let that man cut you." He edges a finger around the gash on my shoulder. "I don't want anything like that to ever happen to you, not ever again. It's the worst thing I can imagine, something bad happening to you. Do you understand?"

I close my eyes, taking in his words like air. It's surreal, magical. I understand him completely. "You care about me. That's what you're saying?" It's more of a statement than a real question. I know exactly how he feels.

"More than you know," he replies.

"Well, if you care about me, then you have to know that I'm always going to be a reporter, and there's always going to be danger. It's who I am, Ty. If you're going to be my friend, you have to know that. I've realized that what I did in that convent was bigger than saving Brady and finding out what happened to Aubree. I gave a voice to the voiceless, found justice for all the bodies they found on that third floor. Do you understand?"

He cups my hands in his. "I understand completely, but next time you're solving a two-hundred year-old mystery that's left other people dead, do me a favor. Don't let me punk out. Use that killer power of persuasion you have and make me go with you, okay? Maybe I could be your photographer or something. Anyway, I've been told I have a pretty brutal sucker punch, so…"

I'll never deny that fact. The boy sucker punched my soul from the moment I laid eyes on him. He's the best friend I've ever had.

"Ty," I say. "I owe you something."

"What do you mean?"

"This." I cup his face in my hands and place a soft, slow kiss on his lips. Shock keeps him still for a moment, but after a couple of seconds, he follows my motions with a gentleness I've never felt. When the kiss is over, I add, "I'm sorry I didn't kiss you that first night, on our friendship date. Thanks for taking me to the dance tonight."

He grins. "Look, this is a friendship thing, okay? Nothing more, nothing less…" His words trail when he can't hold in the laughter.

I shake my head. "Dork."

"Just get your butt in the car," he says. "Meter's running."

****

When we reach the gym, Macey's waiting by the ticket table with Chris. Her hair is in a bun with loose curls draping her neck. Her pink gown is strapless and above the knee, hugging her goddess figure in all the right places. And Chris is all too adoring, glancing her up and down as she chats with some random chick. But the chatting stops as Tyler and I approach the table. It doesn't take long for me to realize that I'm the girl of the hour. The one who drove the vampire legend clean out of New Orleans, and Ryan Grandle out of Ben Franklin High.

"You sure you're ready for this?" Tyler asks when he notices the attention.

I clutch his hand. "You've still got my back, right?"

"Always."

"Hey, Julia, over here," Macey says, tugging Chris with her. "The gym looks amazing. Wait 'til you see. Oh, God, Julia, your dress is incredible. You are totally fabulous."

"You look pretty, too, Macey," I reply.

Macey isn't kidding about the gym. I wouldn't have believed it could be transformed into something this classic and elegant if I wasn't looking at it with my own eyes.

"Macey, Chris, this is Tyler," I say. Ty mock bows.

"Nice to meet you, Tyler. I've heard a lot about you,"

Macey says.

"Yeah, man. Nice to meet you," Chris adds.

Tyler looks down at his feet instead of Chris's eyes. "I know this is kinda awkward, you being such good friends with Ryan and all."

"Well, not as good of friends as I thought, apparently," Chris replies.

In a few seconds the guys are talking, and then they retreat to get Macey and me some punch.

"Got to have you properly hydrated," Tyler says as he heads to the food table, "because we're dancing when I get back."

A few kids are staring and pointing to me, and I feel a little uncomfortable at first. But when they flash me a thumbs-up, I return the gesture and let out a breath. Then it hits me. This is what I wanted all along, to be popular, noticed, somebody. But now that I'm here, standing in the middle of instant fame, none of it really matters. There were only four things I wanted that day in the convent when James's blade was slicing my shoulder and Ryan's words hung in the air. I wanted Brady safe. I wanted Aubree found. I wanted the people I love. And I wanted the world to know the truth. Now that those things are accomplished, nothing else matters.

"Look at Hannah," Macey says, pulling me from my thoughts. "The girl is still a Queen B, but you have to admit, she looks good."

I laugh and Hannah's eyes meet mine.

"Hey," someone calls in my direction, "you're a legend, Julia."

I keep my eyes locked with Hannah's. "Well, fame is overrated."

Ty returns with the punch. "Drink it fast, Julia. I have dibs on that center spot on the dance floor."

"Not if we get there first," Macey jokes, motioning for Chris to hurry up.

But before we make it to the coveted spot, a petite girl with ebony skin and a flowing yellow dress touches my arm. "Excuse me, Julia, you don't know me, but may I ask you something?"

Tyler steps in front of me, his protectiveness refreshing and annoying all at once. "Stand down, Hercules," I say.

"I just have a question," the girl reassures him. "I'm not trying to bother you."

I push Tyler back and then look at the girl. "Go ahead. I'm listening."

She clears her throat, tension lining her face. "My name's Loni. I go to the public school, but my boyfriend goes to Ben Franklin." She points in his direction. "What I need to know is, are you really as good as he says you are? With solving mysteries, I mean?"

I'm intrigued and goosebumpy all at once. "Maybe. Why do you ask?"

"Are you familiar with the LaLaurie House?"

My God. I stand straighter. "I've heard of it. Why?"

"That's good," she replies. "I need your help."

The End

www.leeannward.com

Evernight Teen ®

www.evernightteen.com